MW00648624

Beach Dreams

Rehoboth Beach Reads

Short Stories by Local Writers

Edited by Nancy Sakaduski

A Playful Publisher

Cat & Mouse Press
Lewes, DE 19958
www.catandmousepress.com

© 2019 Cat & Mouse Press, Lewes, DE, 19958

All rights reserved. Published 2019.

ISBN: 978-1-7323842-4-8

PERMISSION AND ACKNOWLEDGMENTS

"The Admiral and the Ensign," Maria Masington. ©2019 Maria Masington.

"All in a Day's Dream," Paula Kotowski. ©2019 Paula J. Kotowski.

"A Beach Story," Suzanne Thackston. ©2019 Suzanne Thackston.

"Booty," Kristie Letter. ©2019 Kristie Letter.

"The Bull, Dogs, and Sleep," Alexander Hood. ©2019 Alexander Hannah.

"The Dolphin Whisperers," Nancy North Walker. ©2019 Nancy Anna Walker.

"Dreaming in Stick Figures," TJ Lewes. ©2019 Tanya Schuler-Koltuk.

"Dreams We've Lived," D.M. Domosea. ©2019 Dora M. Sears.

"Four Corners," Chris Jacobsen. ©2019 Christiana D. Jacobsen.

"Dear Joan," Mary Dolan. ©2019 Mary Irene Dolan.

"Jojo's Diner," Cindy Cavett. ©2019 Cynthia L. Cavett.

"Last Call," Doug Harrell. ©2019 Douglas G. Harrell.

"Lost and Found," Dave Cooper. ©2019 David W. Cooper.

"Memories Revisited," Jean Youkers. ©2019 Jean F. Youkers.

"Mixolydian Dreams," Krystina Schuler. ©2019 Krystina M. Schuler.

"Red Flags, Wrong Star, and a Wagon with a Broken Wheel," Nancy Powichroski Sherman.
©2019 Nancy Powichroski Sherman.

"The Ripple Effect," LJ Brown. ©2019 Lisa J. Brown.

"Shells," Laura Nelson Selinsky. ©2019 Laura Nelson Selinsky.

"Sisters of Land and Sea," Kim DeCicco. ©2019 Kim DeCicco.

"A Summer Carol," David Strauss. ©2019 David Strauss.

"Unstuck in Time," Paul Barronet. ©2019 Paul Barronet.

"Whispers from the Past," Donna Rothert. ©2019 Donna L. Rothert.

"The Waterman's Daughter," Jennifer Logue. ©2019 Jennifer Logue.

"What Would My House Say?" Sarah Barnett. ©2019 Sarah Barnett.

Table of Contents

PREFACE

These are the winning stories from the 2019 Rehoboth Beach Reads Short Story Contest, sponsored by Browseabout Books. Writers were asked to create a story—fiction or nonfiction—that fit the theme "Beach Dreams" and had a connection to Rehoboth Beach. A panel of judges chose the stories they thought were best and those selections have been printed here for your enjoyment. Like *The Beach House, The Boardwalk, Beach Days, Beach Nights, Beach Life,* and *Beach Fun* (other books in this series), this book contains more than just "they went down to the beach and had a picnic" stories. The quality and diversity of the stories is simply amazing.

Most of the stories in this book are works of fiction. While some historical or public figures and actual locations have been used to give the reader a richer experience, the characters and situations in these works are fictitious. Any resemblance to real persons, living or dead, is purely coincidental.

For contact information or other Cat & Mouse Press publications, go to: www.catandmousepress.com.

ACKNOWLEDGEMENTS

Thanks to Browseabout Books for their continued outstanding support. We are so lucky to have this great store in the heart of our community. They have supported the Rehoboth Beach Reads Short Story Contest from day one and continue to be the go-to place for books, gifts, and other fun stuff.

I thank both the Rehoboth Beach Writers' Guild and the Eastern Shore Writers Association for their support and service to the writing community. These two organizations provide an amazing array of educational programming, and many of the writers whose stories appear in this book benefitted from their classes, meetings, and events.

I thank this year's judges, Tyler Antoine, Stephanie Fowler, Lois Hoffman, Laurel Marshfield, Mary Pauer, and Hal Wilson, who gave generously of their valuable time.

Special thanks to Emory Au, who captured the theme so well in the cover illustration and who designed and laid out the interior of this book as well.

I also thank Cindy Myers, queen of the mermaids, for her continued loyalty and support.

An extra-special thank-you to my husband, Joe, who helps on many levels and puts up with a great deal.

I would also like to thank the writers—those whose work is in this book and those whose work was not chosen. Putting a piece of writing up for judging takes courage. Thank you for being brave. Keep writing and submitting your work!

—*Nancy Sakaduski*

Cathy,

Enjoy some light
reading!

Jean

Memories Revisited

By Jean Youkers

The tide roared toward the shore. She dropped her bucket and ran, stumbling to the safety of Mom's blanket on the sand shimmering beneath the hot August sun. Screaming. She'd seen some type of giant sea creature swirling just beneath the foam. The creature was dragging Caroline down—tiny hands flailing, flaxen hair unfurled from its ponytail into a wild flapping mane—below the waves. She could hardly breathe, certain that the creature was pulling her twin away from her forever.

Sweat soaked Abigail's forehead as she awoke from another of the nightmares that had been plaguing her all summer. She bolted upright in bed and wondered why, after four decades, these shadow memories swallowed her during the night. The dreams were sometimes terrifying and other times, well … just beautiful. In blurry visions, Caroline disappeared down hallways or into cavernous rooms with doors that slammed shut before Abigail could follow. In pleasant dreams, the two prepared for their first day of school, choosing matching outfits at a trendy shop on Rehoboth Avenue. They built a sandcastle so beautiful that Mom took pictures of it, pictures Abigail had never seen.

Abigail forced herself into the shower. She had an appointment with Dr. Dearborn and would have to rush to the office afterward, before her boss began clamoring for her draft of the Gallaher brief. She was too busy to ruminate about the idyllic childhood she wasn't sure was real. Was Caroline an imaginary friend, as Daddy always assured her? He never took her back to Rehoboth Beach, where wonderful vacation days had found the family walking along the boardwalk, eating ice cream while watching the incoming tide. They'd played board games in their rental cottage, laughter punctuated by the sound of popcorn popping while swimsuits dried on the porch railing. Despite the vague details, she was certain that the good feelings were real.

First, coffee. She put the K-cup in the Keurig and stood watching it sputter Starbucks' pungent dark roast into her oldest, chipped, ceramic mug, the one emblazoned with "Dad's Favorite Law School Grad." She snatched a container of yogurt from the refrigerator and sat spooning it, untasted, into her mouth. After cleaning the kitchen counter and placing the mug in the dishwasher, Abigail opened the drapes of the floor-to-ceiling windows that overlooked the City of Brotherly Love from her twentieth-floor condo. She took a quick look, as she did each day, feeling satisfied with her world and stimulated by challenges of work and enjoyment of friends; yet of late, she was haunted by the dreams—nightmares entangled with pleasant memories.

After putting on her navy suit, Abigail crammed file folders and the important brief into an extra-large attaché case that also housed her computer. The bag must've weighed twenty pounds, but even with her oversized handbag in the other hand the weight felt minimal compared to that which burdened her mind.

* * * * *

"I'm still having weird dreams," Abigail told Dr. Dearborn. She sat rigidly on the edge of a red plush couch in his comfortable Center City office. "They seem so real that they're pulling me into conflicts I thought I'd resolved long ago, before I moved to Philadelphia."

"What is most distressing about the dreams?"

"The fact that I don't know what's real." Abigail placed her hands on the sides of her head, trying to stop the throbbing, which pain medication had failed to alleviate. "I can picture Caroline and our parents on vacation in Rehoboth as if it were yesterday, even though

I know she was just imaginary. My father equated her to characters like Winnie the Pooh. He said all children have imaginary friends. Sometimes he'd make a game of it, impersonating the voices of Pooh, Piglet, and the three bears."

"Did you feel he was supportive?"

"For a while. When I was in first and second grades. But when I set the table for a tea party with stuffed animals and put out real food for Caroline—in maybe third grade—he became furious, swatted the plates off the table and overturned her chair. That's when he increased the hypnosis sessions from every week to daily."

"Ah, yes." Dr. Dearborn laced his fingers together, tapping them beneath his bearded chin. "We discussed those sessions as being liberating. Do you have some new thoughts about them?"

"I think they were more liberating for my father, because he didn't have to put up with what he called 'my theatrics' anymore. He could be free to enjoy his fame as a scientist and pursue his romance with Nannette, our housekeeper."

"How were the hypnosis sessions for you?"

"They calmed me down, initially. I didn't know what hypnosis was. All I remember is my father talking in a slow, calm tone, asking about my day at school and so forth. His voice would become so quiet that I would fall asleep. After a few sessions, I could remember nothing before first grade, couldn't picture my mother anymore. He told me she'd died.

"The dreams seem so much like memories. I'm *sure* we traveled from Pittsburgh to Rehoboth Beach every summer. I remember being proud when I learned to spell 'Pittsburgh.' But in first grade, I was taught to spell 'New York' and a different last name."

"What did your father say about the beach trips?"

"He eventually admitted I'd been to Rehoboth, along with my imaginary friend, when I confronted him with a souvenir I'd found in a closet—a unicorn with Rehoboth Beach and my name printed on it, mostly worn off."

"You never went back to Rehoboth?"

"We never went on *any* beach vacations because my father thought they were frivolous. Nannette was from France, so they took summer trips there while I was sent to various camps, to get me out of their hair.

"My father traveled all over the world to speak at symposiums. He was a hot ticket—'the famous Dr. Lobotovich.' All he talked about were clinical trials and percentages. He had little time for me."

"So, he was physically and emotionally unavailable."

"Exactly. Nannette was my source of nurturing as I grew up. We'd laugh when Dad was away, but he was always dead serious. She assured me that he loved me but simply lacked parenting skills; she joked that he'd been raised by wolves."

"Was he ever abusive?"

"No," Abigail replied. "He only spanked me once, not violently, just an impulsive smack when I sneaked into his bathroom to watch him dye his hair and mustache silver. My friends said he looked like a 'mad scientist' and I wanted to find out what he did to achieve that look."

"Tell me more."

"My friends were intimidated by him because he was unusually tall and always dressed in suits, but I just thought he was a genius. I worked hard in college and law school to please him in the only way that seemed important to him. After he died, I looked through mountains of research materials from his files. He was studying memories—their formation and retention. I discovered an article he'd published in a medical journal about extinguishing early memories through hypnosis."

Dr. Dearborn raised his eyebrows. "That must have been a shock."

"Yes. I felt like a guinea pig. But since the hypnosis resolved my preoccupation with Caroline, I thought he'd been trying to help me.

I know now that he effectively erased my early childhood. He wanted me to be a serious adult like he was, but he deprived me of being a normal child."

"So now, perhaps the joyful childlike part of you wants to emerge and have some fun." Dr. Dearborn smiled. "Maybe a trip to the beach would help. You could use a break from your responsibilities … and a time to embrace your good memories and make some new ones."

Abigail froze. "I'm too busy at work to go to the beach," she heard herself say. It was like hearing her father's voice.

But that night, a dream had her riding a carousel horse next to Caroline, laughing and singing their own version of "Sweet Caroline." All night long, Abigail waded ankle-deep along the shore, looking at boats on the horizon, feeling sand beneath her toes.

Once awake, Abigail felt an inexplicable compulsion to go to Rehoboth Beach. She pulled two matching suitcases from her closet and started packing. On automatic pilot, she marched into her office and arranged to take a full week off, despite commitments that would have to be reassigned or postponed. She secured an oceanfront room at the Boardwalk Plaza. With Labor Day weekend over most of the tourists would be gone, and it would be the perfect time for a beach trip, a peaceful interlude for relaxation and renewal.

She arrived on Wednesday afternoon, unloaded her suitcases, and checked into the hotel. She loved the charming atmosphere—the compact lobby, complete with two talking parrots.

Abigail stepped onto her balcony and watched the magnificent ocean sparkling in the sun as sounds of waves slapping the shore and boardwalk walkers laughing floated up to her. An unfamiliar relaxed feeling swept over her. Over the next two days, she shed thoughts of work and stormy nightmares. Instead, she bought T-shirts and ate Thrasher's fries, watching seagulls swoop onto the boardwalk, scavenging for food. Walking barefoot on the sand evoked memories of childhood romps on this very beach. It seemed familiar yet unfamiliar.

After enjoying Grotto's pizza the first night and seafood at Victoria's the second, Abigail arose refreshed on her third day of vacation. *Dr. Dearborn was right,* she thought. She had needed a break, and beautiful new memories were in the making at every turn.

At Browseabout Books, she examined greeting cards, laughing at funny ones and smiling at touching ones. Trying on fragrant vanilla hand lotion from a sample dispenser, Abigail noticed the scent of her favorite perfume, Beautiful, wafting by in the wake of a customer who was rushing toward the cashier. As the woman paid for her purchases, Abigail noted that she was wearing an attractive, clunky watch on her right hand. *She's left-handed like me,* Abigail thought.

Abigail wanted to walk on the boardwalk. Stopping to consult the menu posted outside Robin Hood's, she decided to return later for her favorite lunch, a tuna salad sandwich. She noticed two women seated at one of the booths inside. Facing the window, the blonde, whose hair was pulled into a stylish bun, held a coffee cup between her hands as she listened intently to her companion. *Perhaps a mother and daughter sharing a conversation,* Abigail thought. How she envied that kind of a connection.

She walked to the boardwalk and stood facing the Atlantic. The breeze ruffled her hair and Abigail felt a sense of well-being. She stretched her hands toward the ocean and welcomed the sun on her face. The breeze seemed to whisper her name.

* * * * *

Three Months Earlier

Caroline rushed out the door after her session with the psychic, impassioned by the news she had just received. She hadn't cried so hard since the day she had to go off to first grade by herself in

Pittsburgh almost forty years ago. Pulling on oversized sunglasses to hide her tears, she reached the privacy of her car and screamed out loud. Her mind was reeling with new information and her plan.

Caroline took a deep breath. She needed to calm down before she picked up Tad and Tanya from Cape Henlopen High. It wouldn't do for them to see their mother hysterical. She drove carefully down Coastal Highway toward Lewes.

Though Caroline had often passed the little cottage with an enticing sign that read "Mrs. Knowl, Clairvoyant, Fortunes Told, Contacts with the Other Side," she had never considered stopping there. But when her friend Leola from Zumba class insisted that she had communicated with her deceased grandmother through Mrs. Knowl, Caroline put aside her skepticism and made the appointment.

With trepidation, Caroline knocked on the door. Mrs. Knowl wore layers of flowing skirts and blouses, multiple chains around her neck, and a scarf in her hair, like a fortune-teller right out of central casting. Caroline would've laughed had her mission not been such a serious one. Tanya and Tad would have been amazed if they knew where she was while they were in chemistry lab, and Richard would have feared for her mental health. The incense smell within the room masked potential odors emanating from four scraggly, scurrying cats.

"You are here to make contact with someone very close to you, someone lost long ago, no?"

Caroline nodded.

"Please, sit and take a few breaths." Mrs. Knowl fingered her chains and scarf and looked at Caroline expectantly.

"My twin sister was kidnapped on the way home from vacation when we were six," Caroline began. "I was devastated, especially when I had to start school without her. We were best friends. We'd had a wonderful time in Rehoboth. We stopped somewhere for snacks, and when it was time to leave, Abigail was gone."

"What a horrible experience for two such little girls. I know she has missed you just as much over the years."

"Dad called the police right away, then hired a private detective, but Abigail was never found. I studied pictures of missing children on milk cartons to see if her picture was there and cried when it wasn't. When I was older, I checked newspapers at the library and searched online with no luck. I finally gave up. I think the kidnapper must have killed her." Caroline swallowed, struggling for control. "If she is dead, I'd like to make contact."

"Let's see what we can find out." Mrs. Knowl looked grim, focused, then fluttered her hands about a crystal ball and went into a trance. Long minutes passed until her body jolted, as if returning to the room.

"I could not contact your Abigail on the other side," she said, "because she is not dead." Caroline burst into tears.

"I can help, never fear. We must now focus on psychic messaging. You will reach out to her on the twinning telepathic network. The most likely success is to send messages as memories from the last happy times you spent together."

Caroline tried to pull herself together.

"I've seen this work with others closely related, not even twins, so with twins it should be piece of cake. Send images that might reach her while she is dreaming. You two will find a way to locate one another."

"How exactly do I log onto this twinning network?"

"First, locate a space with perfect peace. No TV, music, or cell phone. Close your eyes and focus on images of Abigail. Hold objects that may be meaningful to the two of you and remind her of those times.

"Concentrate for one half hour each session." Mrs. Knowl stood up, signaling that the appointment was over. Caroline hugged the mysterious soothsayer and bolted out the door.

"Good luck!" Mrs. Knowl called after her.

Dizzily, Caroline began. She told nobody, not even her mother, to spare her disappointment in case the process didn't work. Late nights, while her family slept, she held her shell unicorn and photographs. She concentrated on projecting images of beach trips into the atmosphere, messages destined to reach Abigail wherever she might be.

* * * * *

With Labor Day passed and her twins at college, Caroline had time to reflect on her efforts to reach Abigail. So far, no word, yet she remained determined. When she'd finally confided in Richard, he suggested she ask her parents about any forgotten clues. Her parents had retired to Rehoboth, their favorite vacation destination, not long after Caroline and Richard had moved to Lewes. Dad would never discuss the kidnapping, so Caroline was gathering her courage to bring up the upsetting subject with Mom over lunch.

Caroline stopped at Browseabout to buy humorous cards for Tad and Tanya. Now at the University of Delaware, they'd been gone a week and she already missed them terribly. As she emerged from the maze of greeting card displays, she brushed past another customer without looking but enjoyed the scent of vanilla emanating from her. She took her purchases to the counter and glanced at her watch while the cashier rang up her items.

Minutes later, Caroline and her mother sat at a cozy booth in Robin Hood's. She ordered a tuna sandwich and tea. Her mother opted for a Greek salad and coffee.

"I went to see that psychic—Mrs. Knowl," Caroline began. "She said Abigail is alive and that I could contact her through the twinning telepathic network." Her mother listened intently to Caroline's account of the psychic's instructions and her efforts.

"I hoped you might have ideas about where the kidnappers took Abigail," Caroline said. "Did you learn anything at all from the police at the time?"

"She disappeared so fast that the only lead was a rental car found abandoned somewhere near the Philadelphia airport. A witness had described a tall, well-dressed, professional-looking man carrying a sleeping child from the convenience store to a green Buick, and they believed it was the same car. No surveillance cameras then. They speculated that the culprit switched to another vehicle or chartered a plane. They couldn't guess at motive, but it wasn't money. I sometimes wonder if we'd been followed. It sounds crazy, but I remember seeing a tall man wearing a suit and tie, pacing along in the sand outside our cottage."

"I just remember how happy Abigail looked, clutching that little red purse with her unicorn inside. I was doing the same thing—we had each gotten one with our name on it." Caroline sighed. "We were such a happy family."

"Yes, we were. Dad and I tried to keep things normal for you, afterwards, which was almost impossible. I felt so guilty for losing track of you. Two lousy minutes. I thought I saw both of you running around that candy counter, but it was really just one."

"Oh, Mom," Caroline said. "We were identical. It wasn't your fault. You and Dad held together for me for all these years and I know you went through hell. I felt guilty, too, because I'm the one who got to stay in the happy family. Who knows what Abigail endured?"

"We all suffered and did the best we could."

Both women wiped tears.

"Now we just have to focus on locating Abigail," Caroline said.

"Don't get your hopes up."

"Oh, my hopes are definitely up. I'm an optimist. I've been saving her crayons and Mickey Mouse ears." The air lightened and the two sat silently for a few minutes.

Caroline paid the bill and, as if propelled by unseen forces, vaulted up Rehoboth Avenue toward the boardwalk. "I know she's near,"

Caroline said, as her mother struggled to keep up. "I feel her presence."

She headed toward the benches near Dolle's candy store and stopped abruptly, watching as a woman with her back to them reached her hands out toward the ocean, blonde hair swaying in the breeze.

"Abigail," she whispered, then drawing closer, shouted "Abigail, Abigail" until her sister turned around, wide-eyed, mouth open.

With tears streaming down her face, Caroline rushed toward her twin, calling, "It's me, Caroline. And Mom. Oh, Abigail, we have missed you so much."

"Caroline?" Abigail gasped. "You're real or else this is a dream."

Sensing Abigail's shock and confusion, Caroline reached into her bag and held out the shell unicorn that had worked so well. Abigail gingerly touched the unicorn that was in better condition than her own. "Caroline" was spelled out in bright red script. From her bag, Abigail produced the matching souvenir with her own name printed on it.

"You called these guys our magic horses," Caroline said. "Remember?"

"Yes, I remember," said Abigail, and she began to sing, "Sweet Caroline, good times never seemed so good—"

"So good, so good," responded Caroline.

HOCKESSIN RESIDENT JEAN YOUKERS LOVES TO WRITE FICTION, HUMOROUS NONFICTION, AND POETRY. SHE IS A MEMBER OF THE WRIGHT TOUCH WRITING GROUP AND HER WORK HAS APPEARED IN THE *BEACH DAYS*, *BEACH FUN*, AND *BEACH LOVE* ANTHOLOGIES, AS WELL AS IN *THE BROADKILL REVIEW*, *DREAMSTREETS*, AND *CICADA'S CRY MICRO-ZINE*. SHE WAS SELECTED TO PARTICIPATE IN THE DELAWARE DIVISION OF THE ARTS WRITERS' RETREATS IN 2016 AND 2018. JEAN DREAMED UP THE HAPPY ENDING FOR "MEMORIES REVISITED" FIRST AND THEN HAD TO FIGURE OUT THE BEGINNING AND MIDDLE, AN ENJOYABLE PROCESS. SHE IS ALSO AN ENTHUSIASTIC STUDENT AT OSHER LIFELONG LEARNING INSTITUTE AND A HUGE FAN OF CAT & MOUSE PRESS.

Mixolydian Dreams

By Krystina Schuler

Brandon slipped his key into the lock of his jazz and blues club. Everything had to be perfect. He'd waited an eternity for his dreams to become reality and had sunk every dime he had into The Mixolydian Club. If it failed, he had no alternate plan. A thrill shot up his arm as he felt the satisfying click of the bolt sliding open. The slap of construction odor tempered his enthusiasm.

"God, it reeks in here." Brandon passed through the dining room and propped the front door open, then unlatched one of the enormous windows, folding the panes back and filling the space with fresh air. "Better."

Before long, the place was filled with frenetic energy. The soft opening a few nights ago had gone well, but tonight was for real. Nervous anticipation led to accidents and flared tempers. A stack of plates cascaded from a server's arms and exploded on the floor. When the Dogfish Head delivery person arrived, he swerved to avoid the broken ceramic, causing beer cases to tumble from the dolly and bottles to shatter. Now, the pungent aroma of beer joined the lingering scent of latex paint. Brandon closed his eyes and rubbed his brow, wondering if he should have just stayed on the median during his run earlier this morning when he had stopped to admire his picture-perfect success.

Derek, the bartender, jumped into action. "I'm on it. And Brandon, relax. Everything's gonna be fine."

Brandon wasn't as optimistic. Life had caught him up in one riptide after another, and whenever he thought he'd swum free, another one dragged him away again. Why should this time be any different?

A vibration in Brandon's pocket startled him. He removed his phone and read the display. "This better not be bad news," he muttered and tapped the screen to answer. "What's up, Fitz?"

"Are you sitting down?"

"No."

"You should sit."

"Fitz …"

"I was riding my bike this morning when some jackass backed out of his driveway without looking and knocked me across the street. Broke my arm and wrist." Fitz's words rushed from his mouth. "I can't play for at least six weeks."

Before Brandon could reply, a muscular, blue-gray pit bull lumbered into the restaurant, chased its tail a few times, then jumped up on Brandon, pushing him into the support pillar. Brandon clamped his eyes shut, hoping the dog would disappear. Ever since he was bitten when he was fourteen, he'd been deathly afraid of dogs.

From outside, a woman's sultry voice filtered in. "Robee, come back. Here, boy! Get out of the restaurant. Uuuh," she grumbled.

Brandon peered through squinted eyes. The dog's paws pressed against his abdomen. Its head lolled to one side, tongue dangerously close to licking him. The dog appeared to be smiling. As he turned his head, Brandon saw the silhouette of a tall, graceful woman in the doorway.

"Robee, down. I'm so sorry. He's just a puppy, and we're still working on his leash skills." She retrieved the leash, pulling the dog to heel.

Brandon held up his finger and resumed his conversation with Fitz. "You really can't play piano for six weeks?" He hoped he'd just misunderstood the severity of Fitz's injuries. Brandon couldn't open the club without a musician.

"Yeah, sorry."

"I think I'm gonna be sick." Brandon approached the bar and sat on a stool. "Guess I'll call Alex."

"Alex is out of town."

"Shit!" Brandon squeezed the bridge of his nose. "Let me see who I can come up with. Get some rest, Fitz." Brandon hung up and eyed the dog, who was pulling at the leash and looking every bit like a puppy who wanted to play.

The woman held the dog's leash with a white-knuckled grip. "You don't look well," she said, her unusually green eyes showing concern.

Brandon rotated his arm to show her the silvery-pink scars lining his pale brown skin. "I'm not comfortable around dogs."

Stepping back a foot, she whispered, "Robee, sit," and pressed down on his bottom.

"And today I'm supposed to open this club, but I've lost an entire stack of plates, the beer delivery christened the floor, and now my pianist has a broken arm."

Brandon rose from the stool and started setting candles on each table. As he passed the woman, he smelled vanilla and coconut rising from her skin and hair and wondered if she'd taste as delicious as she smelled. But he didn't have time for delicious women—or men. There weren't enough hours in the day for a lover and his dreams. His recent ex-partners were exes for a reason. All of them would say he's married to his dream of a jazz club. Now that The Mixolydian was nearly a reality, he couldn't let anything distract him, not even a woman whose skin looked like the sun never stopped kissing it. She was distracting him already. He shook his head. "What kind of name is 'Robee' for a dog, anyway?"

She chuckled. "It's short for Rehoboth Beach. Someone abandoned this not-so-little guy, and he decided my back porch would make a good home. When no one claimed him, I kept him. Named him after the beach, since he loves playing in the sand. What kind of name is

'The Mixolydian Club'?"

"Mixolydian is a major modal scale often used in jazz and blues music. Plus, I thought it sounded cool." He couldn't take his eyes off her, drawn to her smile and those emerald eyes. Never one to entertain the idea of a dream partner, he was reconsidering. One may have just walked through his door. "What's your name?"

"Zara."

Brandon cocked his head. "Zara?"

"I'm named after my avó, eh, grandmother. She's Brazilian."

She extended her arm toward the glossy black upright piano. "May I?"

"You play?"

Zara responded with a coy grin, then floated to the stage and sat on the bench as if weightless. Robee followed her and lay at her sandaled feet as if he were home. With a thoughtful expression on her face, she flexed her fingers and rotated her wrists. Back erect, her beach-tousled curls cascaded past her shoulders. She lifted the lid off the keyboard and executed a succession of scales and arpeggios that reminded him of waves against the shoreline. Brandon couldn't remember ever being so captivated by a person before, male or female, and he'd had his fair share of both. Then, she dropped her hands down into the first soulful chord and began to sing.

Brandon's heart filled with a strange mixture of joy and melancholy at the sound of her voice, the lugubrious melody of an unfamiliar song. She played as if the piano were an extension of her. Entranced, he hadn't noticed the hostess, servers, and Derek observing, awestruck until the last note reverberated through the room and they applauded.

Zara's cheeks glowed, her expression pure exhilaration.

Brandon approached the piano. "I've never heard that song before."

"No, you wouldn't have," she replied. "I wrote it."

"You wrote it? What are you doing here, then? Why aren't you in New York or Chicago or New Orleans?"

Her smile faltered. "That was the plan. Board a bus to New Orleans after graduation, see what I could make of myself."

He rested his arm atop the piano. An endless list of tasks aside, he wanted to know everything about this woman, this creator of the most sublime, evocative music he'd ever heard. It stirred something in him beyond lust, something deeper. "What happened?"

"My mom had a stroke the week before I graduated so I stayed to take care of her. Moving wasn't really an option."

"Would playing here every night from six to nine for the next few weeks be an option, assuming you've got more than one song up your sleeve?"

She nodded, eyes and smile full of enthusiasm. "I've loads of songs—covers and my own."

"Can you start tonight?"

"I can."

"I don't know what you normally charge, but I can pay you what I was going to pay Fitz."

"I've always just played for the pleasure of it, but getting paid would be even better."

He straightened and stuck out his hand. "You're hired. Oh, and the name's Brandon."

She rose and took his hand. "It's very nice to meet you." Zara reached for Robee's leash. "Come on, boy. I've got a performance to get ready for." She glanced back over her shoulder and tossed Brandon a flirty little wave.

When Zara arrived that night, her eyes darted around the room. Brandon guessed she was nervous. She made herself comfortable at the piano and started to play. After a few measures, her face relaxed, her shoulders softened, and her movements turned fluid. Wherever her music took her, he longed to follow her. He wanted to tell her that, but while he'd been backstage talking to the band that would take the stage next, Zara had finished her set and disappeared like Cinderella.

Late the next morning, Brandon was arranging tables outside when he spotted Robee dragging Zara down the sidewalk. Robee broke free and charged. Brandon tensed, trying to brace himself without looking foolish. Robee skidded to a halt at his feet, danced a few circles, and wagged his tail. Brandon swore the dog was smiling at him.

"Robee!" Zara shouted. "Leave Brandon alone." She caught hold of the leash. "Sorry."

"It's OK. It's a fear I should probably get over." Brandon lowered his hand and Robee sniffed it. A cold nose pushed against Brandon's hand, followed by a wet tongue. Robee nosed the scars on Brandon's arm and whined, like he knew a dog had done that and was sorry.

"He likes you," Zara said. "He usually growls at men."

"Good dog," Brandon muttered through a grin. He tentatively scratched Robee's jowls.

Zara's brows pulled downward, and she pursed her lips. "That's it! You look like that actor ... oh, what's his name?" She snapped her fingers by her thigh. "Jesse ... Jesse Williams."

Brandon grinned. He'd take being compared to Jesse Williams; the man was hot. "Is that a good thing?"

"Definitely. Tall, fit, just the right amount of scruff, and haunting gray eyes? Sign me up."

"Let me go grab a pen," he said.

Zara winked at him, a wink that caused something to shift inside him.

"You were fantastic last night," he said.

"Thanks. All I've ever wanted to do was share my music."

"You're a natural. Did you also get your musical talents from your, what did you call her, *avó*?"

"*Avó*"—she nodded—"right, but, no, my musical gifts apparently come from my dad."

"Apparently?"

She shrugged. "Never met him. He was an Irish tourist my mom had a summer romance with. He went home before she knew she was pregnant. And with a name like Shane O'Connor, you'd have an easier time finding a leprechaun at the end of a rainbow."

Brandon laughed.

"I'm mixed race too: black dad, white mom. Although I lost them both when I was eight."

"How?"

"Earthquake in Haiti."

"Brandon"—she grasped his arm—"I'm so sorry."

He patted her hand. "My grandmother raised me. An old southern belle from Nawlins, who taught English and loved jazz and blues. We'd listen to her old records—Coltrane, Bessie, Ella, the greats—for hours. She hired a piano teacher, and I discovered I had a talent for it. Music saved my life, kept me out of trouble until I was fourteen."

"What happened then?"

"Some of my basketball teammates and I were licking our wounds after losing the qualifying game when our rivals showed up on the boardwalk. Trash talk turned into a fist fight. Someone had brought a dog with them and it clamped down on my arm, tearing it up. That put an end to any ideas I had of performing professionally, piano or basketball." Robee whined and nuzzled his head against Brandon's thigh.

"Anyway, instead of performing music, I provide space for others to do so. My plan is to turn The Mixolydian into a destination."

Brandon stroked Robee's peach-soft ears without thinking, his heart rate slowing until the sea breeze blew Zara's vanilla-coconut scent his way. He locked eyes with her, wondering what it was about her that made him feel comfortable spilling his guts. Her eyes glistened, not with pity, but empathy. Anyone who could create the music she did had to understand the pain of losing that form of expression.

Zara stepped closer to him and rested her hand on his chest. "Then I'll do everything I can to make sure you get off to a good start."

* * * * *

With Zara's help, The Mixolydian exceeded Brandon's expectations. Reservations were backed up for weeks. Regulars came in to hear Zara but stayed to listen to that night's band and sample Derek's drink specials until closing. Brandon should have felt elated, but instead he felt like a hole was burning through his stomach. Tonight was Zara's last night. Tomorrow, Fitz would take her place at the keys.

Brandon spied Fitz at the bar, drinking a pint of his favorite, SeaQuench Ale. As he listened to Zara perform, Fitz scowled, unable to hide his envy, and perhaps his own fears of not measuring up. When Fitz played, he did well, but he was a sparkler to Zara's fireworks. The next time Brandon glanced Fitz's way, he found an empty pint glass in front of an empty chair.

"Thank you," Zara said at the end of her set. "The Mudflat Boyz will be out in half an hour. You should stick around for them." Sadness colored her voice, and she caressed the keys as she descended the platform like someone leaving a lover for the last time.

Brandon met her at the edge of the stage, handed her flowers, and gave her a hug. "Thanks for saving my butt."

"It's a butt worth saving."

"You won't be a stranger, will you?"

"Not if Robee has anything to say about it. We can't seem to go for a walk without him heading straight for your door."

Brandon laughed. Her silly dog had won him over. So had she. "Dog's got good taste in music."

"Among other things," Zara said, smiling.

"Excuse me," a highly polished woman said. "Sorry to interrupt, but my name is Melanie." She thrust her hand at Zara. "I work for a record label in New York. May we talk?"

Zara, a look of disbelief on her face, awkwardly shook her hand and gave a weak nod.

Brandon raised an eyebrow but shoved down the tumultuous feelings roiling through him. He watched the two women walk outside where it was quieter, Zara taking the light and warmth he had come to crave with her. The profound emptiness left behind almost caused him to chase after her, because for the first time he considered maybe his dream was worthless without someone to share it with. He took a few steps toward the door, but decided against it, unwilling to interfere with her dreams, even if it meant sacrificing his own.

* * * * *

Fitz assumed his role as house pianist. His music gave the club a different, less intimate feel. He played technically well, but in a way that came off as rote. Or maybe it was just rote compared to Zara; Brandon wasn't sure he could be objective anymore. His customers could be, though, and after a few weeks, he noticed a downtick in reservations, and fewer people were sticking around after dinner.

Marcy, a regular, waved Brandon over to her table. "Brandon, darling," she said, "you must get Zara back, even for one night a week. This Fitz, he plays well, but he has no soul. Anna and Scott"—she nodded at their tables—"were saying they might stop coming here altogether."

"We can't have that," Brandon said. "I'll see if I can work something out. How's everything else tonight?"

"Marvelous, darling."

Brandon smiled at her over-the-top personality and wove between the tables to his office. He tapped the screen on his phone and sent a text to Zara. "Checking in to see how things are going."

She replied almost immediately. "Just landed in JFK. Spending the week being wined and dined by Melanie and the record label."

Brandon answered. "That's wonderful. Good luck!"

Brandon tossed his phone on the desk and rested his head in his hands. He heard Fitz say goodnight to the audience. A few moments later there was a knock on his door. He looked up and saw Fitz.

Fitz inhaled and flexed his hands. "Bran. I have good news and bad news."

What else was new? "Good news first."

"Caleb proposed. We're getting married."

"Congratulations." Brandon stood, clasped Fitz's hand, pulling him in and patting his shoulder. "What's the bad news?"

"Caleb took a research position at St. Jude's in Memphis. I'm going with him."

Zara was off chasing her dreams, and now Fitz was abandoning him, too. Brandon gritted his teeth and clenched his hands into fists.

Fitz noticed. "Can you get Zara back? I'm not deaf," he said. "She's better than I am."

Brandon shook his head. "She's in New York, probably about to sign a recording contract." He scrubbed his face with his hand. "Don't worry about it. I'll figure something out."

* * * * *

As the days passed, Brandon thought about other musicians he could book. None were quite right as permanent replacements, because none of them were Zara. She brought something extra, something that made people want to gather and stay, the same ineffable quality that drew him to her the day she chased Robee into the club and made his heart smile. He missed her, and Robee too.

He started to wonder how he would survive if she were permanently out of his life. He'd never put someone else's needs above his own before. The club would succeed without her, or it wouldn't. He could live with that, because he realized the club really wasn't the dream. Having someone to share it with, having Zara to share it with, was what mattered, and he was willing to give her up so she could pursue her dreams.

As Brandon unchained the sidewalk seating, he wondered if she'd signed the record deal, if she was trying to figure out how to move her mother to Manhattan, if she would change when she was a star.

"Go get him, Robee." Zara's voice carried on the sea breeze.

Brandon turned and grinned. "You're back!" He squatted to pet Robee, who skidded to a halt at Brandon's feet with that strange dog smile on his muzzle.

"Did you sign to a label?"

"I called Melanie this morning. I told her no."

Brandon jerked his head back. "You didn't sign?"

"It wasn't what I wanted. Rehoboth is my home. My friends are here. My support system is here. Besides, Robee is too much of a beach bum for city living." She rubbed Robee's haunch and looked into Brandon's eyes. "And you're here."

His heart stuttered.

"May I?" she said, pointing through the open door toward the piano with a tilt of her head and a knowing smile.

He grinned, remembering how that question had changed everything. "Can you play tomorrow night?"

"Why wait till tomorrow?"

"Because tonight I'd like to have dinner with you."

Robee barked, licked Brandon's face, then Zara's. They both laughed.

"Silly dog," Brandon said, scrunching Robee's cheeks. Robee licked him again. Brandon rose.

"Good dog," Zara said, and stood. "I'd love to have dinner with you."

Then she kissed Brandon's cheek, too.

WHETHER IT WAS GETTING LOST IN A BOOK AS A CHILD, WRITING A TERM PAPER IN COLLEGE, OR EDITING A LEGAL BRIEF AS A PARALEGAL, KRYSTINA HAS ALWAYS LOVED THE WRITTEN WORD. A FEW YEARS AGO, SHE TRIED HER HAND AT FICTION AND HASN'T BEEN ABLE TO STOP TAPPING AT THE KEYS SINCE. SHE SELF-PUBLISHED HER FIRST ROMANCE NOVEL, *THE GIRL IN THE GALLERY*, IN 2015, AND IS CURRENTLY WORKING ON A SECOND NOVEL. HER STORY "AFTERNOON SHOWERS" WAS PUBLISHED IN *BEACH FUN* IN 2018, AND "ANOTHER DAY AT THE FUCKING OFFICE" WAS PUBLISHED IN THE ANTHOLOGY *WHAT SORT OF FUCKERY IS THIS?* IN 2019. SHE IS THE FACILITATOR FOR THE WRITE TOUCH WRITERS GROUP AND SERVED AS A JUROR FOR THE 2018 SCHOLASTIC ART AND WRITING AWARDS FOR THE DELAWARE DISTRICT.

A NEW ENGLAND NATIVE, KRYSTINA GREW UP IN CONNECTICUT AND NOW LIVES IN DELAWARE WITH HER HUSBAND AND SON. WHEN SHE IS NOT WRITING, SHE CAN OFTEN BE FOUND TEACHING HERSELF TO PLAY PIANO AND UKULELE OR LISTENING TO A RANGE OF ECLECTIC MUSIC. SHE ALSO ENJOYS LONG BIKE RIDES WITH HER FAMILY AND HAS FUN DYING HER HAIR PURPLE. SHE CANNOT WHISTLE, AND SHE DOESN'T LIKE THE TASTE OF HONEY.

Unstuck in Time

By Paul Barronet

Henry Laffer's forty-two-year-old body ached from the long hours in the blue vinyl chair. He'd grown adept at nodding off in it, his head tilted to the right and atop the yellow pillow Lilly had given him. He hovered somewhere between consciousness and slumber when he heard the word said with such utter clarity that it startled him. Henry jerked up, stunned for an instant that his mother's voice had been as strong and distinctive as in the past. Her speech had come and gone during her incapacity the past few weeks, but the utterances had been incoherent mumbles rather than anything comprehensible. Nurses would describe those sounds as a manifestation of his mother's thoughts and dreams coming to the surface, perhaps unintelligible to us but so real to her it was as if she were reliving a past experience in that moment. This comforted Henry. Despite being ill and physically confined to a bed, his mother could wander freely through the images and scenes that comprised the tapestry of her seventy-four years of life.

He stood and studied her beautifully wrinkled face, relaxed and motionless, her head covered with the soft, blue, chemo hat that the ladies from the auxiliary had insisted she wear. His mother was still very much asleep, comatose perhaps, but the word had been unmistakable: *Rehoboth.*

Henry walked from the bed and peered out the fifth-floor window and down onto the half-full parking lot lined with Bradford pear trees popping with healthy, white blossoms. Did this singular word she'd said provide some insight into his dying mother's thoughts? His mind wandered, as it had been prone to do during the past month, when he'd spent sixteen hours a day positioned feet from his mother in the oncology ICU of the DC hospital.

He turned from the window and gazed at the patient, now an empty husk in so many respects, and wondered how much longer. He'd spent so much time in the room that even the pungent institutional smells that bothered him at first had seemingly dissipated. The medical machinery and its serpentine tubes connected to her body droned on, signaling that she still somehow clung to life.

The unpleasant sensation of being an outsider—a "Visitor," according to the lapel sticker he regularly affixed to his chest after checking in—had faded after the first few days. Henry learned the routine and made his best effort to memorize the names of the nurses and the shifts they worked. He'd grown fond of the plump, frizzy-haired elderly lady, Ethel, who served coffee at the stand outside the cafeteria. At first she had seemed almost inappropriately chipper when he peeled dry, worn, dollar bills from his wallet and handed them over, but Henry had come to enjoy the escape that her smile and banter brought. The respite was short-lived; seeing his mother hovering that close to death and looking it head-on sapped his energy and resolve. Even tougher for Henry was the dichotomy that the hospital forced him to see, that while he awaited a dark finality, he'd see smiling mothers clasping new life in their arms while being wheeled out into sunny April afternoons to waiting cars and the future beyond.

That Henry had grown accustomed to his new routine did little to assuage his guilt, a remorse borne from the long hours away from his family and law firm. Shannon had been his bedrock during the ordeal, handling homework and traveling sports leagues and all other things kid related. "What would I do without you, babe?" he'd tiredly asked one night in the dark of their bedroom, as he took her hand and squeezed it hard just to feel the life. She'd brought Lawrence and Lilly to the hospital room twice early on when their grandmother was still lucid, but those days were past, and Henry thought it would only upset them to see their Nanna now. It upset him.

"Hank, the cases, the work, the job. They will all be here for you when you're back," his firm's managing partner, Lester Wickett, had reassured Henry through thick eyeglasses from across the formidable oak desk. "Seriously, you're a producer. You've earned some time away. Just look at the hours you've billed and the clients you've brought in. And a wife and two beautiful kids—I don't know how you find time for it all. Listen, go be with your mom, and we'll hold down the fort."

Henry had given up so much for his career. He recalled the numerous vacations he'd pulled out of at the eleventh hour and pressured Shannon and the kids to go and enjoy without him. He appreciated the partnership's reassurance but feared it would ring hollow if an up-and-coming junior partner stepped in and somehow worked miracles on Henry's caseload. There just wasn't enough time to satisfy all his obligations.

Henry heard a light knock at the door, quiet but enough to reel his thoughts and attention back to the present. He looked up as the door opened.

"I thought I'd check in before heading out for the day." Dr. Elsa Rosenstein, the most regular of his mother's oncologists, strode confidently into the room with a faint smile.

Henry looked forward to his interactions with Dr. Rosenstein. She exhibited objective pragmatism when relaying diagnoses and opinions, but her demeanor conveyed something softer and more human. She injected fleeting happiness into his day.

"How does she seem? I reviewed the records and it didn't look like there've been changes." She walked to the foot of the bed to get a closer look at her patient.

"Yeah, more of the same." Henry joined her. A silence followed. "Though she did say a word. She was still asleep when she did, but she hasn't spoken like that for a while."

The doctor smiled and looked at him. "Really? What word?"

"Rehoboth." Henry paused, reminiscing. "We vacationed there when I was young. My parents rented the same house every July. It was the highlight of my year." Henry smiled sadly as the happy memories and emotions rushed within him. "We started when I was twelve or so. It was really the only family tradition we had. My mom and I kept going after my dad passed, all the way through college and the summer following my first year of law school."

"Ahh, Rehoboth Beach." Dr. Rosenstein placed her hands on her hips. "You know, I've never been. Growing up in the Midwest made it tough for my family to make beach trips, and when we did it was usually to someplace tacky and jam-packed with tourists. Usually Florida." She grimaced and they both laughed. "Were they good trips? Good memories?"

Henry looked at his mother. "Yeah, they were great. In some ways it was the only time that my mom, dad, and I were together. We actually had time to enjoy each other's company without distraction." The doctor nodded. "I miss those trips," Henry continued. "Bittersweet memories. I've been meaning to go with my own family, but I had to cancel the last few years because of work. My mom gave me some major grief for missing those vacations." He hesitated. "But rest assured, she regaled my kids with plenty of beach stories from when she took me long ago."

"Well, look at it this way. Your mom is content right now. I can only surmise that she said the word because she's reliving some old, happy memory—probably the same sort that you have of those beach trips. And to her it may seem real—a dream, but more—as if she were there now."

Henry smiled and looked at the doctor. "Thanks. That's comforting."

"Listen, you've been here a lot—too much over the last few weeks.

How 'bout you go home and get some sleep? Maybe come back with your family tomorrow." She touched his left shoulder. "You're a good son. It's OK to go home." She paused. "It's the right thing to do."

Henry nodded and managed again, almost as if he'd perfected the art, to suppress his tears. "Sounds like doctor's orders," he said as he faked a smile. He walked beside his mother, leaned over, and kissed her forehead. He reached down and took her hand within his and squeezed it hard.

That night as Henry slept, he found himself thirty years in the past. Science and medicine might classify his experience as a dream, but it was as authentic as any reality Henry had ever known.

"Come on, Indy! You can do it!"

From the sandy precipice, twelve-year-old Henry surveyed the chasm he and his beach friends had spent the better part of the afternoon digging. He tried to work up the courage to leap across the pit littered with broken pieces of seashells and rubber snakes—a Rehoboth Beach booby trap meant to thwart even the most enterprising adventurers.

Henry adjusted his soggy, brown, movie replica hat and glanced toward his parents' umbrella. His dad dozed but his mom was watching. This was harder than he thought it would be, but the kids were all watching, and it was too late to back out. His mother stuck her right hand out from the umbrella and gave a combination wave and thumbs-up. He pulled the hat's brim a bit higher to clear his field of vision and then charged, coming to a full sprint and then launching himself over the abyss. As he landed in the sand on the other side, he heard the kids cheer.

Suddenly, he was sitting in a worn wicker chair of the Rehoboth rental house with a *Choose Your Own Adventure* book splayed out on his lap. His stomach felt full and he remembered playing Frog Bog and winning a stuffed blue elephant at Funland. Henry smiled and looked beside him to his mother. "Mom, this is the happiest I've ever been."

His mother chuckled. "Oh, really? Well I'm delighted to hear that, Henry. If this is the happiest you've ever been in your twelve years, then your dad and I are doing something right this trip." She reached out and pushed Henry's bangs off his forehead and tucked them beneath his fedora.

After a moment, his mother grew a bit more serious. "No, for real, Henry, that's good to hear. It's really important to your dad and me that you're happy." She reached from her chair and grasped his hand and squeezed it hard.

Henry smiled and nodded. "I am."

"Good. Then make me one promise, please."

Henry paused and looked into her eyes. "Sure … what's that?"

"Just promise that you make time to care for yourself, for your friends, for your family, for everyone, and if that means vacationing at Rehoboth because it makes you or anyone important to you happy, then you do it."

"Mom, that's easy. I promise."

"Thatta boy, Indiana Jones."

The next thing Henry knew, he was tucked beneath his bed covers, exhausted but still too excited from the day's activities to sleep. Henry smiled and listened to the surf crash. He scratched stray sand out of his hair onto his sunburnt shoulders and told himself that, no matter what, he'd come back to the beach every summer for the rest of his life. It would make him happy, and besides, he'd just promised it.

"Hank, Hank, wake up, Hon. Wake up."

Disoriented. Just a bit longer. "Hank …" He opened his eyes. Shannon lay beside him in bed, wearing the snow-white terrycloth robe he'd given her two Christmases ago. For some reason it always smelled of citrus, an aroma that usually brought him comfort. "Hank, are you awake?" He looked into his wife's eyes. "It's the hospital. It's Dr. Rosenstein." He rolled from bed and took the phone from Shannon's hand as he walked to the bedroom window.

* * * * *

Henry and Shannon walked about twenty yards behind their two children on the wooden-planked boardwalk as the buttery smell of fresh popcorn hung in the humid night. It was crowded, as were most July evenings in Rehoboth, but Lawrence and Lilly knew not to get too far ahead. They'd been planning this excursion for weeks and knew the route cold but were slowed by the unwieldy, stuffed Funland prizes they carried. A distant thunderclap roared slowly across the water, sending the kids running back to their parents. Henry guided them out of the boardwalk stampede and to the walkway's edge. The kids grew silent as they fell spell to the crashing waves and noisy surf.

A bright light from a far-off ship struck Henry in the eyes and lassoed in his gaze. The surrounding sounds slowly sunk below the surface. Perception swayed and uncertainty washed over him. Henry felt off course in the moment.

The last three months since he'd lost his mother had been hard—an amalgamation of tears and sleepless nights and polite responses to endless condolences. It had been a different, foreign time. A chance for a new perspective, or perhaps an old one rediscovered. Another bolt of lightning flashed, this time without a following thunderclap. Henry refocused and looked again out at the sea; the ship's light had turned away from his view and the vessel crested out of sight.

He stared hard at the water. The same water that he'd seen as a child, that he'd spent countless hours splashing in while his parents—his mother—watched. The same water that his kids now enjoyed with Shannon and him.

"Mommy, Daddy, there's the street! Can we please go?" shouted a gleeful Lilly, acting every bit of the precocious seven-year-old princess that she was. Henry pivoted on the boardwalk toward his daughter and found himself back in the moment. "Nanna's favorite place is this way!" she exclaimed, as she pointed to the sign for Wilmington Avenue. "She used to tell us all about it."

Shannon reached out and took Henry's hand, smiling. "We should probably go or the kids will revolt." She bent over and took the stuffed prizes from her children in her other arm, freeing them. Lawrence started skipping with joy as the four of them turned away from the ocean and down the sidewalk. Henry instinctively reached into his pocket for his work phone and remembered, proudly, he'd left it on the rental cottage's nightstand.

Lawrence looked back, frustrated. "Come on, guys. Hurry, *please*!" The children sprinted ahead and then paused once reaching the stairs in front of their destination, waiting an eternal thirty seconds until Henry and Shannon caught up. They inspected the converted single-family home, its distinctive awning and American flag jutting out over the sidewalk. Time hadn't changed the business's appearance in decades so far as Henry could see.

"Ice cream parlor!" shouted Lilly, pointing at the hanging sign and again demonstrating her reading skills.

"The Royal Treat! This was Nanna's favorite, Dad," Lawrence chimed in. "She said she would bring you here when you were a kid."

Henry smiled and nodded. "We did indeed. And we always sat right there," motioning toward an unoccupied corner table.

"Nanna said it was her special place with you. And when you were young, she made you promise that when you had kids you would take us here." Lilly's excitement was evident.

"We asked Mom to bring us here the last few summers but she wouldn't. She said it had to be with you and she made us wait till you were here," declared Lawrence, adopting a formal tone.

For the first time in as long as he could remember, Henry felt at home in the present.

"And now you're here … *we're* here," uttered Lilly. She grinned, took her dad's hand in hers, and squeezed it hard. "Thanks for coming with us, Dad. I've been dreaming about this for so long."

A flood of nostalgia deluged Henry's present. He glanced from his family back toward the ocean. Suddenly, his future felt as broad and limitless as the sea. "Rehoboth," he uttered.

PAUL BARRONET IS AN ATTORNEY AND SPECIAL AGENT FOR A FEDERAL LAW ENFORCEMENT AGENCY. HIS FORAY INTO WRITING BEGAN WITH HIS SUBMISSION LAST YEAR TO THE REHOBOTH BEACH READS SHORT STORY CONTEST, AND HE IS DELIGHTED TO HAVE BEEN SELECTED FOR PUBLICATION AGAIN IN 2019. WHEN PAUL ISN'T WORKING OR WRITING FICTION, HE ENJOYS READING, EXERCISING, MOTORCYCLING, AS WELL AS VISITING REHOBOTH BEACH. HE LIVES IN CHESAPEAKE, VIRGINIA, WITH HIS WIFE, TESSA, AND HIS TWO DOGS, OXFORD AND VANDEVELDE.

Last Call

By Doug Harrell

A sliver of light sliced the dimness as a man in military uniform entered, squinting.

At the bar, a man in a red Phillies cap turned. "Welcome back from the front! Did you sink any enemy subs?"

Military-man delivered a snappy salute, then took off his cap and joined his friend. "We fired on one with the twelve-inch gun from Battery 519 but didn't sink it. Good thing, too, since it was a Navy sub in town for the big celebration. In any event, we were unlikely to inflict damage other than hearing loss with a one-sixteenth charge and no shell."

"I bet the kids loved it. This'll be a Fourth of July they'll never forget," said Phillies-cap.

"Oh boy did they—kids of all ages. We had a vet in one tour group who served at Fort Miles during the war. He must've been a hundred years old and was wearing his old Army duds. I felt like a faker standing next to him in this Halloween get-up."

"I bet he's got stories."

"Don't you know it. He said the Germans sank ships here in '42, before the coastal blackout. The first was a Norwegian tanker only six weeks after Pearl Harbor. A week later they got a cargo ship. Rescued sailors were being brought to Lewes, and the Army Air Corp was flying B-25 sub-hunters out of Dover. Oh, yeah, and he told us the first time they test-fired the big sixteen-inch gun, the concussion broke every window in town. After that, they always gave the town advance notice to open their windows."

"To celebrate not sinking one of ours or breaking any windows, let me buy you a cold one." Phillies-cap waved to the bartender. "Kyle, give us a Yuengling for my friend here and put a new head on my Dogfish."

Kyle drew the beers, but his thoughts were eight miles down the road in Rehoboth. After a few days to cool off, he wasn't so sure anymore. He set the beers in front of the two men.

"How was the turnout?" asked Phillies-cap.

"It gets better every year, and this was the best yet. So much of the fort has been restored and is accessible to the public now. We took kids up the fire control tower to spot the sub, and over to the battery to fire on it. We even took them to the mine control room to throw a switch we told them would activate the minefield that used to run across the floor of the bay from Lewes to Cape May."

"That can't be too interesting to a kid."

"Oh, but it is. We tell them a Nazi sub has been spotted trying to sneak through. When they flip the switch, we play a recording of an explosion and yell 'You got him!' I think they enjoy that most of all."

Phillies-cap pointed at his watch, and both men quaffed down the last of their beers. They paid and walked out, leaving Kyle alone with his thoughts.

Kyle had been tending bar at Pilots' Pub for a few days. The tips were lousy, but Kyle was a lousy bartender. He had needed a place to stay when he left Megan, and his friend Zach had fixed him up with a bedroom upstairs at the Pub in exchange for covering slow times—like the evening shift on the Fourth of July.

In his first few days, Kyle hadn't looked around much. Pilots' Pub felt like it had been there when the British bombarded the town in 1813, and it probably had. The walls were dark wood paneling, and the lights were low. Most bars on water have big glass windows, but Pilots' had none despite its location backing up to the canal.

The somber atmosphere matched Kyle's mood. He didn't like his day job, and he didn't want to marry Megan even if she was having his baby. Kyle didn't know what his life plan was, but he knew what it was not—at least not at twenty-four. He had always pictured himself in a big city like New York, downtown in a high-rise condo, the city lights twinkling below him as he sipped a beer on the balcony. He would be going to clubs, going to games, going everywhere—not hanging around at sea level in the town where he grew up.

All this made perfect sense a few days ago when he walked out the door and started driving. Reality hit when he realized he had no place to go. Shame arrived when he had to go back to pick up clothes and a few other things. He loved Megan. Certainly, he cared about her needs, but what about *his* life? Didn't it matter what he wanted?

He walked over to the old pictures on the walls. There were photos of pilots of various eras waving as they were ferried out to ships and a sepia print of the old, original pilot station. One entire wall was devoted to World War II. Kyle saw photos of the big pillboxes built into the dunes, their enormous guns projecting outward toward the camera. There were also photos of local Lewes boys smiling broadly as they prepared to ship out, many never to return. Pilots' Pub was working its magic on Kyle. It was a different kind of place—a place steeped in history. It made him feel part of something bigger.

Kyle turned and saw a thirtyish man sitting at the bar dressed in an old river pilot's uniform like in the pictures. "Oh, I'm sorry. I didn't hear you come in. What can I get you?"

The man gave a start, "Oh. Howdy, bub. All hail the king!"

"Come again?"

"What hay wagon did you fall off? Pull me a King Gambrinus."

"Sorry, I know we don't have it on draft. Let me check."

Kyle looked in the cooler, but the man objected, "I don't want no bottled sunshine. Gimme a draft of somethin' local."

"Dogfish Head is brewed right here in Milton," Kyle said.

"Milton! Gimme one of those." Kyle pulled it and set it at the man's elbow. Shaking his head, the man said, "No King. I've seen a lot of changes, and I've been against every damn one of 'em!" Then he smiled. "Sorry, bub, it's been a rough war for me. Manny Wiltbank at your service."

"Pleased to meet you. I'm Kyle. You're dressed like a river pilot. Are you part of the festivities this evening?"

"Festivities. That's an interestin' way to put it. Nope. I done my bit." Manny rubbed his chin. "I ain't never seen you before. When'd you start?"

"It's complicated. I don't really work here. I'm just hanging out while I figure out what to do with my life."

"That's a twist—the barkeep spillin' *his* guts."

"Sorry, you're right—"

"No, go ahead. It'd be nice to hear somebody else's troubles for a change. Your girl walk out on you?"

"More like I left her," said Kyle.

"You don't seem too gassed about it."

"To tell you the truth, I miss her already. I'm just not ready to settle down yet and be a father."

Manny huffed. "Go tell it to the Marines. Your girlfriend is pregnant and that's your cue to set sail and find yourself?"

"It doesn't sound too good when you say it like that."

"No, it don't. You ain't the first palooka whose short arm jumped the startin' gun. What I don't get is how you're standin' here. Ain't her daddy got a shotgun?"

"If he did, I'd be married or dead—pretty much the same thing."

"Not on your life! Pour yourself some borrowed brass and sit your rabbit-ass down and I'll tell you the difference."

Kyle was peeved, but if he was going to be abused there was no point in being thirsty, so he pulled himself a beer.

"So, in '44, I get sent out to bring a Norwegian tanker upriver to Sun Oil at Marcus Hook. It'd come across in the latest convoy."

"*1944*? Oh, I get it." Kyle realized that Manny was lecturing him in character.

After a stern look, Manny continued. "Norwegian ships weren't uncommon in those days. When the Nazis occupied Norway, most were at sea, so they just docked at Allied ports and started runnin' war supplies. A lot of 'em made port here on the river."

"Makes sense."

"So, they run me out to the ship, and I go up the ladder. Right away I get this queer feelin'. Somethin' ain't jake, but I can't put my finger on it. I try talkin' to the crew, but they don't speak English. On the bridge I meet the captain. He gives me command of the ship and I get her underway. Funny to think—outside of the U-boats, sailin' all the way across the Atlantic ain't nearly as tricky as sailin' up the Delaware River. Sure, you got storms and all, but on the river we have currents, and shoals, and tides to deal with. Anyway, I run 'er up to what I used to call the startin' line and radioed the password to shut off the mines. Then I start jabberin' like I always do when I'm on the river."

"Where is this going? I thought this was about me having to 'man up' and all that crap."

"Don't blow your wig. I'm gettin' to it. When I'm on the river, I talk whether anybody can understand me or not just to pass the time, and as we're headin' up, I'm just bumpin' my gums hopin' some of the chumps on the bridge might chime in and say somethin'. But only the captain talks, and even he don't say much. I'm comin' to a tricky stretch near Pea Patch Island and I'm tellin' him how we was originally the lower three counties of Pennsylvania, but we're Delaware now and not Maryland 'cause the Dutch had started a colony called Zwaanendael that got wiped out, when all the sudden he snaps, 'Please stop talking about this Zwaanendael.' Only when he said 'Zwaanendael,' he pronounces it *Tswaanendael*. You hear the difference? Tse-waanendael, not Ze-waanendael."

Kyle did, and he didn't care. He was cradling his chin with his elbows on the bar looking bored.

"Well, I heard that right away. Now I don't know Norwegian from Navaho, but I sure have heard a lot of it. Before the war, I ran Germans, too, and they're the only ones I ever heard pronounce a "Z" like that. I start puttin' things together. He's the only one talkin'—it's like everyone else is mute. I ask myself, 'What's a German doin' commandin' a ship of Norwegians who ain't speakin' no Norwegian up the Delaware River?' 'Nothin' good,' I answer myself. So real casual like, I'm reachin' for the radio when I feel a muzzle pressed against in my ribs. 'It will not be necessary to use the radio,' he tells me."

That perked Kyle up. "Damn! What'd he do?"

Manny frowned. "You mean what did *I* do?"

"Oh, right, what did *you* do?" Kyle asked, playing along.

"Well, right away, I don't do nothin'. I gotta think. Now that the cat's outta the bag, the captain starts barkin' orders. Meanwhile, along the shore, towns are shootin' off fireworks, lightin' up the sky—kinda like 'rockets' red glare,' and by the flashes I can see the crew is pullin' guns and stuff outta crates. I'm in a tough spot. Maybe if I do what they want, they'll let me go. But I know what they're after—our refineries. Socony-Vacuum over in Paulsboro is makin' the new crackin' catalyst, and Sun in Marcus Hook is makin' the high-octane aviation fuel. That's the juice that won the Battle of Britain, and that's givin' our flyboys the edge in the skies over France."

"Jesus!" said Kyle. "A whole ship of German commandos! I can't believe I never heard about this. What did you do?"

"At first, I don't know what to do. There's no way I'm gonna overpower four guys on the bridge with a gun in my ribs, but then I get thinkin' about the war, and all the boys over there countin' on us to keep 'em supplied. I realize those Krauts ain't never gonna get that tub up to Marcus Hook without me. They'd get to the moon and back easier. I'm thinkin' I can drift outta the channel and run her aground before they catch on."

"We're comin' up to Pea Patch Island on our port side usin' the Finn's Point light, and I command for a course change to port. Now the channel there runs close to the island, and I'm easin' her over a little too far. It's givin' me a funny feelin' to do it, I won't lie. Meanwhile, the captain is gettin' suspicious. Turns out he knows about rivers, and he sees I'm a few degrees off linin' up the New Castle front and rear range lights. There are flood lights on over at Fort Mott on the Jersey side, so I point to the gun emplacements. No way for him to know they were built to keep the Spanish off the river in '98."

"I don't know how much time I got before he starts tellin' the wheelhouse to correct course, so I ring the engine room to increase speed five knots. Now Fritzie knows somethin's up, and he's tryin' to push me off the controls when the ship runs aground hard and everybody's knocked over but me. I feel a hard punch in my ribs, but I'm still standin'. The punch is a shot from Fritzie's pistol, but he just wings me. While they're sprawled about, I make tracks over the side so fast you'd think I'm Jesse Owens.

"Hittin' the water from that height knocks the wind outta me, but I snap to and start swimmin' toward Pea Patch. Them Krauts open fire, but it's dark and they can't see nothin'. Problem is, I'm hit worse'n I thought. I can't hardly move my right arm, and I'm bein' pulled downriver with the current faster than I'm movin' across it. I must be bleedin' pretty good 'cause I'm gettin' weak. I know if I don't get to the island before I'm swept past, there's no way I'm gonna make it to the riverbank. I give it all I got with my left arm, flappin' like a crazed killdeer, 'til I'm so tapped out it's all I can do to tread water. There I am with water up to my chin, cryin' as I watch the silhouette of Fort

Delaware recede into the distance."

"Why were you crying? Was it the pain?"

"I'm cryin' because all I can think about is gettin' back to my wife and little girl and what their lives will be like if I don't make it."

"Then what happened?"

"What do you think happened, numbskull? I drowned. What's left of me is swept down river and washed out to sea, never to be found."

"How do you know this? Was he a relative of yours?"

"You're a funny guy, you know that."

"What happened to the Germans?" asked Kyle.

"Who cares? You're missin' the point."

"What's the point?"

"Cogitate on it—you'll think of somethin'." Manny stood up. "Time for me to shove off and meet my gal. She's been waitin' on me long enough."

Although he had been the butt of Manny's sarcasm, Kyle wanted to give Manny a souvenir. "Hang on a sec." He went into the back and grabbed a Pilots' Pub logo mug, but when he came back, Manny was gone, leaving only his untouched beer.

Kyle looked at the clock—ten minutes to quitting time. There was nothing he needed to do, so he wandered over to the pictures. Further along the wall, he found a framed article about a Nazi attempt to sabotage the refinery in Marcus Hook. It read in part, "Inspection of the vessel revealed substantial quantities of plastic explosives, incendiary devices, and other commando paraphernalia. This incident serves as a potent reminder of the role all citizens must play to keep our coast safe." At the bottom was a picture of a man named Helmanus Wiltbank with the caption, "Hero of the Bay." The picture was yellowed and grainy, but the man looked a lot like Manny. Kyle figured Manny must be a grandson. That would explain how he knew so much about it.

After closing the bar, Kyle pulled on a baseball cap and went to King's for an ice cream cone. As he strolled along Second Street a sudden breeze came up and blew his cap into St. Peter's graveyard. He chased after it until it came to rest against a shiny gray tombstone behind a fresh grave. The name on the stone read

EDITH PAYNTER WILTBANK
December 5, 1921 – June 30, 2019

Kyle thought it must surely be a coincidence until he saw what was written below.

Relict of Helmanus Wiltbank
Hero of the Bay
May 20, 1907 – July 4, 1944
Rest in Peace, God knows where

Kyle gasped. Manny wasn't *pretending* to be Helmanus Wiltbank. Manny *was* Helmanus Wiltbank. Kyle choked up at the thought of Manny dying on the river when all he wanted was to return to his wife and daughter. As of today, his beloved Edith had been waiting for him for seventy-five years.

Kyle pulled out his cell phone and called Megan. In a clumsy torrent of words, he apologized for being such an ass and begged her forgiveness. She was happy, if skeptical, and she had a right to be. But things were different now. *He* was different now.

A tear rolling down his cheek, Kyle laid his hand on the tombstone. "Thank you, Manny. Welcome home, buddy. Welcome home."

DOUG HARRELL IS ALMOST A NATIVE OF DELAWARE, HAVING BEEN TRANSFERRED TO WILMINGTON BY DUPONT AT THE TENDER AGE OF FIVE. AFTER THIRTY-TWO YEARS IN THE PLASTICS INDUSTRY AND ACHIEVING THE MAGIC AGE OF FIFTY-NINE AND A HALF, HE CHUCKED IT IN LAST YEAR TO PURSUE HIS LIFELONG DREAM OF WRITING MYSTERIES. HIS STORY, "LAST CALL," HAD ITS GENESIS IN A CONVERSATION YEARS AGO ABOUT FORT MILES. DOUG WAS ON CAPE HENLOPEN BEACH WATCHING AN OLD WARSHIP BEING HAULED OUT TO SEA WHEN A NEARBY MAN RECOUNTED THAT HIS GERMAN UNCLE HAD SERVED ON A U-BOAT IN WWII. THEY HAD DONE RECONNAISSANCE AROUND CAPE HENLOPEN FOR AN ATTACK THAT WAS NEVER MOUNTED. THIS GOT HIM THINKING, "WHAT IF …?"

Shells

By Laura Nelson Selinsky

Seven identical seashells left fine white powder on her fingertips. Chalky. Pale and probably as old as she was.

Endless sand had scoured off any hint of sheen, leaving the shells dull against the cover of *Snug Harbor Silence*, the mystery she'd brought to pass the time. Even the shells' scalloped ridges were worn smooth. *Beauty ground away by time and tide*, Ruth thought. *Like every old woman on the beach.*

A boy's impatient *humph* startled her. Ruth dropped her grandson's shells beside her chair, and he scooped them up. Max arrayed them in a line, neatly paralleling the straight shadow line cast by her chair. Her silent grandson, beautiful as a Vermeer and distant as the moon.

"Sorry, buddy. I forgot you were waiting for those." *I forgot you.*

He didn't respond, except to lift and reorder the shells, examining each minutely before repositioning it between its indistinguishable brethren. One he weighed in his hand before placing it last.

"Your mommy and Sophie are in the water," she said to break the sphere of silence that surrounded their umbrella.

Sounds rarely moved Max. Gulls and vendors and children's voices, even his sister Sophie's voice, all the merry jangle of the beach, shut out. She watched her grandson move the seventh shell back three places in the line.

Waves surged and broke, surged and broke, as Ruth waited for a response she knew wasn't coming. Max picked up his shells and moved to the other side of her chair. There the umbrella shade laid down a curve of shadow. He bent to place the shells along the gray arc beside her pallid feet.

Time was when she'd have painted her toenails like shining seashells. Her toes looked especially ashen compared to the florid flip-flops that her granddaughter Sophie had picked out for her birthday. The card had said they were from Max, too. But he did not care about holidays or flip-flops or old women on the beach. She studied him as he moved that troublesome shell from the third place to the sixth. When had she stopped dreaming of a grandson who loved her in the demonstrative way her granddaughter did?

Sophie's sputtering, shrieking laugh cut through sunbathers' chatter and the steady roll of surf. Ruth peered into the glare and made out her daughter Anna and her granddaughter kicking out through the breakers. *Teaching her to bodysurf.* A grin stretched Ruth's beach-chapped lips. Sophie paused, treading water, and waved. Ruth waved wildly in return. Sophie was gulping in breaths, ready to fling her body through the breakers.

"Look! Sophie's gonna ride in on the next big one." *Look up, Max. Just this once.*

Max's grunt of frustration stole her attention from his big sister. He grabbed his shells off the arc of shadow and squeezed them in his fists, rocking for a moment. Then he slithered under Ruth's low-slung chair. She laughed as his little-boy roundness joggled her seat. But he popped out on the far side and returned to his shells without any answering giggle.

Again, he laid out the shells, first through seventh, alike as they could be. As he bent, close beside her, she saw the first scarlet creep of sunburn along the waistband of his shorts. "Mom's gonna have to put some more sunblock on you, buddy. Don't want you burned." Her hand twitched toward the beach bag. But only his mother could put lotion on him. He'd wailed that one time she'd tried.

Suddenly, small wet hands grabbed hers. *Sophie—back already!*

"Nana, I did it! I surfed, like, a hundred miles. Did you see?"

Ruth jerked her head up to smile. "Of course. You were just perfect. The perfect bodysurfer. Practically professional." Drops of seawater streaked down her paperback's cover and flicked across her knees.

Max moved his shells away from the trampling feet and realigned them.

"Now we're going to get ice cream." Sophie pulled away, nudging her brother with a watermelon-pink swim-shoe. "Max, ice cream! Do you want to come?"

Max moved two shells, the third and the fourth, reversing their positions. Ruth bit her lip as she caught her daughter's eye. "Nah, we've got such a good spot here. How about you and your mommy bring me rocky road from Starkey's?" She saw a bittersweet smile flash across her daughter's face as they turned toward the boardwalk.

"We'll bring you some back," Sophie called, tugging at her mother's hand.

Ruth watched them vanish into the colorful cloud of beachgoers. She thought suddenly that everyone else would vanish like a flock of butterflies, migrating into perpetual sunshine. Only she and Max would remain on the beach, silent and solitary as shells.

Seven swift clicks on her plastic chair arm made her turn. At first, nothing seemed changed. Max crouched beside her, tracing the umbrella's shadow with one little hand. He did not raise his head. But seven shells were lined up for her inspection. Each was infinitesimally smaller than the one beside it.

Worn shells, chalk white, but with precious, singular beauty. Ruth stared for a long moment and felt unfamiliar joy rise.

"These are perfect, Max. Just perfect."

At about nine, Laura Nelson Selinsky wrote an opera (libretto and score) about which her elderly parents still laugh. Since then, she's been a naturalist, a pastor, and a teacher of (no surprise) literature, writing, and mythology. After coaching her students to wins in poetry, prose, and public speaking competitions, she thought she should also enter a writing contest. Laura writes both fiction and nonfiction in a variety of genres, and her first novel is scheduled for November of 2019.

Judges' Comments

A tight, finely crafted story. Two children contrasted; one, a perfect little girl, bodysurfing in the ocean waves, a daughter any mother would wish for; the other, a boy playing with his shells, so disconnected, so noncommunicative he is thought to be not quite right. Victory comes to both children. For the little girl, it is expected, a part of growing up. For the boy, it is a simple, yet startling, success and its profound implications resound to all of us. This brief story is an example of how unobtrusively and simply the profoundest of events can be captured in a single unremarkable moment.

What I enjoyed most about "Shells" is the precise, deliberate word choice that carries and bolsters the short piece of prose. Reading it, one can easily tell that the writer spent a significant amount of time editing and tightening up her piece to make sure it fired on all cylinders. This compact story suggests a larger context, which is one of the hallmarks of quality short fiction.

All in a Day's Dream

By Paula Kotowski

My phone died on my morning walk. Looking back, I think that's when it all started. Without the distraction of Pandora blasting Kenny Chesney in my ears, I was left to my own thoughts.

Or maybe it was because I'd changed my usual routine. Start at the Henlopen. Walk the boardwalk two and a half times. Turn at Funland to get in my three miles. What's the temperature on the Thrasher's display? What time does Atlantic Jewelry open? Any dolphins this morning?

But that day, I turned west from the Henlopen parking lot, doubled back the way I had come, and hung a right on North First Street. I couldn't begin to tell you why. Maybe I needed a change of scenery; maybe the rut I felt I was in wasn't just the route.

Anyway, two houses from the corner, the music died. I stopped, fiddled with plugs and buttons, and concluded that 0% charge really does mean 0% charge.

As I stood there, I took a closer look at the house in front of me. It was an older place, smaller than most others on the street. The tan siding had taken on a distinct hint of green, and the blue shutters had faded to dingy gray. One shutter dangled by a single hinge. Trees and shrubs I knew were once lovingly planted were in need of a trim, and the lawn could certainly use a manicure.

I chuckled at my own poor attempt at humor, and I guess that's what got my daydreaming juices flowing. As I decided to walk on, with nothing else to amuse my brain, I began to weave the tale …

The house is owned and inhabited by an elderly lady named Mary.

No, not Mary. Too common. Martha. No. Muriel. Yeah, Muriel.

The house is owned and inhabited by an elderly lady named Muriel. She's eighty-one years old and has lived in the house for fifty-six of those years. Muriel's husband is Henry.

Is Henry or was Henry? Is Henry alive or dead? Or maybe he went for a pack of cigarettes and never came back? Nope. Not the type. Poor Henry is dead.

Muriel's husband was Henry; everyone called him Hank. But he's been gone for almost fifteen years now. Muriel and Hank have a daughter named Constance, Connie for short.

What's Constance's story? I'll have to think about that.

Muriel and Hank met at a Catholic youth dance in Wilmington. Henry was five feet ten inches tall and slender but had a bearing that made him look ten feet tall and had dark, wavy movie-star hair and luminescent green eyes. Muriel was pretty in a girl next door sort of way. She was sweet and shy and smitten with Hank the moment they met.

They married right out of high school and settled into an attic apartment on East Cleveland Avenue in Newark. Hank took classes at the university and worked the occasional odd job, while Muriel ran the cash register at the local drugstore.

Maybe the drugstore was Happy Harry's. When did Happy Harry's open? I should look that up.

Eventually, Hank went to work for …

Not DuPont. Not everybody in Delaware works for DuPont, for God's sake.

Eventually, Hank went to work for a fast-growing electronics company, and they bought a house in Ogletown. Muriel got a job as a secretary in the local elementary school, cooked and cleaned like a good little wife, and waited for babies to arrive.

OK. So far, so good. Maybe too good. Every story needs an unexpected twist.

Hank's job involved some traveling. Some weeks he'd be gone from Monday to Thursday. *It's hard to go about the business of baby-making when your husband isn't around,* thought Muriel. But Hank assured her that the world of electronics was about to explode, "and I want to be the one lighting the fuse."

The first year he was away so much was hard on her, but luckily Muriel made some good friends among the young teachers at the school. Spending time with them helped ease the loneliness. They invited her to birthday celebrations and Tupperware parties, and, when school ended for the summer, they took Muriel on her first trip to the beach. And for the second time in her life, Muriel was smitten.

Which, I think, must have something to do with her ending up in the little house in Rehoboth. Hmmm …

Meanwhile, Hank with his movie-star hair and big personality was making some new friends of his own. Or, at least, one particular new friend.

Uh, oh. Not sure if I like where this is going. Good old Hank, who I already decided wouldn't run off. What's he up to now?

She was a couple of years older than Hank. They met at a convention in Phoenix.

A convention? Really? Oh, well … forgive the cliché.

The affair was brief. Just a fling that weighed heavily on Hank's conscience. But despite the exchange of office addresses, Hank never expected to hear another word from her.

So, he was quite taken aback when a letter landed on his desk about three months later.

And I bet he was even more taken aback by her news!

There was never any question in his mind about what Hank would do. The woman had no interest in raising a kid alone, nor did she have any interest in Hank. Hank knew he had to confess to Muriel; he knew he had to find a way to raise his child.

Their conversation was a hard one. Tears of hurt and anger. Sobs of guilt and remorse. But, gradually, they developed a plan.

No one gave a second thought to the young couple as they moved into the cottage on First Street in Rehoboth. Just another working man with his stay-at-home wife and their adorable baby girl, Connie. After the baby arrived, staying upstate would have attracted way too much attention, so Muriel had chosen to start their new life at the beach she loved.

And that's where they stayed. That's where Connie grew up, Cape Henlopen Class of '81. Hank, of course, is gone now, and Connie married, moved to Colorado, and only gets back east every couple of years.

But Muriel is still here.

* * * * *

I found myself walking past that run-down little house a lot. I'd pause for a moment each time, thinking about Muriel, Henry, and Connie.

One morning, there she was. Well, not really Muriel, of course, but a petite, elderly woman, meticulously sweeping the few steps that led to the front door. The sight stopped me in my tracks.

"Good morning," not-really-Muriel said. "I've noticed you walking by so many times, my dear. You always seem to linger a bit, like you're looking for something or someone. I'm Sarah. Would you like to come in for a bit of conversation and a cup of tea?"

So, Muriel was really Sarah? And was there a Henry? A Connie? Do daydreams ever come true?

"I'd love to," I replied. I could hardly contain myself as I followed Sarah up the short, brick path to her front door. "So," I ventured, "have you lived here long?"

"Oh, my, yes," she answered. "I have lived in Rehoboth my whole life. Born and raised right here in this house. After my siblings all moved away and my parents died, I didn't see much sense in going anywhere else. So now I'm just an old maid with only my cats for company."

Wow, I thought. I missed that one by a mile. I took a deep breath. "Well, Sarah, how about that cup of tea, and you can tell me the whole story."

PAULA KOTOWSKI SOLD HER FIRST SHORT STORY TO AMERICAN GIRL MAGAZINE AT THE AGE OF TEN. BUT WRITING TOOK A BACKSEAT DURING HER TWENTY-SEVEN YEARS AS A PUBLIC-SCHOOL EDUCATOR AND COUNSELOR IN MONTGOMERY COUNTY, PENNSYLVANIA. SINCE MOVING TO THE LEWES-REHOBOTH BEACH AREA IN 2001, PAULA HAS BEEN A CONTRIBUTOR TO THE LEWES HISTORICAL SOCIETY JOURNAL AND HANDLES PUBLICITY AND PRESS RELEASES FOR READ ALOUD DELAWARE IN SUSSEX COUNTY. IN 2006, SHE SELF-PUBLISHED 50/50: A GENERATION OF WOMEN REFLECTS AND IN 2009 CO-AUTHORED (WITH KITTY COLE) COLE'S MEMOIR, SAND IN MY SHOES. PAULA RECEIVED RECOGNITION FOR HER WORK FROM DELAWARE BEACH LIFE AND THE REHOBOTH BEACH WRITERS' GUILD IN THEIR SHORT STORY CONTESTS IN 2009 AND 2010. AS FOR THE INSPIRATION FOR "ALL IN A DAY'S DREAM," PAULA SAYS SHE'S JUST AN INCURABLE DAYDREAMER!

The Admiral and The Ensign

By Maria Masington

My parents packed me up mid-semester from my teaching position at an upstate community college and drove to my snowbird Uncle Walter's Rehoboth beach house while he wintered in Miami. They did this because a therapist had told them that I, their thirty-six-year-old man-baby, needed to change the people, places, and things around me. I'd only been there a few times before, since my family always went to Ocean City, New Jersey, where ironically, they don't sell booze within the city limits.

At first, I thought I'd won the alcoholic lottery this time—not a rehab, not a hospital, not house arrest—a beach town. Then, my parents informed me that my legal fees and three stints in treatment had exhausted their resources and that, unless they started printing money in their garage, they'd be eating cat food in their old age. The joke made my stomach hurt. When the consequences of my disease were brought to my attention, I wanted to numb the shame.

I was being delivered to a beach in Delaware because it was free and, since my driver's license had been revoked, would keep me far from my parents. I thought they would at least take me out to lunch or offer to take me to Peebles for supplies, but they literally drove away the minute I was far enough out of the car not to pull off a limb.

"Thanks for a lovely morning," I shouted, as they tore off. My father gave me the finger. I got it. I was the reason they couldn't retire, and they probably dreaded the sound of the phone ringing. It was all about me, all the time.

I went inside what my uncle referred to as his "bungalow" and made a beeline for the fridge, hoping to find beer. I was sidetracked by a menagerie of magnets including *I heart Dewey Beach* and the oldie but goodie *Delawhere?* Fantasizing about what might be inside, I gingerly opened the door. Debating if I should pour out what I found or drink myself to death, I was dismayed and relieved to see that it held only a box of Arm & Hammer baking soda and condiments that looked like they'd been there since 1993.

I started opening cabinets, searching for a stray bottle or the motherload of an entire stash. Nada. One drawer was stuffed with takeout menus from Grotto's, Go Fish, and other nearby spots and a wine list from a place called The Cultured Pearl. Another drawer contained cooking implements—the very sight of corkscrews and a "shuck it" bottle opener made my mouth water. There were swizzle sticks shaped like mermaids, still-folded drink umbrellas, and beer can cozies from every 5K race he'd run. Uncle Walter also had a Dogfish Head Crafted Brewed Ales opener mounted on the kitchen wall, so I suspected there had been some good parties here.

My last drink was before we'd gotten in the car at ten a.m., two hours ago. I reminded myself that my sole job was to stay sober.

It looked like I was in a little suburb, so I pulled up Google Maps and started toward the beach. I walked in the frigid February air down onto the sand, snow squalling around me like confetti, so dense that I couldn't see the ocean. But I felt the spit of the Atlantic, snowflakes sticking to my eyelashes, and icicles forming in my beard. The frosty sand crunched with every step, and if I were not such a spineless loser, I would have walked into the sea. Who was that author? Virginia Woolf? The one who filled her pockets with rocks and drowned herself. She was a far braver soul.

As I walked, I kept adjusting my gait up and down the sand to avoid the freezing water hitting my leather Toms.

Again and again, like the ocean coming in and going out, how many times had I gone without and then given in—twenty-four hours, two weeks, five-and-a-half months sober—and then blown it? Classes, sobriety tests, relationships, all failed. Where was the unimaginable triumph of driving without worrying when a cop car pulled up next to me? Taking a woman out to dinner and remembering it the next day? Not lying to myself that I would only have one drink? I took a piece of driftwood, cocked my arm, and threw it unceremoniously. It arched in the air and thudded into the water five feet out. Splat. Dead wood like me—controlled by the ocean, unable to manage anything about itself. Eight more hours and then I could go to bed sober. My head hurt, but I walked the shivery, misty beach until I was exhausted. I Ubered home, hoping I'd be too tired to think, but by the time I got to Walter's, I was jumpy and couldn't sleep. My insides felt like the bumper cars at Funland.

* * * * *

I awoke confused and sick. My weeklong, horribly managed, self-orchestrated detox had included two visits to the emergency room, a black eye of unknown origin, body odor that would put a goat to shame, and $850 worth of damage to my uncle's pristine home—and those were the least traumatic parts. I had, however, miraculously emerged from the high drama without having had a drink.

I had decided to spend every single minute of every single day busy. An off-season Uber driver made a killing those first months carting me around for groceries, therapy, and recovery meetings. Not needing to pay rent, a Venmo account and math degrees kept me fed and watered. I created a webpage and left flyers every place that would let me. Parents whose kids were failing calculus or had to improve their SAT scores wanted my services. People will pay a lot of money for diplomas and college admissions, and once the kids' grades improved, so did word-of-mouth referrals. I knew nothing about adulting or being a decent human being, but mastering numbers requires no people skills. I taught at Uncle Walt's kitchen table, while parents played Candy Crush in the living room.

I kept the "evidence" in the bedroom: journals therapists made me keep, reams of recovery literature, and a trashcan brimming with Pepsi cans, sandwich wrappers, and refuse from Candy Kitchen—wadded bags from gummy sharks, pistachio fudge, and chocolate haystacks. When I wanted to drink, I ate sweets. I woke up, called my chauffeur, went to therapy, exercised, went to recovery meetings, tutored, and spent afternoons at the Lewes and Rehoboth libraries.

I also met every day with an old guy the local recovery community called The Admiral. We met when I was texting at a meeting. He leaned over the guy sitting between us, looked me in the eye, and said, "Have some respect." After the meeting he said, "Since you like using your phone so much, call me every day before nine in the morning." Then he put on his US Navy ball cap and walked away.

According to The Admiral, I was attempting a "geographic cure"; I believed moving would fix my problems, but as he pointed out, I was still stuck with myself. I felt bullied and a little bit like a pet project but still wanted a life beyond seventh graders who'd rather be skateboarding than doing math. This dude in the World's Best Pop-Pop T-shirt and sea-foam Crocs was the only person on earth who had not given up on me.

"When we go into the meeting, don't share," The Admiral said. "No one wants what you have."

"But my old life coach told me I need closure."

"OK," he replied. "Sit there and closure mouth." He made air quotes over "closure."

"LOL" I said, to which he told me to shut up.

                    * * * * *

Spring was hard because women showed up at the beach in droves. "No relationships for a year? That's impossible!"

"Oh yeah," said The Admiral. "I forgot what a great catch you are."

"Oh yeah," I said, and once again, shut up.

"Learn how to care for something other than yourself!" he barked, so I bought pothos plants from Giant because, like me, they're hard to kill and, unlike me, they grow fast.

In April, he said he had less free time because his family would be visiting every weekend, so he brought a Rehoboth Animal Shelter cat to the house. "Keep it alive," he said, and drove off. I named her "The Captain."

I expected resisting those of the female persuasion would be the biggest challenge that summer, but it was glassware. On tables outside restaurants, in storefront windows, in tan hands on the beach—beautiful glassware. Sculpted bottles, tumblers, flutes, mugs, and wine glasses filled with frothy ambers, icy silvers, deep rubies, and soft yellows that, if I stayed sober, I'd never enjoy again. It was more than wanting a drink; it was jealousy that other people could drink without disaster and I couldn't. I ran more, bought a pink cat collar and leash from Critter Beach, walked the neighborhood with The Captain, and tried not to romanticize my drinking days.

My parents never contacted me. I emailed, inviting them to visit and got "Thanks, but no thanks." I texted "Hi! Luv & miss u!" All I got back was a thumbs up emoji.

"Who could blame them?" growled The Admiral, his life now a constant barrage of my nonsense and histrionics. My three a.m. texts read, "I think I'm going to pick up!" His seven a.m. responses read, "Don't believe everything you think." My emails explained that recovery meetings weren't working for me. Return emails informed me that they'd happily refund my misery at the door.

Sometimes, he was nicer. When I called, crying so hard that I couldn't speak, he said, "Ensign, don't give up five minutes before the miracle and don't bother reiterating that you don't believe in miracles."

In May, when I was ninety days sober, he had started calling me "Ensign" which, according to Wikipedia, is the lowest officer rank in the US Navy.

* * * * *

Uncle Walter met a lady in Florida, so he spent less time in Delaware that year. He graciously invited me to stay into spring and summer, but when he was home, it was AARP party central. The Admiral decided I needed to be out of the house.

"I'll be fine," I said. "I have a master's degree in pure math. I think I'm smart enough to navigate backyard barbeques and bridge clubs."

"Oh yeah, I forget how smart you are. It's been five whole minutes since you reminded me," said the Admiral. "Ensign, you don't hang out at the barber shop if you don't want a haircut. Also, FYI, you are going to drink again because you don't think of anyone but yourself. You're going to have to start doing service work."

The gall of this guy. But I knew deep down that I could very, very, easily drink again.

Not wanting to give up on the dream of being a functioning, sober adult, I agreed and imagined myself volunteering in a cool hat and apron, ladling soup to thankful needy people like a hero. The Admiral had other plans.

The first week Walter was home, and I was ordered to stay elsewhere for seven days, I lived in his widowed neighbor's guest room and spent the days weeding, fertilizing, and mulching, which is much more exhausting than teaching algebra.

Walter had apparently been instructed not to invite me to anything and the Admiral took it upon himself to give assignments. "Our friend Mary is very pregnant. Go amuse her three-year-old." "Our friend Mitch broke his leg. Go clean his house." "My Navy buddy has cancer; you're sitting with him during chemo."

I worked harder than I had in years and kept my brain active with tenth-grade geometry, but there were still physical and mental cravings I could not extinguish. Some nights I went to bed at eight p.m. so I wouldn't drink. I screamed in the shower because the pain was so raw. I wept when I felt like I needed booze more than air.

Walter was always polite enough to clean the house before he flew south, but I could still smell beer in the floorboards and gin sweating from the bungalow's pores. Each time I tortured myself, inspecting the garbage and recycling for bottles like I was scared I would find my former best friends treated like trash.

Every single, solitary day, in addition to staying sober and helping people, I was also expected to look at my character flaws and consider the monumental task of cleaning up the train wreck of my personal life. This, we both knew, was going to take years. The Admiral hassled me about topics like "sloth" and "gluttony." Then he expected me to think about apologizing not only to my parents, employers, landlords, and students, but also to my ex-wife.

"My ex-wife? The Pitbull? She's a nut job, and she's mean."

"You picked her," said The Admiral. "I guess I misunderstood. I thought you totaling her car, wetting the bed, having seizures, and chasing other women contributed to her insanity and temperament. Forgive me."

I sighed. "Touché," to which he told me, yet again, to shut up.

In January, I got a fulltime gig teaching SAT-prep courses and tutoring at a learning center, where I could focus on the relationships I am best at: the ones with numbers, fractions, and decimal points. Walter said I was a good maintenance man/yard person and could stay six more months if I couch-surfed with friends when he was there. I learned to avoid blocks with liquor stores that called my name and to navigate around restaurant patios where normal people drink normally.

Throughout the year, The Admiral invited me to join his ranks at Easter dinner, Dewey Beach Movie night, Fourth of July fireworks, the Sea Witch Festival, Thanksgiving, Christmas, and the champagne-associated holiday of New Year's Eve. I was sort of a part of his family and sort of like a pet he didn't have the heart to put down.

* * * * *

It's now February again. I bundle up and walk to the beach. I stand at the shoreline, the sea spray glazing my hair. With gloved fingers, I gently open an envelope The Admiral gave me the night before, with "Do not open until 2/17!" written in Sharpie across the front. Inside a Post-It note reads, "Here's to finally figuring out the equation, Lieutenant Junior Grade." I guess I have risen in rank.

The note is stuck to a golden coin with recovery symbols on it and a Roman numeral; I gingerly slide it into my pocket. Then I pick up a smooth stone, cock back my arm, and with all my might throw it ceremoniously into the Atlantic. It arches in the air and then gracefully slips into the freezing ocean. No big splash, no parade down Rehoboth Boardwalk, just me learning to manage my life and make a dream come true. As they say in the vernacular, "Don't believe in miracles? Stick around and be one."

I am five-years sober today.

MARIA MASINGTON IS A POET, ESSAYIST, SPOKEN WORD ARTIST, AND SHORT STORY WRITER FROM WILMINGTON, DELAWARE. HER WORK HAS APPEARED IN MULTIPLE JOURNALS AND ANTHOLOGIES, INCLUDING *BEACH NIGHTS* AND *BEACH PULP*, PUBLISHED BY CAT AND MOUSE PRESS. MARIA IS A MEMBER OF THE WRITTEN REMAINS WRITERS GUILD AND IS ACTIVE IN THE DELAWARE AND PHILADELPHIA ART SCENE. SHE FREELANCES AS AN EMCEE AT LOCAL OPEN MIC NIGHTS, PROMOTING BOTH BEGINNING AND ESTABLISHED WRITERS.

JUDGE'S COMMENT

The Ensign is a man possessed by a demon not of his own making, nor of his own desire. His is in an epic struggle shared by millions. Alcohol is an addiction that rules his life. The Admiral is the unsympathetic, tough-guy guide. It would be easy to dismiss this story as just another addiction piece, but the author skillfully draws us into the life and character of the Ensign and makes us feel his humanity. To some degree or another we have all felt his need and shared his struggle. Success and failure, need and disappointment, are not emotions restricted to the addicted.

Booty

By Kristie Letter

Darla never dreamed she'd be back at the beach off-season, jobless and with impossible hair. Yet here she was, shuffling down the sand in a sports bra and sweat suit. These days, everything looked shinier, there were more chain restaurants, and fluorescent T-shirts seemed to be in style again. The November cold meant that the only people out enjoying the Atlantic were Darla and some old guy running a metal detector over the sand.

Darla thought that walking the beach each morning would help her get back in shape while going through her spiritual transformation. She had only stayed married and working at the bank because she was afraid to make a change. Not anymore. She pumped her arms as the magazine had suggested for maximum benefit and tilted her chin toward the metal-gray sky.

"Darla?"

She turned.

The metal detector man in the full-coverage hat waved and pulled off his headphones. Darla squinted.

"Miko? Is that you?" Beneath the big hat and faded face was a lifeguard she used to know.

"What are you doing here, Darla?"

That answer could take an hour. She could explain the corporate downsizing at the bank or her boss, who reminded her of Biff in *Weird Science*—the boss she had trained, and who had then gotten promoted in record time for his "innovative strides in building culture." She could discuss her divorce and her bad decisions, and maybe even mention she was now living with her mother and having to endure her mother's obsessive television watching.

"Just enjoying the fruits of my midlife crisis."

He laughed. "Me too."

A lifetime ago, Darla and Miko had met in the Silver Dollar, an eighties boardwalk arcade. Although the old-school games offered nothing more intense than spinning plastic soccer players and big, yellow circles gobbling small, white circles on a pixelated screen, the Dollar's low lights gave everything a coppery glow and Prince played from speakers in the ceiling. It had an aura. But the Silver Dollar was long gone, just like those versions of Darla and Miko.

"Are you looking for something you lost?" Darla pointed to the metal detector.

Miko shook his thin, graying hair. "I'm looking for treasure."

No way. Her cute, high-school lifeguard had grown up to be a middle-aged treasure hunter. Not the Indiana Jones kind with a sonar-equipped boat and necklace map found in a dusty attic, but the type with a full-coverage sun hat and a metal detector. Now, he was apparently trying to find real silver dollars.

"Do you really find stuff in the sand?"

"Lots of wrecks around here. My charts put money on the *Faithful Steward* as the one that will pay out," he said. "I've done a lot of tide work and Coin Beach is nothing compared to this area here." He gestured toward the beach in front of where the Silver Dollar used to stand.

Darla had never heard of "tide work," but she let Miko demonstrate various features of the metal detector. The thing reminded her of the Weedwacker she used to keep her mom's yard from becoming totally overgrown. If Darla hadn't come down from DC, her mom's small un-updated beach house would have been entirely consumed by honeysuckle, ivy, and that bamboo her mother planted years ago because someone on TV had said it was a good idea.

"You try it." Miko handed her the metal detector, which was heavier than it looked, and the earphones. She had only been half-listening when he explained pulse induction and multi-frequency, so she just swept it along, trying to keep her face toward the wind so her hair didn't get tangled. The beeping got more intense.

"Slowly!" he said. She moved in smaller circles until Miko nodded. He took the large metal shovel with holes and started to dig.

They found a beer can and some Funland tokens.

For the next few days, Darla made to-do lists and did small projects around her mother's house until the proliferation of ceramic seagulls and Princess Diana memorabilia started to really bother her.

She was not going to call Miko. Definitely not. But if she did call him, it wouldn't be like some kind of booty call.

Back at the bank, she had used that phrase in an attempt to improve corporate culture. After her boss had called her "my girl" one too many times, Darla explained the difference between connotation and denotation, as her Biff-like boss didn't quite understand why calling women "girls" would be a problem since both mean "female." Darla used the "booty call" versus "butt dial" explanation, to show how two things can have the same dictionary definition but wildly different implications. Biff had giggled when she said "booty" but the next week told her "the forward direction of the company led to some difficult decisions."

"You're firing me?"

"We just want you to find a position that maximizes your strengths," he said.

Darla had wanted to maximize her strength to punch her Biff-boss in his smarmy face. Calling her ex-boyfriend who thought he could find beach treasure with a glorified Weedwacker would also would not maximize anything.

After three hours of her mother's too-loud Hallmark movies, Darla had had enough. She stepped out to the cold November porch and called Miko.

As if her intentional call had been a butt dial, she couldn't speak when he answered. All that debating and she hadn't planned what to say.

"Hello? Is this Darla?"

Then again, he knew the call was from Darla. He knew her *breathing*.

"Wanna get Nicola's?"

"Good," he said. "Everyone always wants to go Grotto's."

"No contest."

Nicola's décor of blond wood panels and faded bricks set Darla's nerves at ease. Nothing was as sweet as that sauce. When her father was dying, all he wanted for breakfast, lunch, and dinner were Nic-o-bolis. Darla closed her eyes until the silvery memory became less sharp. Her dad would be perfectly happy if she were a treasure hunter. He told her "bankers are never out for the little guy."

Old places and low lighting made Darla forget she was on a date (maybe?) with a fellow who stored his metal detector under the booth while he ate. With the familiar pizza and the golden glow, she could see the young lifeguard beneath Miko's grown-up persona. They laughed and reminisced, talking about Darla's banking foibles and the summer traffic until the conversation turned to treasure.

"Everyone talks about the *DeBraak*, but that's not the real one." Miko shook his thinning hair.

"The real one what?"

"The real treasure. They've found almost everything from the *DeBraak*." When Miko discussed the ships, his face lit up.

"What is the real treasure?"

"The one from the *Faithful Steward*. In 1785, the ship sank right off Rehoboth Beach with four hundred barrels of British coins." Miko's face changed. "The ship also carried women and children sailing for Philadelphia. Only a handful survived when the ship grounded at the mouth of the Delaware Bay. The survivors stood on the shore watching everyone else go under. In twenty-four feet of water, only a few hundred yards from the shoreline, the ship sank."

"Wait, did you say only seven women and children survived?"

Miko nodded. "Everyone else was close, watching from the shore. They recovered the bodies, I think. Just not the coins. Each barrel had between one and two hundred thousand coins." He detailed the various coins and their values. The banker in Darla did a quick calculation. That was a lot of money for a lot of treasure hunters, considering what each coin would be worth today.

"Mom, I brought you a Nic-o-boli," Darla said, when she returned to her mother's house. She wondered if she and her mother would ever talk about how much they missed her dad. Maybe the Nic-a-boli would bring it all back like that French cookie Marcel Proust ate.

But all her mother's lunch did was garner a few complaints about heartburn.

"Mom, have you ever heard of the *Faithful Steward*?"

"Are they a band?"

"Never mind."

For the next few weeks, Darla and Miko saw each other every day—for movies and a few dinners, but he didn't make any big moves. Miko reminded Darla he knew more knock-knock jokes than any man alive and Darla reminded Miko that she did spot-on impressions of eighties-era heavy-metal singers. Darla talked about her attempts to reframe her life. Miko talked about how tides changed the shoreline.

Then came the booty call, but not quite the one Darla expected.

Miko invited Darla to look for treasure with him on a full-day excursion.

"I've never dug for pirate booty before except that one time on the beach with you," she said.

"Technically, it isn't pirate booty. The British were just trying to offload coins and the ship sank."

"So just plain old booty?"

"Plain old booty."

When he arrived, he had more supplies than Darla thought possible. In his leather bike bag he had handfuls of hand-drawn maps filled with networks of arrows and numbers.

"I don't know what I'm looking at," Darla said.

"These model the movement of the shoreline since 1918 and show the possible paths the barrels of coins might have traveled, so I can figure out the best places to dig."

Darla noticed Miko had said "we." Maybe she should be more open to treasure hunting. What did she have to lose?

Walking on a beach at sunset is the stuff of romance novels, with two figures, hand in hand on the sand. Add a metal detector and the romance dies fast. They spent four and a half hours pursuing what Miko termed a "hot spot," only to find a metal button. Darla was hot, cranky, and unimpressed.

Darla decided. She needed to get a life. A real life, not a Hallmark cliché of meeting an ex in her hometown. "I have to go," she said. Darla was a banker. Bankers made excellent, logical choices.

"Do you want to get pizza?" Miko turned the button over in his hand.

"I don't think we should see each other anymore," Darla said.

When he looked at her, the sun hit his face in a way that obscured his features. Her memory of him superimposed a lifeguard's face over

Miko's features, but then the earnest middle-aged reality emerged. Some ancient treasures weren't worth digging up. They probably weren't even there anymore.

Darla sat on the couch next to her mother. The more time she spent in the too-small, too-many-knickknacks, too-loud-television house, the more she realized she needed to make a change.

"My life is a wreck," Darla said. Her mother kept her eyes on a rapper telling Ellen about his passion for gourmet cooking.

"You exist because of a shipwreck," her mother said.

"What?"

For once, Darla's mother muted *Ellen*.

"Over between Brooklyn and Laurel, there was a retreat for nuns called St. Agnes by the Sea. It's the Star of the Sea now."

"What does that have to do with a shipwreck? Or me?"

Darla's mother closed her eyes and told the story. "In 1918, the steam tug *Eastern* towed two barges in a storm. Strong winds kept the tug from turning away from the shore. Both barges ran aground in Rehoboth. Although one of the barges survived mostly intact, the *Merrimac* wasn't so lucky. The 640-ton ship rode right up on the sand and crashed directly in front of the startled sisters on the porch of St. Agnes by the Sea."

Darla's mother paused, opened her eyes wide, as if waiting for her daughter to take in the dramatic scene.

"I don't get it."

"Your great grandmother was Sister Mary Wendelin."

"I thought nuns weren't allowed to have babies."

Her mother raised her eyebrows. "She thought it was a sign from God."

"She thought her baby was a sign from God?"

"No, the *Merrimac*. The ship that delivered that handsome sailor right up onto her porch. After that, her daughter—your Grandma

Jean—met my dad when he dialed a wrong number and found her voice enchanting. Those were signs, Just like it was a sign when I hit a bike with the car and the rider was the man who would become your father."

"You being such a bad driver was a sign?"

"Exactly," she said. "I miss him."

"Me too."

If weather and gods conspired to deliver a handsome sailor to the door of a nunnery and a handsome biker to her mother's bumper, who could argue with the whims of chance?

Before Darla could think of how to frame a phone call, before she could pull her phone from her purse, she saw him. Her very own faded lifeguard was stepping up onto the honeysuckle-covered porch of her ramshackle family home.

As Darla opened the door, Miko reached into his pocket.

Darla started to talk. "I'm sorry I said I didn't want to see you anymore. I just worry—"

Miko placed his fingertip on Darla's mouth.

He dropped to his knees. Miko looked up at her and the golden bits in his brown eyes sparkled in the late afternoon sun. Also, she could see his bald spot clearly from this vantage point.

His fingers unfurled to show a small circle of metal on his palm.

"I found it," he said. Although the metal in his hand looked like something that could cause tetanus, she saw that it might be coin, maybe even a coin from the *Faithful Steward*. "Will you take this coin and find more with me?"

Like the *Merrimac*, not to mention her mother's bumper, Miko had barreled through the randomness of life to arrive at her feet. He had resisted Darla's best attempts to keep her distance. Who was she to ignore divine intervention in presenting the man of her dreams?

The thin gold light of the afternoon pressed down on the silver glimmer of the ocean. Like Sister Mary Wendelin, Darla decided to accept the treasure delivered to her porch.

KRISTIE BETTS LETTER'S SHORT STORY COLLECTION *FIRE IN THE HOLE* JUST CAME OUT FROM ENGINE BOOKS, AND HER POETRY COLLECTION *UNDER-WORLDLY* (EDITORIAL L'ALEPH, 2017) EXAMINES WHAT LIES BENEATH WITH WHAT *COWBOY JAMBOREE* DESCRIBED AS "FANTASTIC IMAGES OF THE SUBTERRANEAN GRIT." KRISTIE GRADUATED FROM CAPE, BOUGHT ALL HER COLLEGE TEXTBOOKS BY WAITRESSING AT GROTTO'S, AND LOVES NOTHING MORE THAN VISITING EXTENDED FAMILY IN REHOBOTH. SHE NOW IS AN AWARD-WINNING TEACHER IN COLORADO AND LOVES TO PLAY TRIVIA WITH HER HUSBAND AND CHILDREN. FOR MORE, PLEASE VISIT KRISTIEBETTSLETTER.COM.

A Beach Story

By Suzanne Thackston

Mikey loved the beach better than just about anything, except maybe Halloween and (sometimes) his parents. His family's annual summer visit to Rehoboth Beach was just about the best thing of the entire year. This summer, they rented a cottage on New Castle Street, just a couple of blocks from the beach. Now that Mikey was five and had graduated from his swimming class, it was going to be the best summer ever.

After finding their cottage and unpacking, they wasted no time in grabbing their beach stuff and heading out. When Mikey's flip-flops hit the sand, he was off, racing for the line of lacy surf on the far side of towels and umbrellas and coolers and slick bodies littering the beach. When his mom caught up with him, she grabbed his arm hard and yelled, a lot. His dad grinned at him and set up the umbrella and blanket. Mikey never took his eyes off the ocean. As soon as his mom turned him loose, he shucked his T-shirt and baseball cap, kicked the flip-flops onto the beach blanket (prompting more shrieks from his mother), and ran for the water. His dad ran after him, scooped him up, and dived in, holding him tight. They both came up sputtering and laughing.

"Deeper!" Mikey yelled, and his dad obliged. They swam together out past the breakers, Mikey's dad supporting Mikey's belly. When Mikey got too tired to swim on his own, they trudged ashore and got their boogie boards. That was the most fun of all. Mikey only came out when his mom yelled that he needed more sunscreen; but then, he was right back in the exploding surf with his daddy.

Later that afternoon, after they had packed their beach gear and stowed it in their cottage, Mikey and his parents went for a walk along the boardwalk, smelling the popcorn and sunscreen and fried chicken and cotton candy, arguing over what to have for dinner. No one could agree, so Mikey got pizza while his folks got boring grown-up food. They carried it to a bench on the boardwalk to eat and people-watch.

Mikey wiped his hands on the napkin his mom made him get, then finished wiping them on his shorts. He took the napkin and paper plate to a trash can next to a post covered with flyers of missing children. As he threw it in, something yellow caught his eye a little farther along the boardwalk. He walked over to where it leaned against the railing. It was a stuffed bear with bright fur, laughing eyes angled up at him, and a red mouth.

"Hey, Dad!" Mikey called, picking up the bear. "Look at this bear. Can I keep it?"

Mikey's dad glanced over as he chewed his veggie wrap. "Pretty cool, buddy. But it belongs to someone. Better leave it."

Mikey held the bear at arm's length and looked at it. The bear looked back at him, eyes seeming to dance with good humor.

"Nah," said Mikey. "Look, there aren't any kids around here."

He was right. The boardwalk was full of couples mooning in the sunset and teenagers trying to look tough, but there were no little kids.

Mikey's mother made a face. She put down her paper carton of sushi. "Not a chance," she said. "Who knows what germs are crawling all over that thing. You get to go souvenir shopping while we're here, remember? If you want a stuffed animal, you can pick out a nice new one then."

Mikey put the bear down. Its laughing eyes looked a little sad. As they walked away, Mikey looked back. The children in the missing-kid flyers were all looking at him. So was the bear.

The next morning, Mikey and his dad raced into the ocean and had a bodysurfing contest. There was a moment of heart-pounding excitement when someone yelled, "Shark!" but the lifeguard quickly identified the fin as belonging to a dolphin. A whole pod of dolphins. Mikey's mom even waded into the water, shading her eyes to get a better look at them as they rose and dove gracefully out past the breakers.

"Look at the fins, Mikey," said his dad, holding him up high so he could see them better. "See how they curve backward in an arc? That's how you can tell. Sharks' fins are triangles with straight sides."

When the pod was out of sight, they went back to bodysurfing.

His dad got tired long before Mikey was ready to quit, but they dried off and had a drink of water. Then, they joined Mikey's mom, who was lying on a blanket, reading a book.

"Why don't you build a sandcastle?" Mikey's dad suggested. Mikey really wanted to go back into the ocean, but he picked up his pail and shovel, took them over to some nearby rocks, and got to work.

Mikey's sandcastle was a masterpiece. It had turrets and moats and drawbridges and lots of finger-poked windows. Mikey climbed over the rocks to get some seaweed to decorate the ramparts when he saw a familiar yellow object leaning against an outcropping of stone, looking out to sea.

"Hey!" Mikey cried. He picked it up and ran over to his parents. "Look," he said. "I found that bear again."

Mikey's dad frowned. "Can't be the same bear."

Mikey scowled up at him. "It is so. I know it!"

Mikey's mom picked it up. "It's remarkably clean for being on the beach. It's not even damp." She handed it back to Mikey. "But this is somebody's woobie, Mikey. Put it back where you found it."

A Beach Story

Mikey kicked at the sand. He dug a toe into the soft pile. "I like it," he said, but his voice was low. His parents didn't reply. Slowly, he walked back to the rocks and replaced the bear, but he set it so the bear could see him as he continued to work on his sandcastle. He knew it made the bear happy to watch him. When they left the beach, the bear was smiling hard at him with its red mouth.

The afternoon was cooler, and the sun hid behind clouds. Mikey and his parents wandered in and out of the shops on the boardwalk. Mikey looked at Pokémon trading cards and plastic tigers and hats with shark fins and light-up laser wands, but nothing seemed quite right.

Toward the end of the boardwalk, right before Funland, they approached a narrow shop with a picture on the window of a sun with dark glasses smiling over bright-blue waves. The sign read "Sun Dreams."

"Let's go in here," Mikey said, tugging at his mom's hand.

She eyed the dark doorway dubiously.

Mikey's dad shrugged. "Why not?"

Mikey saw rows of toys at the back of the little shop and made a beeline for them. In the middle of a shelf packed with stuffed crabs and sharks, down low where Mikey could easily reach it, was a yellow bear. He picked it up. The bear smiled at him with its happy eyes.

"Mom! Dad!" Mikey yelled. "Look!" He brandished the bear at them. His parents exchanged a startled look. Mikey's dad reached out a hand, but Mikey snatched the bear back and held it tightly.

"You told me I could pick out my soobeneer. I want this!" His grip on the bear tightened. It felt like the bear clung to him too.

"Let me see that," his mother said. Mikey hesitated, then handed it to her. She examined it, eyes narrowed. "Must be a popular style this summer. I can't see why, myself."

Mikey's dad glanced at the bear. "If you want it, buddy, it's your souvenir for our vacation. Sure you don't want to wait? You might find something you like better tomorrow."

"I want this," Mikey repeated, reaching for the bear in his mom's hand. She held onto it, but he pulled it from her grip. "It's my soobeneer." Mikey carried the bear up to the counter, hesitated, then handed it to the salesclerk.

The teenager looked at it, puzzled. "Don't remember seeing this before." He shrugged. "Got a tag, though," he said, and rang it up.

That night Mikey slept with his yellow bear snuggled into his neck. He dreamed that he and the bear were at the beach, leaning against the rocks, just as when he built his sandcastle. Then, the bear was gone. Mikey was in the ocean, beneath the surface, but he could breathe just fine. The dream was fun at first. He liked walking on the sandy bottom like SpongeBob. But soon the bright water darkened. Mikey was trying to find his home, a home he knew was under the water, but he couldn't find it. His parents weren't in the dream and there was no one to help him. It was cold, and he was scared. Dark shapes moved in the water above him. He woke up crying. His mom and dad let him get in between them in their bed, holding his bear, and he slept fine for the rest of the night.

Mikey brought his bear to breakfast the next morning and sat it next to him in his chair.

"What's your bear's name?" asked Mikey's dad.

"Teddy," said Mikey.

Mikey's dad laughed. "We can think of a better name for him than that. How about Ace? Or Dagger? He can be your guardian bear."

Mikey's mom wrinkled her nose. "How about Sunshine? Or Snuggles?"

"His name is Teddy," said Mikey. "He told me so."

Mikey took Teddy to the beach with them that day. His mom didn't want him to. She said Teddy would get wet and sandy and gross, but he didn't. His fur stayed clean and dry, bright-yellow and cheerful. When Mikey came out of the sea, breathless and laughing with his daddy, Teddy was there on the blanket, his eyes laughing at how much fun Mikey was having.

They stayed on the beach all day long. At sunset, Mikey and his parents went for a walk along the surf line, Teddy dangling from Mikey's hand.

"Look! Oh, look!" cried Mikey's mom, pointing out to sea. Six or seven curved fins cruised along the surface, just beyond the line of breakers. One of the dolphins leapt high, silhouetted against the pink-and-purple sky.

That night, Mikey smiled up at his mommy as she tucked him into his blankets, Teddy snuggled into his neck. "Thank you for letting me get Teddy, Mommy," he said sleepily. "I love him."

Mikey's mom smiled back at him. "Well, I love you more," she said. But Mikey was already asleep.

Mikey woke crying in the middle of the night. His mom was there in an instant, wrapping her arms around him.

"It's OK, honey," she soothed. "I'm right here. Did you have another dream?"

"Yes," Mikey sobbed, clutching Teddy to his chest. "There was a little girl in the water."

Mikey's dad picked him up in his strong arms and brought him to the big bed. Mikey's dad and mom got in on either side of him and put their arms around him. His mom moved Teddy so she could hug Mikey close, but Mikey reached out and clutched Teddy to his chest.

"Was the little girl swimming?" asked Mikey's mother softly.

"No. She was walking along the bottom of the ocean. It was all muddy and mucky. She was crying. She said she was lost. She wanted her mommy and daddy." Mikey started to cry again.

Mikey's mom and dad exchanged a look over Mikey's head.

Mikey's dad began to sing softly in his deep voice, a lullaby he hadn't sung to Mikey since Mikey was a baby. "Go to sleepie, little Mikey. Go to sleepie, little Mikey. When you wake, we'll patty-patty cake and ride a shiny little pony."

By the time he had sung it twice through, Mikey was asleep.

Mikey didn't feel well the next morning. His mom put her hand on his forehead. Then, she took his temperature and frowned.

"His temperature is normal, but he's a little pale," she said to Mikey's dad. "I wonder if we should pick up some Tylenol."

Mikey sat up in their bed, where he and Teddy were covered in blankets. Teddy's nose was right in Mikey's ear. His smiling eyes looked up at Mikey's parents.

Mikey put Teddy on the pillow and pushed himself out of bed. "I feel better," he said in a thin voice. "I'm hungry for breakfast," he added, speaking up a little. He smiled at his parents. But it wasn't quite his usual smile.

After a day spent at Funland, Ryan's Mini Golf, and the arcades, they went for another sunset walk on the beach. Mikey's parents sat on a towel in the sand, while Mikey and Teddy played near the shoreline.

As the sunset cooled and a waxing moon brightened in the eastern sky, Mikey's mom lifted her head from where it had been tucked under her husband's chin, watching Mikey at the water's edge. He stood perfectly still, Teddy hanging loosely from one of his hands. He was staring out over the water.

"What are you looking at, honey?" she called. "Do you see dolphins?"

Mikey didn't reply. After a few minutes he began walking slowly into the ocean.

"Hey, buddy!" Mikey's dad yelled. "That's far enough."

But Mikey kept walking. He didn't seem to hear his dad.

Mikey's mom cried out, her voice shrill, "Mikey! Stop right now!"

Mikey was up to his knees in the surf. Teddy's feet were getting wet. Mikey kept walking.

Mikey's dad catapulted from the towel and ran into the water. He picked Mikey up under the armpits. "What are you doing?" he yelled, staring into Mikey's face. Mikey's eyes were glazed. He turned his head back out to the open sea. "Mikey?" his dad said, more softly. He cradled his son in his arms and carried him out of the water.

Mikey fell asleep early that night, snuggled with his Teddy. In the middle of the night he woke, gasping in the dark, but did not cry out. His parents slept on.

"What is it?" whispered Teddy into Mikey's neck. "Did you have a bad dream?"

Mikey pulled Teddy closer. "I was on the beach," he said in his quietest, littlest voice, right into Teddy's ear. "There was a huge wave coming, high as the sky. I could see sharks swimming in it. There were crabs, too. They waved their claws at me. I was so scared."

Teddy made damp, comforting noises. Mikey fell back asleep.

The next morning, Mikey said he didn't want to go to the beach. His mommy and daddy exchanged a look and agreed. They spent the day in the cottage watching videos and playing Snakes and Ladders and Trouble. Mikey dozed off while they were watching *Alice in Wonderland*. Teddy fell off the bed when Mikey rolled over.

Mikey's mom picked Teddy up. She looked at him, a line between her brows. Teddy looked back, smiling happily at her with his red mouth. She started to put him next to Mikey, but then, tossed him onto a chair.

Mikey woke from his nap screaming, crying desperately for Teddy. When his parents rushed to him, he could only reply in broken, stammered words that he had been at the bottom of the ocean. Crabs were taking bits of him away.

"That's enough," said Mikey's dad. "We're going home tomorrow."

"And we need to leave that damn bear here," added Mikey's mom.

Mikey began to cry and scream again. Mikey's dad picked Mikey up and rocked him. "We'll talk about that later," he said, looking over Mikey's head at his wife. He gave an almost imperceptible nod. She nodded back.

Mikey was dull and disinterested when his mom and dad tried to get him to play a game or watch another video. He wouldn't eat more than a few bites of pizza. He sat on a chair, holding Teddy, and watched as they began to pack up their things.

"Look, sweetie, there's a full moon rising," said Mikey's mommy as she stood by the window, ready to close the blinds. "Come see."

Mikey got up slowly and walked over to the window. He stood there for a long time, watching the moon slide up over the edge of the sea.

Late that night, Mikey's mommy and daddy didn't feel Mikey wiggle out from between them and walk to the door, moving softly in his bare feet. He carried Teddy in his arms. Very quietly, he slid back the chain and unbolted the door.

The bottoms of Mikey's pajama legs were heavy with sand by the time he reached the ocean. Teddy sat in the sand where Mikey had put him, watching. Mikey walked into the water, following the path of the moonlight. After a while, his head disappeared under the water. Teddy watched as a great triangular fin appeared. There was a swirl, then nothing.

* * * * *

Later in the summer, after the hullabaloo had died down, a family of five strolled out onto the boardwalk to eat their ice cream. The youngest, a girl of about four, pointed to something yellow near the bench.

"Hey!" she said. "Look, Mommy! There's a toy bear."

SUZ THACKSTON IS A STRANGE OLD BIRD WHO LIVES ON A LITTLE FARM IN WESTERN MARYLAND WITH HER NICE HUSBAND, A SWEET DOG, A COUPLE OF SPOILED-ROTTEN MARES, AND TOO MANY BOSSY CATS. SHE GREW UP IN BERMUDA, SO SHE HAS THE BEACH IN HER BLOOD. SHE CAN BE FOUND MUTTERING TO TREES, LEAVING HONEY FOR THE FAERIES, AND STEPPING ABSENT-MINDEDLY THROUGH LOOKING GLASSES.

JUDGE'S COMMENT

Funnily enough, "A Beach Story" was the first story I picked out of my magnificent stack of short stories to be judged for this contest. I was delighted when what started out as a sickly sweet, slightly off-kilter description of a child's time at the beach quickly became something entirely different, and far more sinister. The author's careful use of tone and pointed use of monotony conjured, for me, a sort of daze that transformed into a chilling piece of indelible horror when I least expected it. I think it took a lot of guts to write a macabre story like this one—to be unafraid to take the idea of a "beach dream" and force readers to watch as it slowly shifts into a nightmare.

Red Flags, Wrong Star, and a Wagon with a Broken Wheel

By Nancy Powichroski Sherman

You wish that you were anywhere but here. Even a dental appointment seems better—at least, you could easily cancel that. But a wedding? *Your* wedding? *Today*?

Try to distract yourself by rearranging toiletries into squares and triangles, but the luxurious amenities provided by this four-star hotel simply remind you that this isn't a beach vacation—it's the once-in-a-lifetime (maybe) event on which you will be judged. Why don't bridal magazines spend less time promising dream weddings? Instead, they should offer advice to the bride-to-be about the terror that hits when the time draws near.

You wish that you had kept your blonde hair pulled back into a French braid like you usually wore it. But your soon-to-be mother-in-law, Celeste Harrington Miller, insisted that you get the "royal treatment," which in her opinion meant a mani-pedi and having your hair styled by Jacque and makeup applied by his partner Dave, the top artists at her favorite Rehoboth Beach day spa. The results stare back at you from the bridal suite mirror. Your blonde hair has been pinned into what is described as loose curls but, in reality, the hair is held so tightly that you're surprised your scalp isn't bleeding. And the makeup seems as thick and artificial as an oil painting. You wonder if your fiancé will recognize you when you walk down the aisle.

The melody of "Here Comes the Bride" startles you and, for a brief moment, sends you into panic mode—you're still in your bathrobe. Quickly, turn toward the quilted surface of the king bed where everything has been laid out for you: the gown, the veil, the crinoline petticoat, the accessories. Peeking through the veil, you see your iPhone blinking for an incoming call and realize it's just the ringtone your fiancé Marcus downloaded for you last summer, right after he popped the question and you accepted.

Consider ignoring the call but realize that, if you do, he'll show up here at the bridal suite to check on you. A knight in shining armor. What girl wouldn't want that kind of careful attention? Dumb question, especially today. You don't need a knight in shining armor; you need a therapist.

"Yes?" Your voice sounds snappish. You should apologize, but for what? Being an emotional wreck? Don't all brides feel this way? None of the bridal magazines offered any insight into the inner bride; they were too busy filling the pages with photographs of costumes for canine ringbearers and diagrams for creative napkin-folding with not one word of solace for the stressed-out bride-to-be.

"Mara? Are you OK?"

You aren't, but give him a break rather than the truth. "Today is our wedding day. Of course, I'm OK."

Marcus, who organizes every detail of his life—and yours, recently— must have just discovered the feeling of not being in control of his world. "Are you sure?"

Sure about what? About being OK, or about going through with the wedding? Provide an answer that could fit either question. "I'm fine. Just relaxing."

You wish that were true. How can you relax when you're about to swear eternal union, a forever until-death-do-us-part oath? How do you make this leap when there's still that nagging whisper in your mind: Are you making the right choice? Did you miss any red flags through the haze of infatuation with Marcus?

While you're in mid-thought, he suggests that he stop by the room. "You sound like you need a hug."

"No!" Then lighten up your tone and deliver a reasonable excuse. "It's unlucky for the groom to see the bride before the wedding."

"OK, Mar-Mar, request withdrawn." He makes a kissing sound. "I love you."

The silence tells you that he's waiting for you to return the sentiment.

"Ditto," you say, like the Patrick Swayze character in the movie *Ghost*. But guilt causes you to add the kissing sound before your quick hang up.

* * * * *

From the balcony door of the fourth-floor bridal suite, you look down at the beach where Dallas, the event coordinator, is waving his arms at the staff, who are putting the archway, chairs, and floral arrangements into proper alignment as shown in the wedding brochure. White folding chairs. A center aisle. Simple. Traditional. A rust-kissed white, wrought-iron archway under which the ceremony will take place, with the ocean as the backdrop. You wonder about the wisdom of this. Doesn't it keep the bride and groom (and perhaps the officiant) overly conscious of whether the ceremony will be finished before the tide comes in?

As you watch the florist decorate the arch with greenery and wildflowers, muse over the choice of iron rather than some other material. Where else iron is used? Window bars at an insane asylum, doors on prison cells, gates of cemeteries. Perhaps symbolism more than practicality inspired the choice.

Suddenly realize that the interlocking wedding band design on the unity candle looks much like silver handcuffs. Until death do us part. With the bridal couple so close to the water, you wonder how many of them face their demons of doubt and, without speaking the words of assent, make a run for it, leaping into the waves to swim far out to sea and die in the arms of Poseidon rather than say, "I do."

Someone knocks at the door. Sprint across the room, shouting, "Marcus, that better not be you!" Through the peephole, see a gray eye peeping back. Your maid of honor. "Did Marcus send you here, Deedee?"

"Nope." She giggles and takes a stumbling step backward. Her party-girl face, as well as a half-empty bottle of Smirnoff in one hand and two shot glasses in the other, shows that she's already started celebrating. When you open the door, she hands you a shot glass with the word *Bride* written in gold. "Medicine for bridal nerves," she says, pouring vodka into your glass and hers.

You toss down the vodka in one gulp and hold out the glass for more.

Deedee fills the glass. "I knew it. Scared of the ceremony, or are you finally coming to your senses? It's not too late to cancel, you know."

"So, you think I shouldn't get married?"

She rolls her eyes. "I was kidding. Of course, you should get married. Why not?"

Remember Judge Judy's warning about choosing a spouse: *Don't hitch your wagon to the wrong star*. But what if your wagon had a broken wheel, and what if it hobbled past the right star, and what if you missed red flags along the way?

It's no use explaining Judge Judy's advice—you've already said too much to Deedee. Even when she's sober, she blurts out private confessions like a stand-up comic.

Toss down the second shot. You look forward to the numbing that might follow. In just a half hour, you'll lose your identity. Mara Spenser will be replaced by Mrs. Mara Miller, wife of Marcus Miller. Ohmigod! All those *m*'s will follow you through every document you sign. Think of all the future receptionists, insurance agents, and bankers who will point out the M&M connection as though it had never occurred to you before that moment.

Deedee downs her own shot of vodka and then holds the bottle upside down. "All gone. Time to get ready."

"Is it too late to at least keep my maiden name?"

"Yes, it's too late! The marriage license is official. You are going to be Mara Miller." She giggles.

You turn your back to the mirror and stare at the ocean as Deedee dresses you. Petticoat. Gown. Jewelry. Veil. Deedee oohs and aahs throughout the process, and when her work is finished, she says, "Beautiful. Look in the mirror. You're a bride."

You don't want to look. You don't want to see the results. It won't be the image you dreamed of. Marcus's mother picked out this gown, not you. Remember looking into the three-way mirror at the Kleinfeld Bridal shop in Manhattan and seeing a bride doll looking back at you. It had your face, but the gown and veil seemed more like a theatrical costume. You had wanted a simple lace shift and a beaded headband, but your future mother-in-law "just loved" how you looked in the corseted ball gown with full tulle skirt and a pearl-studded cathedral-length veil, both by Elandra Enchanté, the current in-vogue designer. Excessive and expensive, but your soon-to-be mother-in-law was paying for the gown as a wedding present, so you surrendered. Remember hearing Marcus's mom announce to the salesperson, "We're saying yes to the dress," as though she were on the TV show.

Tell Deedee, "I'll have plenty of time to see myself. Dallas arranged two photographers and a videographer."

"Come on, Mara. I have my cell phone all ready to catch the moment when you see yourself for the first time as the future Mrs. Miller."

"Maybe it's unlucky for the bride to see herself before the wedding, too."

Deedee makes a game-show-buzzer sound. "Good try, Mara, but not good enough. You only get one chance to see yourself as a bride before the rest of the world does. You might regret it if you throw away the opportunity to memorialize that moment."

You pose in front of the full-length mirror, pretending to admire yourself, but the reality is that you're focused on the mirrored image of the wall behind you. "Wow!" you say with fake enthusiasm. Then, quickly turn away from the mirror lest you actually catch a glimpse of yourself. "Now, don't you dare share that video with Marcus before the ceremony. Promise?"

You can tell by her reaction that he had set her up to do this in the first place, so you make her swear on your friendship. You doubt that she'd break that kind of promise, but who knows; sometimes vodka talks before Deedee thinks. Give her a hug and lead her toward the door. "Thanks, Deedee. Now, I need a little alone time before the big walk down the aisle."

"But as maid of honor, I'm supposed to be by your side," she insists, as you guide her into the hallway and shut the door.

* * * * *

Gaze over the empty room. You wanted "alone" time, but the silence makes you feel lonely instead, and the Enchanté wedding gown is so full you can't sit down. Now what? Maybe you should have let Deedee stay with you.

Step out on the balcony that overlooks the Rehoboth boardwalk. The ceremony decorations are complete, several family members and friends are already seated on the white chairs, and Dallas stands with Celeste beside the archway, admiring his efforts. To you, the overall look has morphed into a very different setting. Although the greenery and flowers woven through the scrollwork of the arch are designed to imitate a classic cake topper, the effect looks more like a funeral arrangement to you. The rows of white chairs are as straight and even as grave markers.

Maybe it's just bridal jitters, but you do wonder if any bride ever threw herself over this railing in an effort to escape getting married. Whether it's the vodka or your own quirky sense of humor, you become genuinely curious about the logistics. The railing is short enough to hoist yourself and the billowy skirt of the wedding gown over it.

Try it out. See if you're right. Four years of gymnastics in high school and a great sense of balance assure you of the safety of this little experiment.

Lift the skirt. Put one leg over the railing. Straddle it for a moment like the bar of a boy's bicycle. Then bring the other leg over the railing, too. Now, you're standing on the thin ledge of the balcony, leaning back against the railing like you're on a bar stool at Irish Eyes, where your bridesmaids took you for a girls night out earlier this week.

Feel the wind blow the fabric out and up into the air. You're Marilyn Monroe in that famous poster of the steam billowing from the subway grate. Quickly grab a handful of fabric and pull it tight against your legs. Your lacy bikini thong is meant for the bridal night, not for the entertainment of passersby.

Suddenly, you notice Marcus walking toward his mother. You'd better duck inside the bridal suite before he sees you.

You start to climb back onto the balcony, but the railing catches layers of the tulle skirting. Your right foot slips, you gasp, someone on the boardwalk screams, and now the wedding gown becomes a $9,999 Elandra Enchanté rescue harness as you dangle in the air like a pendulum.

Wedding guests join the crowd that is forming on the boardwalk.

You watch from an upside-down position as Marcus runs across the sand and toward the hotel. Whatever buzz you had from the vodka shots is rapidly dissipating.

He calls out, "What are you doing?" Without waiting for an answer, he rushes into the hotel.

The smart-ass part of you announces, "Just hanging around."

Nervous laughter rises from the crowd below. Cell phones appear. You're being live-streamed. The YouTube video will probably go viral, but you might not be around to relish the limelight; if the fabric in the gown breaks free from the railing, you'll land on your head, break your neck, and be paralyzed or dead.

Don't panic. Slow your breath. Pretend that this is an aerial yoga pose.

Your soon-to-be mother-in-law—that is, unless you fall to your death—breaks through the crowd. "Mara! How did this happen?"

You prepare to lie, but Celeste barely takes a breath before continuing. "And where's that party-girl drunk you picked as maid-of-honor? This wouldn't have happened if she were doing her duty."

You hear your fiancé shouting, "Mara, don't move!" He rushes onto the balcony and grabs the section of wedding gown that has attached itself to the railing, holding the fabric tightly, with his hands acting as clamps. "Mara, please don't fall."

"I wasn't planning to," you say.

Another round of uneasy laughter rises from the spectators on the boardwalk.

Marcus shouts to the crowd below, "For God's sake, someone dial 9-1-1."

Dallas calls up to him. "Already done. The fire department is on its way with a hook and ladder truck."

"I'm not *that* heavy."

Hear Marcus say, "You're perfect, Mar-Mar."

"No, I'm not. No one's perfect." Try to do a stomach crunch to lift your head in an effort to look up and see your fiancé. The movement twists the gown a bit, and everyone hears the sound of a rip.

The crowd gasps.

Try not to cry. Hold still.

You hear syncopated clicks and realize that both of the wedding photographers are capturing this part of the story to include in your wedding album. Do they really think you want to remember this mess? Consider the future when you and Marcus are parents. Imagine your children finding the book and thinking their mom is a crazy lady. You can't help but laugh until tears run down your forehead.

The laughter eases your fear—that is, until you hear a crack of thunder in the distance. The weather forecast gave a zero percent chance of rain, but the way this day is going, a ninety-nine percent chance seems more likely.

Listen as the boardwalk crowd debates heat lightning versus pop-up thunderstorm. Really? Who cares about the weather!

You're getting dizzy from being upside-down. With as little movement as possible, try to lift your head a bit.

Another ripping sound. Everyone—Marcus, the wedding party, the guests, the vacationers on the boardwalk—scream, "Don't move!" in unison.

Declare, "Marcus, I love you."

"And I love you, Mara."

Say, "I want to get married right now."

"Now?"

From below, the wedding officiant begins, "We gather this day to join in matrimony these two young people ..."

You plead, "Cut to the important part. The 'do you take' and the 'I now pronounce you.' I don't know how long I'll be here."

Dallas rushes up to the clergyman. "No, no, no! We're all set up on the beach. It's what everyone wants, right?" He looks around.

In the background, the sound of a siren gets closer and closer until the hook and ladder firetruck reaches Olive Avenue and stops beside the hotel.

"See? Everything is going to be all right," Celeste declares. "The wedding ceremony will take place on the beach—as planned."

Police move the crowd back as the truck's aerial ladder is raised to the corner room balcony from which you're dangling. One firefighter rushes into the hotel lobby, while another climbs the ladder and joins the first, who is now standing beside Marcus. Despite the volume of tulle, they manage to lift you into an upright position and deliver you safely to the balcony.

Throw your arms around Marcus, and say, "I do," loud enough for everyone to hear.

The crowd cheers.

"That's not official," Dallas informs the crowd. "There will be no 'I now pronounce you' until everyone is seated and the bride walks down that aisle." He herds the guests toward their chairs on the beach, and the bystanders follow along, as though they're now invested in this exchange of vows.

As the firefighters exit and the ladder descends, Marcus holds you tightly and whispers in your ear, "What made you climb over the balcony rail? Is getting married to me so horrible that you'd rather die?"

Look into his eyes and say, "No. It wasn't that. I was feeling overwhelmed. I guess I just lost my mind for a moment."

"Should we postpone the wedding?"

"No way. I don't want to wait another day to become your wife." Feel the tears welling in your eyes. "I love you, Marcus."

He kisses your forehead, your nose, but before he reaches your lips, the bridesmaids dash into the bridal suite.

Deedee, who seems remarkably sober now, takes charge. "Go away, Marcus. You're supposed to be standing under that arch, so shoo!" She grabs his arm and leads him from the balcony to the room entrance.

As he steps into the hallway, his mother rushes in. She is gasping for breath and dabbing her face with a lace handkerchief. She examines your gown, tsk-tsking as she rummages around the skirt. Then she surprises you with a bear hug and a smile. "Saved by the dress!"

Without further discussion, Deedee and the bridesmaids surround you. While two of them fix your hair and straighten the veil, the others do their best to disguise the ripped netting of the gown, while Celeste supervises.

* * * * *

Ten minutes later, you are at the doorway that leads to the ceremony. The curtain of clouds parts, revealing a clear, blue sky and a glorious, sunny day, surely a good omen. The string quartet begins to play Handel, and the bridesmaids take their measured steps down the sandy aisle.

When the music transitions to Bach's *Jesu, Joy of Man's Desiring* and you step onto the sand, your bridal jitters are gone. Maybe hanging upside-down and being in imminent danger put everything into perspective: Your love for Marcus. The future you planned together. And the absolute trust that it's what you both want.

He waits at the wedding arch with a wide smile. You lock eyes and close the distance between you, only mildly aware that Marcus isn't the only one looking at you—everyone is. But your soon-to-be husband is the only one that matters.

Judge Judy would be pleased. You've hitched your wagon to the right star—Marcus—and the only flags you see are on the back of a lifeguard chair. Symbolic? You bet.

Nancy Powichroski Sherman is a storyteller. Her award-winning short stories have been published in literary journals and several anthologies. Her own collection of stories, *Sandy Shorts*, was awarded a regional first place (2015) by Delaware Press Association and a national first place (2015) by the National Federation of Press Women. Her follow-up collection, *More Sandy Shorts*, was launched in June 2019. Nancy fondly remembers her participation in the first Rehoboth Beach Reads competition, *The Beach House*, where both stories she submitted received honors: "Why You Trashed Vera Wang" (second place) and "No Magic Words" (judge's award). That book was her first introduction to Cat & Mouse Press and to Nancy Day Sakaduski, who later became her editor and publisher.

Judge's Comment

The humor in this story is contemporary, historical, (nearly hysterical) as well as universal. The voice of doubt, directed at the reader is wry, dry, and spot-on. The narrative arc rises and falls in a smooth manner, although the main character does not, (so nicely done). The tongue-in-cheek monologue and dialogue works well. The bird's eye view of the outdoor beach-side wedding is cleverly executed. Everyone reading this story will chuckle, then cast their eyes from the water back to the hotel balconies. Great title.

The Waterman's Daughter

By Jennifer Logue

"Miss Meri, Miss Meri, I'm going to take you to the window now, so you can feel the breeze."

The voice startles me. It takes me a moment to realize it belongs to the woman who had promised to take me to my favorite place in the house after lunch. She is the newest of the small team tasked with my personal care each day. Though I don't know her well, I like the way she smiles without reservation. It also doesn't seem to bother her that I never say a word.

After rolling me across the room to the window facing the ocean, she sits down on the window seat in front of me. "Miss Meri, the other girls say you love the water. They say it calms you in a way nothing else does. Is that true?"

Her smile is kind and her hair moves with the breeze that floats through the window behind her. I let my eyes shut. I don't need my sight to connect with the water. The beach smell that is carried in with the breeze is enough to take me back.

* * * * *

My father was a waterman, as was my grandfather, my great grandfather, and many others before them. The Nordic roots of my family tree ran deep, and my father named me *Meri*, the Finnish word for "sea." He knew I'd be as much a part of the water as he was.

We made our home in a small cottage in Lewes, Delaware. He used to cradle me in his arms in front of our old stone fireplace and tell me stories of the things he had seen on the water. When I grew older, I'd join him on his boat as he fished on the Delaware Bay. Nestled between bait buckets, rods, and crab pots, I'd watch my father work, waiting for the warm smile that would come when there was a lull in activity. "Meri, you see anything interesting in the water today?" he would shout over the roar of the waves and the wind.

I always saw something interesting, not just in the water, but also in every place else connected to it. "Daddy, look at all the colors," I'd exclaim, rubbing damp beach sand across the palm of my hand. Together, we'd stand on the edge of the sand dunes in hopes of spotting a lizard or rabbit among the grasses. Watching little crabs emerge from their holes in the muddy banks of the estuaries entertained me for hours. I was called to observe these places in a way I could never explain in my waking hours. Only in my dreams did it all make sense.

There was a green-eyed woman in my dreams, the mother rarely spoken of in my home. My father would only say she had died when I was an infant. But I knew the truth. She was of the water. Most nights I dreamed she rose from the water, her long hair the color of sand like mine, drying in the breeze. She would enter our tiny cottage in the night and visit me in my room with the whitewashed plank walls. In my dreams, she ran her hand across the quilt until she found mine. Then she would watch over me in the night, our fingers intertwined. As the sun rose over the water, in my half-awakened state, I'd reach for her with my warm hand as she slipped quietly from my grasp.

I never told my father about these dreams. I didn't share that I swept beach sand from my floorboards each morning, or that the smell of salt air lingered in my room. These were the secrets I hid deep in my heart.

As a child, I kept to myself, exploring the local beaches and estuaries that rose and fell with the tides. I was a frequent visitor of our town's little library, and each day I'd read books about the water and the creatures who lived in it. In the evenings I would sit on the shore and envelop myself in the essence of the water. The bay, sand, and grasses that swayed quietly in the dunes behind me embraced my soul.

But it was the old Brownie camera my father gave me for my fourteenth birthday that changed my world.

"Meri, show the world the way you see life along the water," my father said as he presented his gift.

I quickly grasped the process of taking, then developing, photos of life near the bay. I spent hours each day photographing the water, along with shorebirds, oysters, horseshoe crabs, and many other creatures. The essence of the bay came alive in my little darkroom when I hung my photos up to dry.

By the time I graduated high school, I had gained the attention of local museums and galleries. Sharing the beauty and wildness of the water and beaches along the Delaware coast seemed to be what I was created to do. I was grateful for the notoriety and for the income that allowed me to buy a home in Rehoboth and care for my father after he docked his boat for the last time.

When he died, I turned the small cottage in Lewes into a haven for beach visitors who wanted a quiet sanctuary. Now, bicycles and kayaks sit ready for use, books fill the shelves in the front room, and my photographs on display inspire nature exploration. The old stone fireplace stands ready for those who seek a retreat during the cooler seasons.

* * * * *

"Miss Meri, are you cold?" she asks, as she stands to close the window. *No. I'm not cold at all.*

Her eyes must have registered the slight turn of my head because she stops and sits back down. She smiles, seeming content in knowing she can understand my desires without my speaking. I return to my memories.

* * * * *

It was the afternoon of my fifty-fifth birthday when everything changed. The late spring sky was darkening as I headed north toward Kitts Hummock beach with my camera in the passenger seat.

The wind had picked up by the time I arrived and the air that greeted me was alive and fierce. The briny smell of the water and screaming of the gulls fighting their way against the wind created an electricity in the air that delighted my soul. I stepped over a line of horseshoe crab shells. Though some were empty shells from molting, the stench suggested that many were crabs that had stranded on the beach and died. But closer to the water, the ones that were alive were making the most out of their limited time for spawning. I've always felt awe in the presence of these prehistoric creatures and that day was no different.

As my hair whipped around me, I bent low in the surf to catch the glisten of the sunlight on the shells, the surf tugging at my ankles. Gray sky and equally gray water contrasted with the sparkling, pebbly, beach sand. While water droplets and sand pelted my skin, the crabs carried on, unconcerned with the fury around them.

I was so intent on capturing the wildness of my surroundings that I barely noticed the pain building behind my eyes. I didn't question why everything around me blurred. I felt myself drop to my knees, then fall on the sand next to the subjects I'd been photographing. Was I dreaming? The last thing I remember was a set of green eyes and sandy-colored hair whipping in the wind.

When I awoke, the air was painfully still. Gone was the damp, briny air. Gone was the roar of the wind and the waves and piercing cries of the gulls. I heard voices say words like "aneurysm" and "stroke." I felt needle sticks and cold stethoscopes. Hands did tasks to care for me and the beeping of machines echoed in the room. *What happened?* I'd ask. But I never got an answer. It took me several days to realize the words weren't leaving my lips, that they were locked up tight in my head.

The early days were painfully difficult and discouraging, but my dreams of the woman rising from the water kept me going. Images of those green eyes looking deep into mine filled my head and the smell of salt air settled around me. Each morning, the housekeepers would look puzzled by the sand that came up when they cleaned the floor and the nurses would note that my room smelled briny. Even for a hospital near the shore, this was unusual.

After weeks of rehabilitation, I returned to my home in Rehoboth. My ability to control my legs remains limited. Words float from my head but never quite leave my throat. I sit by the window and watch the water. I contemplate whether the woman of the water was real or was nothing more than the dream of a woman longing for her mother.

The ladies who care for me often take me to the boardwalk, and my camera sits comfortably in my lap. People still speak about how I capture the shades of gray in the water right before a storm and the unique glimmer of the sand that pours onto the beaches where the ocean meets the bay. Photographs of Rehoboth Beach icons such as the big, orange, Dolle's sign, the bandstand, and the white benches that line the boardwalk continue to be bought by postcard and magazine publishers. My photos still hang on gallery walls and are included in regional publications sold at Browseabout Books. I wouldn't have chosen to be like this, but it's not a bad "rest of a life" for a waterman's daughter.

* * * * *

"It's dinnertime, Miss Meri. I'm going to take you to the dining room now." My dreams blink away as I feel her let go of the hand that I hadn't even noticed she'd been holding. The gentleness in her tone beckons me to look more closely. Green eyes. Sandy blonde hair. When I dare to take a breath, I inhale salty air that comes not just from the window, but also from her. As she pushes me down the hall, I open my hand and sand streams slowly from my palm.

THOUGH A NATIVE OF COLORADO, JENNIFER LOGUE HAS SPENT THE PAST TWELVE YEARS EXPLORING DELAWARE AND THE SURROUNDING AREA WITH HER HUSBAND AND CHILDREN. HER WORK HAS BEEN INCLUDED IN *BEACH FUN* AND THE VETERAN'S ISSUE OF *THE ALMAGRE REVIEW*. SHE ALSO HAS PUBLISHED ARTICLES ON THE MIGHTY AND THE DOWN SYNDROME ASSOCIATION OF DELAWARE WEBSITES RELATING TO HER SON, WHO HAPPENS TO HAVE DOWN SYNDROME. HER STORY "THE WATERMAN'S DAUGHTER" WAS BORN AFTER SHE VISITED KITTS HUMMOCK BEACH TO WATCH THE HORSESHOE CRABS SPAWN ONE WILD AFTERNOON. IN THE CRACKS OF HER DAY, SHE MERGES HER PHOTOGRAPHY WITH THE WRITTEN WORD ON INSTAGRAM @STORYUNFOLDING.

Dear Joan

By Mary Dolan

It is the summer of 2019, and I see an eighty-something woman typing on a portable Royal that is every minute her age. With eyes hidden behind rhinestone-studded sunglasses, her face is shaded by a frayed straw hat. Moving nearer, I take in a faded umbrella, itself having covered a lifetime of beach dreams, then edge in closely enough to read over her shoulder. On heavy white stationery that has yellowed at the borders is the simple salutation, *Dear Joan*. Beneath it, a letter unfolds:

I am back in Rehoboth and musing under this tattered old umbrella (yes, the same one) as I reflect upon the unfinished business of my life and try to find harmony in the closing years I'd yearned to spend with you. There is little reason for *you* to recollect so deeply, but I long for the clarity and peace that come from telling the tale of our younger days. And where my eyes can drift to the horizon of sea and sky, I also grasp the long view of my story. This writing day is for truth telling. What better prompt than this old umbrella?

The year was 1948. You were a seventeen-year-old junior in our Catholic girls' school and had just completed singing *Ave Maria* on the auditorium stage. I was a fourteen-year-old freshman who stood up to applaud you, then sat down in love with you.

I knew I had to meet you. The chance came one day during lunch. I can still see myself springing from a cafeteria table and pushing into line next to you. Reaching for a chocolate milk, I casually asked whether you vacationed in Rehoboth Beach over the summer. It was a wild guess, but it connected. You said yes, and I named St. Edmond's as the place I had seen you. Being the only Catholic church in Rehoboth made this assumption genuine enough, and we became acquaintances during the following months.

I soon joined the school choir just to be near you, even though I didn't know how to read music, play an instrument, or carry a tune.

The old woman sits back in her beach chair and smiles as she puts a fresh page into the typewriter. Rolling her shoulders and flexing her fingers, she continues.

Today they'd call it stalking, but I simply timed my comings and goings with your schedule. As the trolley approached your corner, my heart raced when I saw you waiting. I always contrived to sit up front next to an empty seat, and you never failed to join me, more out of kindness to an obviously besotted schoolgirl than for adult conversation. One morning I asked what scent you were wearing, and from that day to this, White Shoulders has been my signature fragrance.

After your graduation, we kept in touch with birthday and holiday cards, and especially with postcards I sent from Rehoboth while summering there with my family. You working a full-time office job and me still in high school prevented our meeting often during those years, but you encouraged and applauded all of my achievements at school. Working an entire year to be elected to the student council was worth the effort just to earn your congratulations. And you will never know the joy it brought me when you stopped signing your letters "As Ever" and replaced those words with "Love."

After my graduation, I resolved to forge a closer connection between us. I encouraged you to join my employer's glee club and to attend USO dances with me on weekends, all so I could be near you. I certainly had no interest in the servicemen. Yours was the only name on my dance card. And I was delighted when our parents insisted we take cabs home because of the late hour. How well I recall those winter nights when you put your arm through mine and we'd snuggle in the back of the taxi to keep warm. An insistent need inside me yearned for more, but naiveté kept it at bay.

During those years, I made sure you were invited to every party and encouraged overnight sojourns at each other's homes. Both of our bedrooms had double beds. Being so near you those nights made for endless unfulfilled longings of a true innocent. Movie dates became routine, but my most precious memories were our weeks together in Rehoboth, and the joy of sharing that attic room with skylights in its old dormers. How many stars we wished upon.

What joy those summers brought. Endless days on the beach, with no thought to the dangers of sun to our fair Irish skin, led to night strolls along the boardwalk. Candy corn and french fries, saltwater taffy and fudge, heightened the pure enchantment of being together. Rainy days were spent with jigsaw puzzles on the wraparound porch or splashing in the town's notoriously deep puddles following a downpour. On the best days we'd walk hand in hand along the surf's edge in contented silence broken only by the crashing of the waves and the calling of the gulls.

When I see the "Life is Good" T-shirts so popular today, I think *you have no idea*. No life was ever as good as mine during those years when we became and remained best friends. We were inseparable and, given your irrepressible good nature, we laughed all the time.

I watch as the old woman looks up at the pale underside of her beach umbrella, her eyes closed, and appears to sink into her memories. I sense a sadness in her as storm clouds slowly approach from the east. Finally, though, she begins again.

My dear Joan. How pure and wholesome were those years. Would they have ever ended were it not for the inevitable pull in the post-war 1950s toward traditional marriage, children, and anchoring oneself to the confines of the home? I cared nothing for those things. In my mind I was married to you and I loved our life of friendship, fun, and, yes, love. It was enough for me. I'd read the literature available at the time about what were called "Boston Marriages" and pictured us living that life. One whole summer, under this very umbrella, I dreamed of you becoming a famous vocalist while I managed your affairs. We would share a home and work, travel together, and make my dreams come true.

Looking back, I wonder whether you knew how seriously I took to heart your continuing comment, "If you were a boy, I'd marry you." I truly believed you meant it. I loved you, and had the legal option to marry come sooner, I would have formally proposed. From the instant I saw you, I saw us. I saw us as the carefree teens we were and the devoted young women we became. But my heart saw beyond those years to a shared adulthood, middle-age, and finally, waning days, together on Rehoboth Beach.

I absolutely expected us to grow old together, and had the nineties come sooner, who knows what might have been?

Naturally, we never discussed this possibility and, inevitably, along came the genuine stalkers who threatened to take you away from me. Predators with names like Bill or Bob or Jack. When my older brother, Jack, developed a crush on you, I often teased that if you two married we could live next door to each other, hanging our laundry on adjacent lines, cooking meals together, remaining best friends for the rest of our lives. But you didn't love Jack. Pulled along by the culture of the times, and less endowed with my rebel spirit, you married Frank.

The nearest I came to standing with you at the altar was serving as your maid of honor, and silently affirming, *I do*.

I feel, more than see, weariness creep over the woman as she pauses to remove the sheet and replace it with what would be the last page of her letter.

So, Joan, there rests the misunderstanding of our youth. Now I find myself overwhelmed by what I hold within: the words *I love you*, forever unspoken, my frustration at the absolute absence of intimacy, dreams of happily ever after shattered. Emotions so freely expressed in this day and age, so cloaked in disgrace then.

No one on this beach of many memories would guess that I write about such force of feeling, feelings forbidden decades ago, decades when I was forged and shaped by first love. Other chapters have woven in and out of other years, and happiness has not eluded me altogether, but like Rehoboth's ocean wildly rushing in and ebbing out, my sustaining life force has always been our love story.

Respectful of her privacy, I step back and wait for her to finish the letter, but she doesn't resume typing. Rather, she stares out to sea, as her reverie carries her back to that fourteen-year-old girl, seated in her high school auditorium, listening to the soaring beauty of the *Ave Maria* and falling in love all over again.

MARY'S JOURNEY HAS TAKEN HER FROM PHILADELPHIA, WHERE SHE RAN A MARKETING COMMUNICATIONS FIRM, TO THE COAST OF MAINE WHERE SHE LAUNCHED A SECOND LIFE'S CHAPTER SELLING HER PHOTOGRAPHY ON THE EAST COAST ART SHOW CIRCUIT.

SETTLED NOW IN EASTON, MARYLAND, WITH HER PARTNER, JUDY, AND HAVING TRADED HER SHOW TENTS AND DISPLAY RACKS FOR A LAPTOP, SHE SHARES THE KEYBOARD AND HER ACCOLADES WITH FIVE RESCUED CATS. LAST YEAR'S STORY FOR THE REHOBOTH BEACH READS SERIES WAS FOLLOWED BY A FIRST-PLACE AWARD THIS YEAR. ALSO THIS YEAR, MARY RECEIVED SECOND-PLACE HONORS IN DELAWARE PRESS ASSOCIATION'S PROFESSIONAL COMMUNICATIONS CONTEST, WAS AWARDED RUNNER-UP BY A WOMEN'S ONLINE PUBLICATION, AND SAW HER HAIKU PUBLISHED IN A JOURNAL OF NATURE POETRY.

"DEAR JOAN" IS NOT A STORY YOU CAN WRITE WHEN YOU'RE YOUNG. AND MARY WAS RELUCTANT TO SUBMIT IT EVEN NOW. EIGHT DECADES LATER, RECALLING CHERISHED MEMORIES STILL ECHOES THE OLD HEARTBREAK. THE WRITING WAS DIFFICULT, THE MELANCHOLY GENUINE, AND THE PASSAGE OF TIME UNSETTLING. READ IT GENTLY.

JUDGES' COMMENTS

"Dear Joan" is a modern tragedy in which fate rules. The 1950s were the times, and the author, in true Greek fashion, makes us feel that in that narrow-minded, segregated culture, the story could have turned out no different. Expressed through an ever-shifting point of perspective, this short story poignantly describes the pathos of lost love. Filled with ache and longing, this finely woven tale was a no-brainer for first prize.

Lost and Found

By Dave Cooper

Ben knew little about the man on Rehoboth's boardwalk except that each year his wrinkles grew deeper, his back was more bent, and his body leaned more heavily on a cane. The strangeness of noticing this one person didn't escape Ben. He pushed up from his towel and tightened the belt of his swim trunks.

Even when lying on the beach, he was able to spot the old man among the hundreds of vacationers swarming the end of Rehoboth Avenue. Some thought the railroad's end to passenger service would slow migrations to the "Nation's Summer Capital," but they were wrong. DeSotos and Pontiacs just replaced the railroad cars.

The old man had to be part of this migration. He appeared only in June, sat each night on the same bench in front of the Belhaven Hotel, and stared across the sand with the porch-lined Victorian's window-eyes watching over him.

"Why does the old man come here?" Ben asked aloud. With a sigh, he stretched his neck turning his head from side to side. "And, why do I care?"

* * * * *

Alex closed his notebook, glanced at the smartphone propped in his beach chair's cup holder, and tossed his pen into his bag. He liked the gradual build leading to Ben meeting the old man. The story flowed so well it seemed to be writing itself, as if the characters had stepped from the pages and whispered words into his ear.

Alex brushed sand from a sepia-toned postcard and turned to face the boardwalk at the end of Rehoboth Avenue. He lifted the worn and dog-eared picture of the Belhaven to fill the spot where the hotel had once stood, within the Candy Kitchen's footprint across from Dolle's. Writing period fiction posed new challenges for Alex, especially since history had never been one of his strong points, but he felt he had done his homework for this story. Lots of homework. For now, though, Ben's questions about the old man would have to wait. No more time to write.

Alex navigated through vacationers hovering around the caramel corn window at Dolle's and the line forming outside Nicola Pizza with the deft movements of a local. He worked his way back to the Sea Mist Motel, the blocks passing as quickly as dusk passed into night.

The thought of owning the Sea Mist had appealed to Alex more than the reality of owning it. Too bad this realization had come only after signing the mortgage papers and a decade struggling to survive from one summer season to the next. He wished the world would just leave him alone to write.

Alex ambled up the motel's creaking and rotting front steps to the lobby where a middle-aged woman with dark red hair sat behind a Formica counter.

"Hey, Sandra," he said.

"We had a cancellation for room seven," she replied.

Sandra had been a more-than-loyal employee, staying with him through the rough financial years and the even more difficult personal ones, yet he couldn't shake how her high-pitched voice traveled his spine like a cheese grater.

"How are the scholars in four and five?" he asked.

"I saw a few stumbling around a little while ago."

"OK, thanks." Alex felt her gaze on his back as he walked through the door to the pool. Sandra wanted more from him. He knew that. Her smile would warm any other man, but she wanted something he just couldn't give her—an optimism he lost long ago with a marriage gone horribly wrong. He kept telling himself she would someday stop waiting. Give up. Move on.

Pale-green light rose from the pool's water. Undulating reflections, ethereal ripples, bounced among scattered and empty plastic chairs. A fence of peeling white boards provided a backdrop for the hypnotic show.

Alex sat at the nearest plastic table, fished in his pack for his notebook, and began writing, the words an escape from his reality.

* * * * *

The old man sat on his bench with his head sunk to his chest and his hands thrust deep within a yellow gabardine jacket's pockets. The Belhaven seemed to retreat from the old man and give Ben permission to approach.

Ben motioned to the bench and asked, "May I?"

"Of course, son." The old man moved his cane. "You on vacation?"

"No. Used to be stationed here. Fort Miles. Decided to stay after my discharge."

The old man said, "Thought you might be military."

"Hair gives me away." Ben ran his hand over his crew cut. "And you, sir? Vacation?"

The old man nodded. "Come here every year."

Ben gazed out to sea. A small boat's light bobbed like a firefly on the water. The boardwalk lamp above the bench hummed slowly to life, giving the old man in his yellow jacket a faint golden glow.

Ben glanced over his shoulder. "The Belhaven, they just finished painting it. Looks real nice."

"Yes, it does."

"Do you stay there?"

The man nodded. "This place is … special."

"Certainly has some history," Ben said. "I thought you might have some kind of connection to it."

"The best and worst of my life happened right here. I was about to start a new chapter—we were about to start a new chapter in our lives." The man looked out to the water, where a few amber streaks lingered. With much effort, he grasped his cane and pushed himself to his feet. "If you'll excuse me, I'm going to turn in."

Ben stood. "I hope I didn't offend you."

"No. Not at all. I'm glad we met."

The old man left Ben to his thoughts.

* * * * *

Alex forced himself to close his notebook. Ben and the old man's first encounter, a key scene, had been put to paper, yet this would have to be enough, for now. Even an inspired writer had to eat.

Alex left the pool and walked to his apartment behind the motel. He tossed his bag on a tattered leather chair and groaned at the slim pickings in his kitchen cabinet. The refrigerator's contents were even less promising.

A half hour and a bag from Grub Grocery later, Alex crossed Rehoboth Avenue toward his apartment. A sudden breeze stroked his body. The sensation of a thousand needles ran up and down his arms and legs. He shivered and readjusted the bag in his arms.

Alex took a few more steps toward his apartment, but the breeze pushed him the other way, toward the boardwalk. More pins and needles. He yielded and let the gusts take him to the end of Rehoboth Avenue.

A thick bank of ocean fog diffused the lights from storefronts into glowing plumes. Luminous white clouds tethered to lampposts hovered above vacationers' heads. Gulls floated between fog banks, ghostly creatures blinking in and out of existence.

The breeze nudged Alex's back, directing him onto the beach toward the sounds of waves crashing on each other and against the jetties. He sat and pushed his bag into the sand to keep it from spilling, stretched his arms above his head, and took a deep breath. Perhaps an hour passed before a new sound rose above the metronome of waves and whispering wind.

Crying?

Alex stood and tried to see through the fog. The moon shone above the ocean, but the fog made it a pale, useless disc.

The crying grew louder. Alex lifted his grocery bag and followed the sobs to a kneeling figure, a young nightgowned woman with wavy brown hair draped over alabaster shoulders. Skin luminescent despite the light-starved beach. She sifted sand through her fingers handful after handful.

Alex knelt. "Miss, can I get you some help?"

Without looking up from her chore, she pleaded, "My ring, I have to find it. My fiancé worked so hard. Saved for so long."

We couldn't find a lost pickup truck in this fog let alone a ring in the sand. "Are you sure you lost it here?"

She clawed her way through the sand again and again.

Alex set aside his bag and started digging. *I can help until she calms down enough to see reason.*

Night-cold sand ran between his fingers, grains spilling and covering others, most never to be touched again. He brushed against something. Carefully, he grasped the small object. He lifted it slowly, holding it up to the pale disc moon. *The ring.* A few beams struck a humble diamond. *I'll be damned.*

"You found it!" The woman's eyes shined.

Alex placed the ring in her outstretched palm.

She slid the band across her knuckles and melded into a rolling veil of fog.

"Miss?" Alex scrambled to his feet. "Where are you?" He willed himself to the fenced path through the dunes and onto an abandoned boardwalk.

No woman.

No one.

Only silence, thick fog, and lampposts illuminating what should have been a circus of parents, kids, junk food, and arcade sounds.

"Is anyone here?"

Alex felt his way through the fog and across the boardwalk to where he knew a row of benches faced the large, round bandstand at the end of Rehoboth Avenue. He found the benches but no bandstand.

"No, this can't be right."

He shuffled along the benches moving to his left toward the Candy Kitchen, or at least to where candy-lined windows should have been spilling bright fluorescent light onto the sidewalk, but he found instead a three-story Victorian hotel with green trim, steep gabled roofs, and a wrap-around porch.

"My God, it's the Belhaven."

He rubbed his forehead, squeezed shut his eyes, and steadied himself using the bench. The Belhaven had been destroyed by a horrendous storm in 1962.

"Thank you," he heard the woman say, again.

Alex raised his gaze and saw her watching him from the hotel's porch. She turned and disappeared inside its dark doorway.

Alex crumpled to his knees. A wave of cold mist rolled over him. *None of this makes sense.* The wave subsided, the air cleared, and the boardwalk burst to life with laughing children, chatting adults, and dizzying motion. The world spun with Alex as its axis.

"What's happening?" he yelled.

Alex didn't remember walking back to his apartment. Sleep didn't come, and he couldn't shake the woman's image from his mind. Couldn't rationalize what he had seen. Had no one to tell.

He did the only thing he knew to do. He took up a pen and opened his notebook.

* * * * *

Ben found his usual spot on the beach but lay with his towel facing the boardwalk. Every few minutes he scanned the vacationers until he saw the old man standing in front of the Belhaven, hunched and leaning on his cane.

Ben gathered his things and hurried to the boardwalk. "Sir," he called.

The old man smiled and tapped his cane. "Good morning."

"Good morning." Ben extended his hand, which the old man took warmly. "Do you have some time?"

"Can't say I have much time left, but I can spare a few minutes." The man motioned to the bench.

They sat.

Ben said, "You told me this place was important to you."

The old man nodded. "Still is."

"Why?"

The old man turned as much as his frail body allowed and pointed with his cane at the Belhaven. "I brought my girl here years ago. Sarah. Took the train all the way from Philadelphia. Asked her to marry me." He looked down at his shoes. "I gave her … well, the ring wasn't much. And then … I was so mad at her." He turned and looked up into the Belhaven's windows. "Some things seem so important, at the time, then your world turns upside down."

"Did she—" Ben stopped when he noticed the man nodding.

"She got a fever just before we were to go home. Even now, it still helps to talk about what happened here. My Sarah. What could have been." The man groaned as he rose.

"Will you be back, tomorrow?" Ben asked.

"No. No, I don't think so. Regret is a hard devil to shake, but I got up this morning and something felt different." The old man smiled. "I haven't felt this way in many years." He said goodbye to Ben, then crossed into town becoming lost among those milling about Rehoboth Avenue.

* * * * *

Alex woke at his desk. The story of Ben and the old man lay beneath his folded arms. Despite a scrawled, *The End*, he felt this draft had yet to be finished. One of the character's conflicts had yet to be resolved, but Sandra would already be covering his shift at the front desk. He showered hurriedly.

No more writing today.

Alex stopped just outside the motel office door, his eye having caught a flash of bright pink from a small bunch of flowers in a wooden planter.

Sandra looked up from her perch behind the counter and smiled at him through the ripped screen door. "Good morning."

"Hey, Sandra," he said through the screen. "You put these flowers here?"

"Two days ago."

Alex nodded and opened the door.

Still smiling, Sandra watched Alex enter and said, "The girls in room eleven told me the bathroom faucet is leaking."

Alex grunted. "Can you stay a few more minutes, so I can look at it?"

She nodded. "The room is empty. They checked out."

Alex opened room eleven with his master key and shook his head at what awaited his poor maid. He stepped over a pile of wet towels, picked his way through a mosaic of pizza boxes, and glanced at a leaning tower of beer cans and scattered wine bottles.

"Thank you," a woman said.

Alex suddenly felt the pins and needles of last night, stopped, and turned toward the bright rectangle of the open doorway.

A woman crossed through the light. Long dark hair. Alabaster complexion. Wearing a light color. Maybe white.

The pins and needles became a chill. Alex kicked through the towels and boxes, clutched the doorjamb, and leaned into the parking lot.

Sandra stood outside the office holding a stack of mail.

"Did you see someone pass by?" Alex asked her.

Sandra looked around then shook her head. "I just went to the mailbox. Didn't see anyone."

Alex closed his eyes and rested his forehead on the back of his hand. *What's happening to me?* After a deep breath, he stepped from the room and into the sun.

"Who was it?" Sandra asked.

Sandra's voice sounded different. No longer shrill. Her eyes sparkled in the sunlight. Green. Beautiful. He thought, *Thank you for not moving on*, and it surprised him.

Sandra continued, "Someone you know?"

"Maybe someone I met on the beach."

Alex thought about Ben's line, *What could have been*, and said, "Someone returning a favor." He stepped toward Sandra. "Someone trying to help write *my* story."

DAVE COOPER IS A HISTORY AND MARTIAL ARTS TEACHER WITH ALMOST TWENTY-FIVE YEARS OF EXPERIENCE IN EACH FIELD. HIS FIRST ARTICLE APPEARED IN THE NATIONAL MIDDLE SCHOOL ASSOCIATION'S *MIDDLE GROUND* IN 2003. SINCE THEN, HE HAS CONTRIBUTED TO A VARIETY OF PERIODICALS INCLUDING *TEACHING HISTORY*, *MIDDLE LEVEL LEARNING*, *FAMILY CHRONICLE*, *BOY'S LIFE*, *COLLEGE BOUND*, AND *PENNSYLVANIA EDUCATIONAL LEADERSHIP*. HIS FICTION AND POETRY HAVE APPEARED IN *TIMBER CREEK REVIEW*, *YORICK MAGAZINE*, *NFG*, AND IN THE CAT & MOUSE PRESS ANTHOLOGY *BEACH PULP*. DAVE CONTINUES TO TEACH AND WRITE IN LANCASTER, PENNSYLVANIA. MORE OF HIS WORK CAN BE FOUND AT DCWRITING.WORDPRESS.COM.

Jojo's Diner

By Cindy Cavett

"Sweet dreams are made of this …"

The Eurythmics song resonated through the speakers of the old Jeep's stereo system. Jo Kowalski and her daughter, Arianna, were on their way to Rehoboth Beach for a fresh start.

"Mom, you know there are modern cars with surround-sound speaker systems and touch screens that do way more than play cassette tapes, right? We need to get you a real car and a real stereo."

Jo shrugged a shoulder at her twelve-year-old daughter. She still remembered when *her* mom used to play vintage vinyl records long before they became a trend. She also recalled telling her mother to get with the times and buy an eight-track stereo deck so they could listen to what the cool kids were listening to: Styx, Journey, and the Eagles.

Arianna flipped through cassette tapes stored inside an old shoebox. Jo already knew which one she'd pick. Her daughter was obsessed with eighties movies, just like her parents. Sure enough, Arianna popped a tape into the cassette player and they immediately heard the inspired keyboard crescendo at the beginning of "St. Elmo's Fire (Man in Motion)." Jo and Arianna sang at the top of their lungs.

Jo's heart was overflowing with anticipation as she and Arianna drove down Baltimore Avenue toward the sea. They had desperately needed something to look forward to after Joseph's death.

Arianna changed out the tape as they arrived at a stop sign with a yellow tulip planter base. Tiny pink flower petals blew in on the ocean breeze and landed on Jo's khaki capris. She lifted them in the palm of her hand and blew them toward Arianna, who giggled.

They pulled up to a colonial-style, two-story building on the corner of First Street and Baltimore Avenue. The vinyl siding was a bright summer-yellow with black shutters and black entryway doors. Jo had been able to buy the building, which had housed a small restaurant, from an estate trust for a steal. As soon as they parked, Arianna let out a long whistle of surprise.

"This place is huge, Mom. Are you sure about this?"

Jo unbuckled her seat belt and nodded. She had never been so sure about anything in her life.

"Yep. Come on, honey. Let's check it out."

The sun was high, with the weather being a perfect seventy, warm for the end of March.

"I hope we can get everything done in time for the Memorial Day weekend," said Jo.

The real estate agent had mailed Jo a rusty, old key. Orange marks smeared her fingers as she struggled to unlock the front door. It wouldn't budge. After several jiggles and a nudge, the warped wooden door finally opened. They stepped into the darkness and sneezed in unison. Opening the shades and curtains didn't help their sinuses, but once the sun poured in, it seemed like a different place.

"Well, what do you think?" asked Jo.

Arianna looked around.

"Not bad, not bad. Maybe we can paint the oak paneling white? Make it brighter in here. What do you want to do with these old booths? Some of the seats have holes in them."

Jo stuck a finger two inches deep into a cushion. "We need to upgrade these. I'm thinking new booths around the outside and in the center."

The wall next to the front register was hidden behind postcards, photos, and thank-you notes from patrons over the years. Jo glanced at a few and saw that some were over thirty years old.

"I think we'll keep this keepsake wall," said Jo. "This is too good of a collection to take down. I'm sure customers will love seeing that their old memorabilia is still here."

Arianna smiled. "I love it already."

Jo beamed. Soon, her dream of owning a beachside breakfast diner would come true. Having a pre-teen daughter support that dream was priceless.

Next, Jo showed Arianna the apartment above the restaurant. She slid the vertical blinds back from a set of sliding glass doors on the second floor. Dust danced in the sun's beams as they shone through the glass.

"Arianna, look at this deck. You can lie out and tan with your friends when you're not helping in the restaurant."

Arianna followed her mom onto the deck. Baltimore Avenue was alive with shoppers, dog-walkers, and beachgoers heading to the Atlantic Ocean for a relaxing day with the surf and sand. Seagulls laughed as they flew overhead.

"This is perfect," said Arianna.

Back downstairs, Cyndi Lauper was singing "Girls Just Want to Have Fun" through Arianna's Bluetooth speaker. They decided to prepare the place for cleaning and painting. While Arianna took down Venetian blinds, Jo removed curtains. Jo could already smell the pancakes and French toast she planned to cook for her customers.

There was a small knock, and they heard someone push open the door with a "harrumph." Arianna dropped an armload of blinds on the floor. "Can I help you?"

The man glanced around the dining area, obviously looking for someone. He seemed to be in his late thirties or early forties with a goatee that matched his salt-and-pepper hair.

"Hi there, I'm Nick. You must be Arianna. I'm looking for Jo— is she here?"

"Maybe. Who are you?"

"I'm your mom's real estate agent. I wanted to stop by and make sure everything was going alright."

Jo pushed her way through the swinging door into the main dining area, carrying a stack of curtains that went up past her chin.

"Oh, hi. It's great to see you again, Nick," she said, passing the curtains to Arianna and then realizing she was still wearing a kerchief on her head. She grabbed it off her dirty-blonde hair and scrunched it, wishing her fairy godmother would appear and magically make her hair behave. "Thank you for helping us get such a great deal on this place. It really is a dream come true."

Nick smiled warmly, displaying adorable dimples.

"It sure is. How is everything—any problems? You getting settled in OK?"

Jo took in Nick's crisp, blue chinos, fine-leather shoes, and a button-down collared shirt with a logo on the pocket and suddenly felt out of place in her T-shirt, capris, and Converse sneakers.

"Actually, aside from a lot of dust, everything seems to be going fine, knock on wood." Jo rapped on the wooden counter that held the cash register.

Nick smiled and did the same.

Another believer in superstitions. I like him already. "Arianna, would you mind grabbing the final draft of the menu from the trailer? The keys are on the counter."

"You got it, Mom."

Nick walked into the main dining area. "So, this is going to be a breakfast place?" he asked, taking a seat in one of the booths.

Jo sat down across from him, gleaming with happiness but wincing as a spring poked into her leg. "Yes, that's right. A seaside breakfast and brunch diner. I want folks to come in and enjoy themselves—people on their way to fish, families on vacation, retirees heading out for a morning walk—pretty much everyone."

"You are too sweet," said Nick. "Please tell me you'll be changing up the colors in here. Or do you want it to continue screaming for help?"

Jo laughed so loudly her voice echoed against the paneled walls.

"Obviously make it a bit brighter, but I want to add a bit of vintage flair—eighties and nineties memorabilia—tasteful, not tacky."

Nick and Jo chatted like old friends until Arianna arrived with the menu.

"Good afternoon. My name is Arianna and I'll be your server today. Here is our menu. We have absolutely no working appliances, and no food, water, or plates, but I can get you a fresh bowl of seaside air if you wish, courtesy of Rehoboth Beach."

"I see we have a comedic waitress," said Nick. Jo winked at him and played along, looking at the menu.

"Well then, dear waitress," said Jo, "I suppose I'll take a bowl of seaside air, with a side of cleaning crew to help us. How does that sound?"

"Now that sounds like a good order, Mom!"

"Our agency has a cleaning company we recommend," Nick said. "I'll get you hooked up."

"Seriously? That sounds great," said Jo. "I can use all the help I can get. Memorial Day is the unofficial start of the summer season in Rehoboth, and I need this place open for that weekend."

After the cleaning company finished, Jo assembled a painting and decorating crew comprised of young people Arianna had met and an older woman named Pat who had stopped in several times to see their progress. The space was being transformed from an outdated restaurant to a fresh, new diner with vintage tributes to eighties and nineties pop culture.

Jo brought in some of her favorite finds. She placed a *Miami Vice* police badge in a display case beneath the cash register by the front door and laughed when Pat hung a framed print of Dorothy, Blanche, Rose, and Sophia from *The Golden Girls* over a booth. Arianna arranged a couple of Smurf figurines wearing sunglasses in the case alongside a suction-cup Garfield that previously held tight onto the back window of her dad's 1986 Nissan Stanza wagon.

Jo hadn't completely resisted the tacky, but the restaurant was now bright, beachy, and full of character. It felt like home.

One day, after the afternoon had waned and most of the crew retired for the evening, Jo found Pat hovering near the memorabilia wall by the front door. Pat's hand grazed the photo of a couple. The picture had to have been at least fifty years old.

"Do you know them?"

Pat let her fingers linger a few seconds longer, then turned to smile at Jo as she opened the door to leave. "Oh, yes," she said quietly. "Goodnight."

Jo was happy to have found friends so quickly in Rehoboth Beach. If she wasn't shopping for supplies and decor for the diner with Nick, she was listening to local artists at the monthly night of songs and stories with the local writers' guild. Arianna had made friends quickly as well and joined the high school drama club. Nights and weekends revolved around the diner, rehearsals, and beach living. It was everything Jo had always dreamed of. The only thing missing was her late husband, Joseph.

With only two weeks left to prepare the diner for its grand opening, Jo worked long hours into the night, repeatedly going over every detail. On the last Friday before the diner's opening, Jo went over things one last time with the staff she had hired.

Arianna pecked Jo on the cheek before leaving with one of her theater friends for their latest rehearsal. "Love you, Mom," she yelled, as she ran out.

Love you, too, sweetheart. Jo stopped going over the inventory list and closed her eyes for a moment to listen to the sounds of the night. The din of the boardwalk was heating up with vacationers. The ocean's waves spilled into her mind and filled her with calm, even if for just a few moments.

She opened her eyes and sighed at the brightly lit laptop in front of her. Piles of notebooks, receipts, and a thick budgeting book begged her to dive back into Adulting 101.

Jo's cell phone buzzed with a text from Nick telling her to stop working and meet him at the Purple Parrot, pronto. She grinned but put the phone down and went back to the spreadsheet on her laptop. Her phone buzzed again. He told her to stop ignoring his texts and said she better not make him dance all by himself. Jo laughed and went back to work. Pat sat down in the booth across from her.

"Pat! Holy crap, you startled me. You're like a ninja. I thought you left with everyone else."

Pat chuckled.

"No, honey. I still had some woodwork to touch up in the ladies' restroom. The mural looks great in there, but it ain't gonna look good if the woodwork around the door is a righteous mess."

Jo took off her glasses and relaxed. A couple of times a week, for the past few weeks, Pat had stayed behind to chat. Jo loved hearing her stories.

"You know there isn't a lot more work to be done here, don't you?"

Jo nodded. "Pat, what would you say if I asked you to stay on and help out around here? You could do whatever you like—wipe tables, keep the customers company, help with receipts. I know you enjoy being here and we'd really love to have you stay."

Pat smiled, her gaze lingering on the photos by the front door. She put her hand out and patted Jo's.

"Little lady, why are you working here on a Friday night when the doors aren't even open yet? You need to get out and enjoy yourself while you still can. You live at the beach for Christ's sake."

Jo sat back and sighed.

"You want to know the truth? I'm scared. I want to make this dream of owning a beach diner come true so badly. I have a business degree and a master's in marketing. I worked in the hospitality industry for twelve years. But owning a business is completely new and utterly terrifying. Joseph and I always wanted to make this dream happen together. This was *our* dream, and I don't have him here to help me. I can't fail and I can't let Arianna down either."

Pat patted Jo's hand again, then held it tightly.

"Jo, I want you to take a deep breath, and then listen to me. I know you've got the weight of the world on your shoulders, but I've got a story to tell you."

"I'm ready."

"A long time ago, a man and his wife built a little restaurant from the ground up. I mean actually built it, like with their own hands as well as their blood, sweat, and tears. It took over a year. But with the help of his dad and brothers, and her cooking and organization, their dream came true. They called it the Sand Dollar Restaurant. It was nothing fancy, just a little place that served home-cooked meals to locals in the winter and tourists in the summer."

Jo nodded for Pat to go on.

"Now, this man and wife, they were mighty in love. The kind of love that people wish on stars for. And try as they might, and boy did they enjoy trying, they just could not produce a family. You see what I'm saying? So, they poured their hearts and souls into their Sand Dollar Restaurant, giving their love to everyone who came through the door for almost fifty years."

Pat squeezed Jo's hand.

"Eventually, the man started to get tired. He couldn't cook in the kitchen anymore, so he took care of the cash register. He started a collage on the wall next to his seat. Over the years he posted pictures of customers, postcards, and trinkets. It was such a hoot that people kept giving him more and more things to put up. One day, the man couldn't get out of bed. His wife stayed with him every day, while the staff took care of the restaurant. And then, just like that …" She snapped her fingers.

"He was gone," said Jo.

Pat nodded. "He was gone."

Jo wiped a tear from her cheek before it fell from her chin and kept listening.

"Jo, this is the Sand Dollar Restaurant that my husband and I built back in 1970. Before he died, we put the restaurant into an estate trust to make it easier to sell when the time came. You bought it from our trust."

"Pat, I had no idea. I'm so sorry I didn't realize this sooner."

Pat waved her off.

"Pish-posh, girl. You've been busy getting your diner ready for its grand opening. Besides, I kind of hid who I was from you."

"Yeah, that's true. Why *did* you hide your identity?"

"I wanted to see who we were leaving the Sand Dollar to. You remind me a lot of me at your age. And from what I hear of what your husband was like, he reminds me of my Tom. And you know what? I now know that the Sand Dollar is in good hands and our legacy will live on. You've already achieved your dream, girl. Now you need to learn how to enjoy the moment."

Jo got up from the booth and hugged Pat.

"Thank you, Pat. I will take good care of your restaurant."

"All right, all right, now you got my eyes leaking. Go on girl, git. Go join that man at that club and make some noise. The night's still young."

Jo kissed her on the cheek.

"Lock up for me?"

Pat nodded. "You got it."

The grand opening of Jojo's Diner, named after Jo and her late husband, Joseph, was held the Wednesday before Memorial Day. In front of the mayor, new friends, and the local media, Jo and Arianna cut a massive red ribbon on the steps of the diner. The first crowd of customers enjoyed breakfast while listening to Billy Joel sing out, "It's Still Rock and Roll to Me." Jo loved talking to her customers and found that they enjoyed reliving their memories of growing up with the movie stars, TV actors, and childhood toys displayed at Jojo's Diner. It was exactly what she had hoped would happen. Joseph would have been delighted.

Pat wound up staying on at Jojo's. But instead of having Pat bus tables or waitress, Jo asked for her help in the kitchen, especially during the morning rush. And on busy Saturday mornings, Arianna helped out as well. Her favorite job was the one Pat had taught her—how to pour the batter for the diner's specialty: sand dollar pancakes.

Cindy Cavett is a business professional, freelance writer, and award-winning author. Cindy's work has been published by Cat & Mouse Press and Running Wild Press and has appeared in broadcast media, newspapers, magazines, and online. Her story "Rehoboth Beach Break" was given to nominees for the 2019 Golden Globes, SAG Awards, and 2018 Emmys.

"Jojo's Diner" was inspired by and in memory of Cindy's mom, Jo Demay-Guenzer. Jo had a lifelong dream of owning a diner at the beach. She enjoyed cooking French toast and sand dollar pancakes and loved the sea.

Cindy is grateful to the Rehoboth Beach Reads judges for selecting "Jojo's Diner" and to Nancy Sakaduski for her extraordinary editing talents and guidance. She would also like to thank Kristeen Gillooly-Gonzalez and Kimberly Chesser for their help and guidance, and her husband, Jason, for his love and support and for walking the dogs when she's up writing at five a.m. Learn more at SeasideCindy.com.

The Bull, Dogs, and Sleep

By Alexander Hood

June

I laugh hysterically as the bull runs after me. I can't stop myself; I almost fall over in the soft sand of the beach as I walk on, quickly as I can. My knees hurt. The bull slowly gains on me, and I turn to see his giant red eyes leering at me.

The space between the crowd and me has expanded. The only one still nearby is my friend Carol, who is staying with me; we are getting out of this alive together. We must be quite a sight—two eighty-year-old women, dressed in white, with red bandanas, walking relatively quickly as the "bull," made up of two drunk, twentysomething males, chases us across the sand.

The annual Running of the Bull is a Dewey Beach tradition I have watched with envy many times, but before this year I never imagined I would participate.

The crowd starts to chant "Go, beach grannies, go!" as we slowly "race" away from the staggering bull. Debra and I hold hands as we speed up, spurred on by the positive energy of the crowd.

The Starboard is getting closer. The bull moves in slow circles, making moves as if to catch up, but lets us finish the footrace to a giant "hooray" from the crowd.

We step aside as the bull enters the crowded bar, eventually to meet its fate at the hands of the "matador"—a local celebrity with a wooden sword.

A group of kids makes room for me as I breathlessly sit down on one of a few chairs. I look around at the rowdy crowd and laugh to myself. *Finally. After all these years.*

July

It's always so hot during the summer, and the soft, metallic clanging of my air conditioner is getting on my nerves. I do like July, though, because school gets out and my granddaughter Megan comes down to spend a week with me. She's a great kid; occasionally there's a temper tantrum, but for the most part she is thrilled to be at the beach with grandma, bodyboarding in the surf and catching up with the friends she made last year.

The high point, of course, is the fireworks that occur around the Fourth of July. We bring out the chairs and sit on the beach to watch. It's completely dark before the fireworks start; we have to use our voices—plus the occasional flashlight or sparkler—to navigate to my group of friends.

I used to think the Rehoboth fireworks were too long, having seen them year after year, looking somewhat similar, explosion after explosion. I take a deep breath, inhaling the faint smell of gunpowder, and look around. So many people, so much laughter, so many colors and people, all coming together. *I may miss this the most*, I think, as I walk Megan back into our house and hear the familiar sound of my cottage's creaking screen door as it shuts behind us.

August

Pontoon boats might as well be named "party boats." Every August, the Clayton gang rents two pontoon boats from Rehoboth Bay Marina and heads out into the bay. I'm in charge of the guacamole and chips; the others take care of the heavy stuff and bring the alcohol. I get a laugh from the group when I tell them I tried to buy the beer at the Dewey liquor store, but they thought my ID was fake.

Just as in the past several years, we have lucked out with gorgeous weather. We glide across the bay, headed to our favorite sandbar. After purposely running the pontoon aground, we hand over the beach chairs and set up our own island paradise. The wind blows across the water. We toast to the "best summer ever."

September

I wake up from my dream alone, shivering and sweating at the same time. It's 3:30 a.m. and the house is silent.

Wide awake. It's time to start. I came across an article online that talked about "death cleaning." The concept is depressing, but it stayed with me. I kept thinking about what the family would find if they came to my house and I was not there. Instead of my homemade strawberry cobbler, they'd be faced with the piles of paperwork and mail that I never seem to want to focus on.

It just wouldn't be fair to leave those things to others, so my first room is the study. In the coming weeks, I'll take care of the more personal things that might shock—letters from lovers long lost, clothes that might make everyone blush—but for now, I focus on the paperwork I've never discarded. I always hated the dentist's bills, often for some small amount that wasn't covered by my insurance. Why did I save them? I add the folder to the shred pile and sigh at the work ahead.

October

It starts with my granddaughter Megan's question: "Has Chester ever seen the beach?" Although Chester's a cat, it's a fair question, especially since he only lives a few blocks away from the shore. Chester— indoor explorer, adventurer, scaredy cat— has never touched sand or heard the ocean. With that in mind, early one Saturday morning Megan and I scoop up Chester, put him in his brown travel carrier, and head to the Rehoboth beach.

As we trudge down Queen Street to the shore, Megan takes Chester in his carrier and runs ahead excitedly. The cat carrier bangs against her little knees.

"Be careful!" I yell, trying to catch up as I stumble down the beach with my newly purchased cat harness.

I smile to myself as Megan puts the carrier on the sand and bends down to unzip it. Chester pokes his head carefully out of the carrier. I catch up to Megan, put my arm around her, prepare the harness, and smile.

Then we hear a bark. I look toward the boardwalk and see a group of people surrounded by lean, muscular-looking racing dogs. Megan looks up at me, and I swear under my breath. "Greyhound Weekend."

What happens next is slow-motion chaos. Chester springs free and runs toward Dewey. The dogs come off the boardwalk, heading in my direction on their way to chase Chester. My granddaughter runs after Chester. Without thinking, I turn to face the dogs, raise my right hand as if a traffic cop, yell "stop," and pretend to have a treat clenched in my left hand. The diversion, something I'd seen on TV, causes the dogs to slow down and look back at their owners in confusion. Thankfully, it's enough. Megan catches up to Chester, grabs the agitated cat in her little hands and makes her way back. I look to the owners, thankful for well-trained dogs, and run over to help Megan get Chester into the harness.

The cat carrier is still on the beach; I'll have to get it tomorrow. But today, a little ice cream, some Neosporin for the scratches from terrified Chester's claws, and a can of expensive cat food will solve everything.

Later that night, with both Megan and Chester sound asleep, I share one of the best laughs I've had in a long time with my son, Michael, and his wife, Samantha. I ignored the concern in their voices about the fact that I'd forgotten it was Greyhound Weekend, one of my favorite weekends of the year.

November

Thanksgiving this year falls on November 24, which is three years to the day since Joe passed. I wake and, for a few minutes, forget where I am. The edges of the curtain let in the bright sun. The gentle rocking and murmur of a giant engine confuse me. It's not until I'm out of bed, my feet shuffling across the floor to the tiny bathroom, that I remember I am on a cruise with my son's family.

I always think of Thanksgiving as an occasion for a big table full of turkey, family, and friends. But this new tradition of being in the Caribbean is working out fine.

I think Michael enjoys it, too. But today I'm not looking forward to being holiday happy. Of course, I will join the group for the required dinner, but I've already told them I'm going to do my own thing during the day.

I step off the boat, past the crew taking photos, and into the crowd, when I get that nervous feeling again and start forgetting everything at once. Why is it hot out here? Where did this crowd come from? And most terrifying, who am I? The only thing I remember is breathing deeply with fear.

December

Over Christmas, Megan asked—as only a child could—what it's like to be old. I thought for a minute, tried to put on a warm smile, and said, "You know when you wake up some days and you're not feeling really good? Maybe you have a fever, or a headache, and everything becomes a little tougher, you forget some things and are a little more grumpy than normal?" Megan nodded. "It's like that," I say. "But imagine it a little worse."

I still feel bad about answering so honestly, but I never want to lie to her. The truth is, it's a *lot* worse—entire swathes of time are dropping from my memory and the pain some days is unbearable.

It is time. I put on my thick jacket to walk down to the beach to see if I can see the gray dolphins.

January

It was a pretty good birthday, as far as old people birthdays go. My son and his family came from DC to visit for the day. I know it's hard for them to get away, and it's not the easiest drive, especially with the black ice on the highways; I always get nervous with them crossing the Bay Bridge. That was why I had told them not to visit—we would see each other later —but they came anyway.

They arrived in the late morning and took me to lunch at the Summer House in Rehoboth. As always, we had good discussions and some laughter.

Even in the January cold, Megan wanted to see if the Ice Cream Store was open and what crazy, awesome, or disgusting (depending on who you asked) flavor she could try. As she ran down to the boardwalk with Samantha trying to keep up, Michael and I finished our coffee. I asked him how work was going, how they liked their new house—all the topics we normally discussed.

I had the chance to tell him about my plan. I knew he would try to talk me out of it, but the reality is that it's my decision.

They left in the afternoon, hoping to get home before it got dark. I could see the concern in their eyes as they left. They had found a plate with crumbs on a random shelf, a remote in the microwave, a spilled glass of juice from a while ago that I'd forgotten to clean up—all small things that bother me as much as them, as I notice what I've done for the first time.

February

I missed the appointment today to pick up my final prescription. My appointment was at eleven o'clock and I slept through it. I can't decide how I feel.

I think I was ready—I had long, handwritten letters for Michael, Samantha, and Megan, telling them how much I loved them and how proud I was of them, with a few wise insights drawn from eighty-plus years of living.

I had paid my bills, completed my death cleaning of the entire house—save the garage. Let the kids deal with cleaning the plastic chairs and seldom-used kayak.

Last night I had a great dinner and a bottle of wine—my favorite wine, a nice big cabernet that I had let breathe all day. Maybe I had a few sips during the day as well.

With it unusually warm for this time of year, I sat on the porch and ate an entire Grotto's cheese pizza. It was a fabulous dinner. And then I drank too much wine and slept as late today as I can remember.

The physician's office in DC has only called once, to see if I'm OK and if I want to go ahead. My lungs are hurting more than normal today, and I can't find my reading glasses. Right now I feel like just sitting on the porch and thinking about the last time I had Grotto's with Michael and his family. They cheered when I said, "Pizza for dinner!" We walked down to the restaurant. Grotto's didn't need to, but they arranged the pepperoni slices in the shape of a smiley face. It was a great day.

I walk over to the wine shelf and open another bottle of wine, but plan to only drink half today.

I remember that it's Megan's birthday in a few weeks and she loves it when we go to Zelky's Arcade, spending hours giggling as we try to win enough tickets for just one of the big prizes.

It can wait, I think, as I walk out onto the patio, close my eyes, and welcome the sound of winter birds chirping.

ALEXANDER HOOD WORKS IN WASHINGTON, DC, SO THAT EACH WEEKEND HE CAN FACE THE DIFFICULT DECISION OF WHETHER TO SPEND THE MAJORITY OF HIS TIME IN REHOBOTH OR DEWEY BEACH. HE FEELS INCREDIBLY LUCKY TO HAVE AN AMAZING, LOVING, AND SUPPORTIVE WIFE, AN ADORABLE WATER-OBSESSED DOG, AND A CAT THAT TOLERATES HIM.

AFTER SUBMITTING STORIES EACH YEAR FOR THE PAST FIVE YEARS, ALEXANDER HAS BEEN SELECTED TO PUBLISH A SHORT STORY TWICE IN THE REHOBOTH BEACH READS CONTEST. HIS RECORD IS NOT A TALE OF WARNING, BUT ENCOURAGEMENT TO THOSE DAYDREAMING ABOUT BEING AN AUTHOR TO WRITE FREELY, SUBMIT OFTEN, AND SEE EVERY SETBACK AS AN OPPORTUNITY TO EVOLVE AS A WRITER.

The Ripple Effect

By LJ Brown

The ocean in the early morning had a calming effect on Susan Anderson. It always had, ever since she was a child. On the rare occasion her family took a vacation, it always involved the beach. The humid sea air gave her a sense of new purpose with every breath she took. She let go of any negative feelings she might unknowingly be harboring and inhaled deeply. Every morning, this was Susan's ritual, whether she was home or visiting her favorite vacation spot in Delaware.

Rehoboth Beach had become her second home in the last few years. One of Susan's coworkers had offered to rent her beach house to Susan for a week each summer and Susan had jumped at the chance. On a single teacher's salary, she didn't have many opportunities to get away. But once a year, in the middle of July, Susan traveled to Rehoboth. She looked forward to the relaxation and sun she craved.

After her parents died eight years ago, Susan had no living relatives. An only child of two only-child parents, she'd had a boring childhood with no cousins to play with on Christmas mornings and no siblings to terrorize. Growing up, Susan was often forced to sit with her parents and their friends and listen to them discuss their political views. She was seen and not heard, which caused her to become a wonderful listener and an incredible dreamer.

Her parents found Susan's creativity inspiring. They praised her for her good grades and marveled at her imagination. They were shocked when Susan told them she wanted to be a history teacher.

"There's no money in that," her father had told her.

"Honey, you have such a brilliant mind, you could do anything you wanted," her mother had added.

Susan's response had been, "Everyone has a story to tell. When you study someone's life and learn their story, they are not forgotten. I want to teach my students stories they will remember and then pass along to someone else—a sort of ripple effect.

As a teacher, Susan's history class was anything but boring. She changed the classroom's decorations with each major event she taught. Students looked forward to Ms. Anderson's tactile teaching style. She gave each class her full energy and attention. "Ready to start some ripples?" she'd say each time she started a new lesson.

Spring break was an excellent source of downtime, but summer gave her enough time to fully recharge. Now, in the middle of July, Susan wore her army-green bathing suit, and her ginger-colored curls fell loosely around her shoulders. By the end of the week, despite going through two bottles of a high-intensity sunblock, she would still gain enough freckles to have what looked like a constellation of stars on her skin.

Susan was familiar with quiet; she was comfortable in her own thoughts or reading a book, but she often missed the everyday banter of a companion. Her colleagues only invited her to outings during the academic year, and even then, she figured they asked her out of a sense of obligation. The only times Susan genuinely felt satisfied was in a classroom with dozens of eyes watching or in a lounge chair on the beach with her eyes in a book.

It was midmorning when Susan stopped reading and looked around. She saw families scattered throughout the beach. As she gazed out to sea, she saw a ship sailing parallel to the shoreline. It was more party boat than cruise ship, but it made her think of the Titanic and she immediately began thinking of lesson plans for her students. It was a historical event with many stories. She was surprised that nearby, children continued to build sandcastles and splash in the waves rather than watch the boat pass by.

Susan searched her backpack until she found her Mega Zoom binoculars. She slowly scanned the deck of the ship.

"How cool!" a little boy next to her exclaimed.

"It's fascinating, isn't it?" Susan lowered her binoculars to converse with the child.

"Ellie, come here quick!" The boy yelled. "I found a hermit crab."

"A *hermit crab*? Look out into the ocean. There's a cool boat passing by." The boy only stared deeper into the sand, then glanced over at Susan but didn't respond. "Oh, I get it. You aren't supposed to talk to strangers. I'm sorry. You really should check out the boat though," she said, returning to her binoculars. "I would love to be a passenger on something like that. I bet it's loads of fun. Oh, I wish I had my camera. My students would love to see this." Susan reached into her bag for her cell phone, but remembered she had left it on the kitchen counter to charge. "I'll just have to commit everything to memory."

Susan studied the boat. "Strange." She shifted her eyes to study the people on the deck. "The passengers are dancing." They seemed to be enjoying themselves. Susan fed off their energy and found herself smiling.

Susan's eyes locked with those of a passenger who stood alone near the stern of the ship. The empty stare caused Susan to look away, but she quickly stole another glance. "Why does she appear to be so gloomy, when everyone else is having such fun? If I were on that ship, I would be having the time of my life." The woman looked oddly familiar.

Susan zoomed her binoculars to get a better look. For a moment, time seemed to stop. The woman shared the same reddish hair as Susan. Maybe Susan was dehydrated, but the woman on the boat could have been her reflection in a mirror.

Susan rubbed her eyes in disbelief, took a few deep breaths, and concentrated on clearing her mind. She drank from her water bottle, spilling cool droplets onto her burning legs. When Susan's gaze returned to the ocean, the boat was almost out of view. As she began to reapply her sunscreen, she noticed an abrupt change in the weather. The sky had become dark, and the beach was becoming a wasteland. Her dream vacation was turning into a nightmare.

"I just heard on the radio that a storm's heading this way!" a man called out.

Susan answered over the roar of suddenly angry and restless waves, "The Weather Channel didn't mention anything like this."

"We need to get off the beach," the stranger yelled.

Susan grabbed her bag and chair and sprinted toward the boardwalk, with the binoculars still in hand. She looked back to try and see a glimpse of the mysterious ship, but it had vanished from the horizon. The sky opened up and a hard rain pelted her face. Susan squinted, trying to find her way off the beach. Stumbling over an abandoned bucket, Susan nearly fell and her backpack spilled its contents onto the damp sand. Her binoculars went flying and hit a rock.

"Come on, Susan, get it together," she mumbled. Her hands shook with trepidation and were slippery from the rain. She clumsily gathered her belongings and made it to the boardwalk, cradling her broken binoculars. Disheveled, she sat on a bench, under an awning, near a group of others who had sought refuge. The rain blew sideways and Susan realized she had begun to cry. Her tears mixed with the rain on her cheeks. She tried to smooth her curly hair, but it was frizzy and uncontrollable, and it stuck to the back of her neck.

"Did you hear that?" a woman nearby asked her friends.

Susan clamped her mouth shut, unsure if she was the cause of the whimpering. She stayed frozen on the bench, eyes closed, trying to be invisible.

"Hear what?" another woman asked.

"It sounded like crying."

"How can you hear anything over this thunder, Margaret?" the man from the beach asked.

Lightning flashed over the ocean, causing the group to jump.

"There it is again. You can hear it, Anna, right?" Margaret snapped. "I can hear a woman crying; but this storm is so violent, I can't see what's in front of us."

"I can barely keep my eyes open with this wind," Anna said.

"I don't hear it," a man replied. "You know what, though? Margaret, even though I can't hear it, I believe you can."

"Really, Frank?" Margaret sounded hopeful.

"Yes," Frank answered. "Eight years ago a beautiful party boat sunk because of storm just like this one." Both women gasped.

"Quit trying to scare us, Frank," Anna said. "We aren't going to fall for it. He's probably just making it up."

"It's true, Anna. The ship was struck by lightning and caught fire. Everyone on board died. All the passengers were accounted for and laid to rest, except one."

"How sad," Margaret said.

"The legend says that every year on the anniversary of the tragedy, the lost woman returns to be reunited with her family."

"Does her family live in Rehoboth?" Margaret asked.

Frank answered casually, "As far as I know, her parents died that same day. I don't know if she left anyone else behind."

"Did she cause today's storm?" Anna asked. "It was supposed to be sunny all day."

"Don't be silly," Margaret said.

"I wouldn't be so quick to judge, Margaret," said Frank. "Many people in Rehoboth say they have experienced unnatural occurrences each year around the time the ship sunk. I've never encountered anything strange, except for today's freak storm, but you never know.

Hey, the rain is slowing. Let's grab a bite to eat."

Frank walked to a bench close to where they were huddled and called to his friends. "Come look. I've never noticed this before. This bench was dedicated to that ship's lost passenger."

"Really?" Anna asked.

"How heartbreaking." Margaret sighed, touching the inscription as she read it aloud.

IN MEMORY OF

SUSAN ANDERSON

A TEACHER WHO *INSPIRED* HER STUDENTS

Lost but not forgotten
May her story have many ripples

COLLECTING LIFE LESSONS FROM HER PARENTS, FUNNY MEMORIES WITH FRIENDS, AND TENDER MOMENTS WITH HER HUSBAND, LISA "LJ" BROWN INCORPORATES THESE KEY CONCEPTS INTO HER STORIES. CREATIVE CONFLICTS, THEMES, AND UNIQUE CHARACTERS CAN FILL HER HEAD NOT ONLY DURING EVERYDAY TASKS, BUT ALSO WHEN CHECKING INTO A HOTEL OR RELAXING ON THE BEACH. A VACATION IN OCEAN CITY, MARYLAND, INSPIRED "THE RIPPLE EFFECT." SINCE SHE WAS A SMALL CHILD, SHE HAS FILLED A THREE-RING BINDER WITH PLOTS FOR FUTURE BOOK IDEAS. LISA FEELS HONORED TO BE A PART OF THIS CONTEST AND HOPES THIS IS A FIRST STEP IN MANY GOOD AND EXCITING THINGS TO COME. HER CURRENT PROJECTS INCLUDE WRITING A YOUNG ADULT NOVEL AND A CHILDREN'S SERIES.

Whispers from the Past

By Donna Rothert

The beach had always been her safe harbor. But something was different today. And it made no sense. Hope could not explain her restlessness that early Wednesday afternoon. She was preparing to head for South Bethany, Delaware, a short drive from Rehoboth Beach, a trip that had become part of her weekly routine. Yet today, she was troubled by a growing disquiet. But she ignored it.

She loved the southernmost part of the Delaware coast. Growing up, her family had spent vacations on its beaches and each summer she earned college tuition money waiting tables, first at Summer House in Rehoboth and then at Bluecoast Seafood Grill on Coastal Highway. In South Bethany, she could avoid the traffic jam from Dewey to Rehoboth, so full of the noise and chaotic energy that ramped up on Memorial Day and dissipated after Labor Day. She preferred the quieter Bethany beaches, where even during the busy summers, tempers were kept in check, parking could be found, and restaurants had not abandoned the civilized practice of taking reservations. She knew it was just a short drive to Rehoboth Beach if she craved nonstop vitality and amusements.

Years earlier, Hope and her husband, Mark, had invested in a second home as a weekend getaway, an escape from the political reality and rigors of Washington, DC, where Mark was a captain in the Metropolitan Police and she was an executive with Lockheed Martin.

While they had fantasized about an oceanfront beach house, they soon learned bayside property was a better fit for their budget. They had found the perfect house, tucked away on Little Bay, a fifteen-minute walk to the ocean. And then, two years ago, Mark had lost his battle with cancer, so Hope returned each week to what had become a needed sanctuary.

For some reason, this Wednesday afternoon drive was different. Hope was normally self-confident, but as she left her home in Reston, she was inexplicably weighed down by a strange darkness of spirit. This obscure dread only intensified when she crossed the Bay Bridge onto the unbroken flatness of Maryland's Eastern Shore.

There were no tangible signs of trouble, nothing to warrant this puzzling anxiety. The trip from northern Virginia was as expected—an hour of unmitigated mayhem on the beltway that changed to flowing traffic once she got onto eastbound Route 50. Even the weather was promising—no storms threatened the remaining eighty miles as she turned onto Route 404. Her Audi hummed along, the tank three-quarters full, rolling smoothly on new tires. It was early fall and she was looking forward to some downtime at the beach. She resisted the feeling of indeterminate dread that continued to build as she turned onto Route 26, drawing ever closer to South Bethany.

As Hope pulled into her driveway, she felt the wind suddenly intensify, heard the waves slapping the bulkhead, and saw the darkening clouds racing northward. The house, one of four lots at the end of Victoria Avenue, rose to three stories under a nautical-blue roof with stretches of floor-to-ceiling windows waterside. Her trash can, emptied by the trash service two days earlier, skittered to rest among the overgrown ornamental grasses bordering the steps. Hurrying to unlock the door, she inserted the key only to realize it was already unlocked. She knew, with unwavering certainty, that she had locked it on her departure last week.

Not easily frightened, the years as a police captain's wife steeling her resolve, she cautiously pushed open the door, fearing the worst—a ransacking, a theft, a violation of privacy. The dread was overwhelming. Initially, she could see nothing unusual except that the welcome mat she kept on the porch was missing. As she cautiously entered the house and began to inspect each room, a shadowy darkness lingered like a low-lying cloud. She edged slowly from hall to doorways, displaying fraudulent confidence as she flipped light switches in each room, checking the upstairs bedrooms, then the kitchen and dining room. But it wasn't until she moved out to the three-season porch that an icy sliver of fear snaked across her shoulders.

Evening dusk had cloaked the bayfront community. Her usual sweeping view of the bay and the homes on the distant shore was hidden behind a veil of haze, thicker than fog, as if thousands of spiders had spun fine webs from shore to shore, hoping to trap an arrogant boater challenging the threat of bad weather. No light shown through from any direction. The solitary fullness of the early evening moon cast a gray spectral light. *It's only fog*, she assured herself, but immediately called Peg O'Reilly, her neighbor two doors down.

"Hey Peg, it's Hope. I just got in. Have you noticed anything unusual around my house? When I got in tonight, my front door was unlocked, and—really weird—my welcome mat is gone."

"No. Is anything else missing?"

"Not that I can tell so far."

"Well, it's been quiet since Labor Day. Only news here is Dave Parson's Jack Russell terrier is missing."

"Oh, no. What happened?"

"Evidently, it took off while Dave was washing his car today. He's putting posters up but keep your eye out. With this murky weather, Bandit could wind up anywhere."

"OK, thanks. And will do."

Hope knew Dave doted on his dog. He had named him Bandit for his habit of hiding small objects like dog biscuits, toys, and keys under sofa or chair cushions. She found it odd that the dog hadn't been found already, since there was only one non-water exit from the small community and everyone knew Bandit. The neighborhood was surrounded by the waters of Jefferson Creek leading into Little Bay, and much like Venice, canals divided the streets like fingers of a hand.

Still uneasy about the unlocked door and the missing mat, Hope committed to a good night's sleep and an early morning search for Bandit. Making sure all doors and windows were secured, she headed for bed, catching her reflection in the landing window as she mounted the stairs. Was someone watching her? She couldn't ignore the unexplained chill on the back of her neck. She looked out her bedroom window and stared at the roiling waters, sensing an unexplained presence riding toward her on the night wind. She turned to bed, tired of worrying, and atypically longing for the noisy, hot streets of Coastal Highway and Rehoboth Avenue and the cacophony of vacationing tourists strolling the boardwalk. She finally fell into a troubled sleep, hoping that the nameless fear would disappear.

Before dawn, she was jolted from a fitful dream by a loud sound. She awakened from visions of young Native American men navigating five canoes on overflowing streams through tunnels of trees while women, children, and elders lined the shores, silently watching. What was that sound? The doorbell. *The doorbell?* Her iPhone indicated 5:22 a.m. The house was silent.

Against her better judgment but much like Pavlov's dog responding to a sound, she hurried downstairs, robe flying. Early morning gray light filtered through the door panels. She could see no one and there were no shadows on the porch or steps. Hope opened the door. Victoria Avenue was still. There were no sounds at all, even from surrounding streets. Just the residue of the gloom from the evening before.

Confused, she turned back from the door. Her fitful night's sleep had done little to assuage her disquiet. Still tired, she headed into the kitchen to prepare coffee, hoping to restore her normal daily rhythm. She loved to sit quietly, in any weather, gazing over the calming waters, her spirits buoyed by the timeless spectacle of the early morning sky. Her plan was to search for Bandit, so she moved to the three-season porch, waiting for the coffee to brew.

In the early morning, it was common for fog to engulf the bay, temporarily hiding from view the three tiny islets clustered less than forty yards from her bulkhead. Irregularly shaped, they morphed from year to year, season to season, expanding or contracting based on the whims of storms, wind, and surging tides. She had always enjoyed watching the subtle changes in the configurations of these tiny islands but as she watched the fog's wisps of vapor shift and surge along the shoreline this morning, she became unnerved.

One islet had nearly disappeared and was now no larger than a coffee table, while a second was half the size it had been just last week. She realized no storm had interfered. Were the waters slowly encroaching westward, beginning to gnaw at the land?

Her dream brought to mind the Native Americans. She knew that the Nanticoke people had been forced from their tidewater homes in the early 1700s, to land near Laurel, Delaware, the ancient "wading place," a ford near Broad Creek. Were these winds today carrying retribution? Were ancient spirits hovering over land that had been stolen centuries before? The extreme change in these tiny islands was the first eddy in a stream of unsettling events to follow.

She turned back toward the stairs, forgetting the coffee and instead heading for her bedroom, where she threw on a T-shirt and jeans and headed out to look for Bandit. She searched methodically, weaving throughout the small community, street by street, peering into the crawl spaces under the waterside homes. It made no sense to her that

Bandit had just disappeared.

After an hour, she returned to her house, but as she approached the door, she was again overcome with unexplained apprehension. She had eagerly awaited the crisp autumn air after what had been an unusually rainy and humid summer, but that morning's menacing weather had dampened her spirits as well as the air. As she reached for the doorknob, she was overpowered by the odor of decay—damp, heavy, oppressive. *Now what?*

She stumbled down the steps and circled the house. Perhaps crab traps had not been emptied or a bag of leftover party garbage had blown into the crawl space. Nothing. In the sky above, three ospreys dipped and soared, talons ready, seeking a glint of fish but disappointed in their search. Odd. Osprey are usually solitary hunters.

As she walked toward the bulkhead, Hope felt her usual optimism waning, challenged by thoughts of even more unusual phenomena. For the first time she noticed that the familiar armada of bufflehead ducks, which had frequented the edges of her community waters for years, had not returned. Every year before, they had reappeared on schedule to forage in waters off the bulkhead, their diving antics offering her hours of quiet amusement. Where had they gone? Why had they not come back?

She turned to enter the house, paranoia now surging. Something primitive had entered her awareness. This surprised her, as she had never been short on courage. She enjoyed the local legends of supernatural occurrences in nearby beach towns—wandering sailor spirits, ghosts rattling the floorboards, supposedly haunted rooms in the Addy Sea. Now that she was possibly encountering unnatural phenomena herself, she was troubled.

She had heard the stories of unusual events that had plagued Sussex County over the years. Decades earlier fires had raged for more than eight months around deep pools of water in the nearby Great Cypress

Swamp, often called Burnt Swamp. Then there had been multiple mishaps slowing construction of the Indian River Bridge. A fire in February 2011 followed by strong tremors from the Virginia-based earthquake that same year plagued the long-awaited opening.

But she forced herself to brush these thoughts aside and busied herself for the rest of the morning cleaning closets, doing laundry, sending emails, hoping to shake the sense of doom that seemed to permeate the house.

Around two p.m. Dave stopped by. "Hey, Hope, when did you get in?"

"Late yesterday," she replied. "Peg told me about Bandit. I've been looking for him."

"Yeah, I'm in the middle of distributing lost-dog posters along Route 1. You know, McDonalds, Fins, Cottage Cafe—restaurants that get lots of tourists. I just don't understand … he's never run off like this."

"He'll probably make his way home soon," Hope assured him. "By the way, did you notice anything unusual around my house over the last few days? The door was unlocked when I got in last night and I know I locked it when I left. Plus, my welcome mat is missing."

"No, nothing. Just more fog than usual for late September. Electricity was out for about an hour on Tuesday. Probably something with global warming."

Later that afternoon, Hope was overcome with a sudden fit of yawning and fatigue, unusual for her. Unable to fight the crushing exhaustion, she grabbed a light quilt and reluctantly lay down on the sofa in the three-season porch, her mind ruminating on nameless fears. She had always heard that fear has a real scent. Perhaps Bandit had detected impending calamity. Around three p.m., she finally drifted into a restless sleep.

Less than two hours later, crescendos of thunder and heavy seas crashing against the bulkhead woke her from another disturbing dream. Under a pallid moon, a Native American warrior had been seated beneath the drooping branches of an enormous willow, silently stroking a great horned owl perched on his forearm. He sat beside a mound of freshly turned earth and whispered slow syllables in a language she could not understand, as if he were admonishing her. She awoke sweating in the now cold, clammy room, unable to grasp at the edges of the dream.

Coming out of that dream, Hope was overcome with fear and realized she had to leave and leave immediately. Grabbing her keys, iPhone, and purse, she dashed for the door, clambering down the four steps to the driveway, rain pelting her T-shirt and jeans, hair plastered to her head, drenched as she slid into the driver's seat. Hitting "start," she was grateful for the immediate roar of the Audi's engine, the headlights flooding the end of her driveway and the beginning of her retreat to Virginia.

She immediately headed north on Route 1 and west on Route 26, fearful that the rain and wind would force the closing of some of the low-lying roads. As she travelled west, her panic began to subside.

Her thoughts turned to her memory of the land's early history, her sense of dread, the disturbing unnatural phenomena, and her two perplexing dreams. It occurred to her, as she navigated her way through the storm debris, that Native American culture had stamped the Delmarva geography with their names—Assawoman, Nanticoke, Choptank, and even the state's name, Delaware. She recalled reading that the Delaware nation claimed they had learned powerful witchcraft from the Nanticoke in centuries past.

She sped on, navigating the two-lane roads through the continuing downpour and avoiding fallen branches strewn across the pavement by the heavy winds. Then, gradually, she detected a faint haunting chant layered on top of a rhythmic drumbeat hovering in the wind. Suddenly, her car pulled violently to the right, and she felt the hard thumping of a flat tire. She slowed, pulling to the shoulder next to an open field and turned on her hazard lights.

She was relieved to find a cell signal and punched in the number for AAA. A young woman informed her that because of the storm it would take two to three hours to get a truck to her.

Hope resigned herself to the wait, welcoming the time to consider the strange events of the past twenty-four hours, starting with the unexplained sense of foreboding she'd felt throughout the day and including the disappearances of her welcome mat, Bandit, and the buffleheads, and then the two strange dreams. Questions flooded her mind. Was the anger of ancient ancestors still riding on the night wind? Had blame and guilt seeped into the soil? As she waited, the storm continued to rage.

Finally, she saw the lights of the AAA truck in the distance, coming from the opposite direction, slowing as the driver saw her flashing hazards. As he made a U-turn to pull in front of her car, Hope felt, for the first time that day, a sense of release. With his flashlight sweeping a lighted path in the darkness and rain and wind, he approached the driver's side. Hope rolled down her window and explained that her right front tire was flat. He rounded the front of her car, kneeling out of sight to inspect the damage, only to return three minutes later with a sharp stone in his hand.

"Lady, I don't know how you managed it in this weather, but you ran over an Indian arrowhead. It was stuck deep in the tread of your tire. City visitors spend weekends looking for these things and you run over one in the middle of a storm." He shook his head. "But maybe it makes sense, cuz see that field over there? Some say part of it was an old Indian burial ground. Must be your lucky day." And he turned to his task of replacing her flat with the spare.

After he finished, she thanked him and insisted he keep the arrowhead, but he refused and was quickly back in his truck, pulling away, off to assist another stranded motorist.

Finally, the storm was beginning to abate, now only a light rain in the aftermath of the wind and thunder and lightning. She sat, thoughtful, slowly turning the arrowhead over and over in her hand. She put it on the seat and began to pull back onto the road. Only then did she realize that in her haste, she had forgotten to lock the front door of the house.

And in that moment, she reversed her journey, to return that night to the house in South Bethany.

Early the next morning, Hope received a text from Dave and learned Bandit had been discovered trotting up Coastal Highway and had been returned home. Hope was also relieved when Peg called with news that the welcome mat had been located on the Thompson's deck. Evidently, their six-year-old had used it in the fort he was building.

Sipping her coffee on the three-season porch, Hope gazed across the unbroken waters of Jefferson Creek and reviewed the other events of the past twenty-four hours. As she had forgotten to lock the door in her hasty retreat last night, it was possible she could have been distracted and failed to lock her door the week before. And she realized it was early in the season. Perhaps the buffleheads would still return.

As for the dreams and the arrowhead, while she could never be sure, Hope believed that she had sensed whispers from the past, a haunting reminder of our obligation to honor this land and its creeks, inlets, and bays. She had always been an avid recycler, but she realized she had to do more. A humble start would be a donation to the Delaware Seashore Preservation Foundation. And she would sign up for an eco-cruise to learn more about the ecology of the estuaries near her. This would be just the beginning of a continued commitment to careful stewardship of the land and the tidewaters. In this way, Hope felt she would be honoring the Native American belief: *We shall be known forever by the tracks we leave.*

DONNA ROTHERT IS A RETIRED CORPORATE EXECUTIVE AND FORMER HIGH SCHOOL TEACHER, WHO HAS ALWAYS LOVED WORDS: PUZZLES, FICTION, NONFICTION, POETRY, AND DRAMA. A NATIVE MARYLANDER WHO HAS LIVED AND WORKED IN TEXAS, CONNECTICUT, AND VIRGINIA, SHE HAS TRAVELED TO FORTY-EIGHT OF THE FIFTY STATES. SHE DIVIDES HER TIME BETWEEN RESTON, VIRGINIA, AND BERLIN, MARYLAND, AND IS CURRENTLY WORKING ON HER MEMOIR WHILE MAKING INTERMITTENT FORAYS INTO SHORT STORIES AND FLASH FICTION. UNTIL RECENTLY, HER WRITING HAS BEEN EXCLUSIVELY NONFICTION, HER ESSAYS APPEARING IN THE THIRTIETH ANNIVERSARY ANTHOLOGY OF THE MARYLAND WRITERS' ASSOCIATION, *THIRTY WAYS TO LOVE MARYLAND*. TRAVELS THIS YEAR TO PARIS, BRUGES, MARRAKESH, AND CHINA LAKE, MAINE, ARE PROVIDING NEW SETTINGS FOR PLANNED FICTION. SHE IS LOOKING FORWARD TO FUTURE TRAVEL TO IOWA AND OREGON WITH HER TWO NEW YORK-BASED GRANDCHILDREN, THUS FULFILLING HER GOAL OF TRAVEL TO ALL FIFTY STATES.

JUDGE'S COMMENT

The author shares a gripping tale of Indian spirits from centuries ago haunting her usually tranquil beach home. Weaving history and nature throughout this modern-day story, she makes a compelling case for reverence and care of both. Her thoughtful prose and deft hand at suspense make this a captivating read from beginning to end.

A Summer Carol

By David Strauss

The surf was dead calm, to begin with. There is no doubt whatever about that. The old sea was as flat as a pond on a windless day.

Eddie Scroops scowls at the jammed-up traffic on Route 1, the line of stop lights near the outlets bottlenecked with the comings and goings of tourists.

"Bah."

His son, Tim—they call him Tiny Tim because he's six-four and still growing, calls out from the backseat, "Guess what tomorrow is, Dad? June twenty-first, the first day of summer. That makes today Summer's Eve. Cool, huh?"

"Bah. You know what tomorrow is, son? It's just another day someone has to get up and go to work while all of these slackers"— Eddie waves his hand in a circular motion—"sit on the beach, doing nothing. That someone being me."

"It's called vacation, honey, and you should try it." Eddie's wife, Mary, chimes in from the front passenger seat, a smile crossing her pretty face.

Scroops pulls his black SUV up to the stoplight where 1 turns into 1A and waits again as the light turns red. Mary turns around toward the backseat and smiles at Tim.

"What's the first thing you're going to do when we get to our rental?" Mary taps her boy on the knee, playfully.

Tim shrugs. "Check the surf to see if there's anything worth riding out there."

"Oh, would you look at this"—Eddie motions toward the stoplight—

"some loser asking for money."

The light turns green and Eddie inches the vehicle through the intersection, window rolled down. As he passes the beggar, Scroops yells, "Get a job, slacker!"

Mary scrunches down in her seat. Tim looks away, out the side window, wanting to be anywhere but in this car with his father.

After the chaos of checking-in, finding the rental, parking, and unpacking, the family of three sits at the small kitchen table in the oceanfront condo, exhausted.

Tim disappears to his bedroom for a minute and returns in surf trunks and flip-flops. "Gonna take a walk to the beach, check the surf, scope things out. Anybody wanna come along?"

Mary grabs her husband's hand. "No, thanks. We're going to take a little stroll along the boardwalk. You have fun."

"We are?" Eddie is already busy opening a laptop and grabbing a briefcase from the floor. "I thought I'd get some work done."

Mary frowns. "Work? That can wait. C'mon, you're taking me for a walk through town."

"Bah."

As they walk along Baltimore Avenue, Eddie thinks about the company and how he could be making money instead of wasting time. He is surprised when he finds himself in the Harry K Jewelry store along the boardwalk. Scroops didn't even realize they'd left Baltimore Avenue, had no clue they'd wandered this far.

As Mary meanders through the store, pausing to look at several pieces, Eddie is approached by a well-dressed man, who introduces himself as the owner. The gentleman smiles warmly at Eddie, handing Scroops his business card.

"If you need anything, call me anytime—anytime. I'm here to help."

The owner shakes Eddie's hand and walks back to check on another customer.

Eddie frowns and shoves the card into his back pocket. "Bah."

Later that evening, Eddie Scroops sits alone with his laptop, briefcase open, typing away. Mary approaches her husband, "Ready for some mini-golf?"

Eddie looks up for half-a-second. "Nah. I've got work to do. You guys go on without me."

"Dad, you know tomorrow is the first day of summer. How about we get up and go surfing together? I mean, if the waves pick up." Tim is standing head and shoulders above his mother, their two faces almost identical.

"We'll see, we'll see." Eddie waves his family away, sucked into the soft white light of his computer screen.

Eddie Scroops wakes up alone at the kitchen table, his computer screen flashing blue. He taps the power button and begins to close the laptop when a small dot in the center grows into the life-sized face of a man. A man with brown skin, a scraggly beard, and long dreadlocks.

Scroops slams the laptop shut and rubs his eyes wearily. "Bah."

Deciding he must need some fresh air, Eddie wanders down to the beach and sits alone in the sand, breathing deeply of the salty breeze. As Eddie stands to make his way back to the condo, a ghostly figure emerges from the waves, his dreadlocks dripping with ocean water.

The guy on the computer screen? "No. NO! Can't be—this can't be."

The figure strolls toward Eddie, a glowing orange surfboard under one arm. "Oh, it be, mon!" The specter laughs, a hearty laugh from the soul. "In life I was Bob Marley, mon. And I be here to warn you of what is to come if you do not change your evil ways."

Eddie Scroops falls to his knees in the sand, hands over face.

"Why—why me?"

"It be Summer's Eve, mon. And I tink you know why."

Eddie looks up at the reggae legend, terrified of what is to come. "Will I be visited by the ghosts of summers past, present, and future?"

Marley smiles, his white teeth shining in the moonlight. "Nah, mon. Jus' me. Bob Marley be your tour guide for this little adventure. Now, you best hop on and pay attention, 'cause this ride can get a little gnarly."

Against his better judgement, Eddie finds himself on the back of a surfboard with Bob Marley in front of him, the two heading straight into the face of a breaking wave. Eddie Scroops shuts his eyes as tightly as possible, and when he opens them …

A bonfire glows brightly on the beach, and a small crowd of young people gathers around, laughing. Music is playing from somewhere in the dark, the faces of the kids glow like lanterns in the night.

Bob Marley steers the surfboard toward the group, Eddie Scroops hanging on tightly. "Look, mon. Look. Tell me what you see."

Eddie watches as the group banters back and forth, the playfulness, the innocence of youth. And then he sees it … sees them … sees himself. Eddie, there on the fringe between light and dark, a teenager again, crouched in the sand with a girlish Mary. *My God, look at us!*

"Do you know what night this be?" Marley turns and smiles at Eddie.

"It's the night I helped Mary find her lost bracelet. The night I first told Mary I loved her."

"That's not all, mon. Listen. Listen!"

Eddie strains to hear the conversation, the words he'd spoken over twenty years ago. "And when we get married, I'll shower you with jewels, Mary. You'll never have to worry about a lost bracelet again … I'll …"

The image vanishes. Eddie finds himself riding the surfboard back out to sea—an even bigger wave getting ready to break on top of them.

They are alone in the corner of a bedroom, the surfboard leaning against the wall. A young man that Eddie does not recognize is sitting on the floor. His son, Tim, enters the room.

"What is this, Marley? Where are we?"

Bob raises a finger to his lips. "Hush, mon. We be in the present. Watch and listen."

Eddie watches as his son sits on the edge of the bed. The other boy slides a shoebox from underneath and removes a small pipe and a baggie. He watches the other boy show Tim how to fill the pipe with what he realizes is marijuana. The boy demonstrates how to light it, inhale, and hold the smoke. Father watches son getting high for the first time, just two days before their trip to Rehoboth.

Marley leans in and inhales deeply, "Ahhh, that be some good sensimilla, mon." Bob wags a finger in Eddie's face. "But, your boy, he best be careful, mon. Every little ting, it not going to be alright."

And then they're back on the surfboard again, riding away, riding a wave down the center of a crowded street in Eddie's hometown. Marley pulls him off the board outside the front door of the local coffee shop.

"You best listen up, mon. Listen good." Marley escorts Scroops inside, the aroma of coffee pungent in the air. Mary sits on a counter stool next to another woman. Eddie recognizes her immediately—it is his own sister.

Mary is crying softly, shaking her head slowly. "Twenty years. Twenty years married today, and I don't even get a hug. No card, no nothing. Not one single piece of jewelry in twenty years. When we met he promised me jewels. What he gave me was nothing."

"Oh, shit. I forgot our anniversary again." Eddie shakes his head. He turns around to see a look of disgust on Marley's face.

"There are no words, mon. No words. You ought to be ashamed."

As Marley begins to usher Eddie back to the surfboard, Eddie can hear Mary's voice trailing away, "I'm not sure how much longer I can take this …"

The third wave rises up before them like the watery claw of some mythological beast. Marley turns and nods at Eddie. "You best hold on for this one, mon. I told you it gonna get a bit gnarly."

Eddie and Bob are seated in a courtroom, the surfboard plopped against the wall behind the judge.

"Let me guess—the future."

Marley nods.

The two sit, side by side, and watch as a door opens to the right of the judge. A young man, hands cuffed, is escorted into the room by two officers and taken over to a desk where a lawyer is waiting for him.

Eddie gasps, "Tim! That's my boy, Tim."

"All rise."

Eddie looks toward Marley, who stares straight ahead, his gaze fixed on the surfboard against the wall behind the judge.

The next minute is a blur of procedural mumbo-jumbo. It is not until the judge begins to read the sentence that Eddie is able to comprehend what is happening.

"Twenty years. Twenty years of your life, young man. Possession with intent to distribute, armed robbery, grand theft … so much promise, so much potential. Wasted."

And then they're surfing again back down that same road in Eddie's hometown. Back to the neighborhood and the tree-lined street, back to their three-bedroom home with the manicured lawn.

"I'm not sure I want to go in there." Eddie tries to back away.

Marley stands firm, his bony finger pointing toward the door.

Eddie enters a home he barely recognizes. The house has been remodeled and strange modern art paintings hang everywhere. Mary sits alone at the kitchen table, pouring vodka into a juice glass. Her neck and wrists hang heavy with gaudy jewelry. "Babe, you almost ready?" Mary calls loudly.

Eddie shrugs, "Doesn't look too bad."

Marley points his finger toward the stairs.

A young man, not yet thirty, bounds down the steps. "Hey, sugar mama, how's my kitten?"

"Ohh, kitty be just purrrrrfect." Mary laughs haltingly. "You look gorgeous, Johnny."

The young man pauses. "William. My name is William."

Mary gulps down the vodka. "Yes, that's right. William. That's what I meant."

Eddie looks at Marley, pointing to the scene. "Where am I? What the fu—"

Suddenly, it's after dark and they're back on the board, surfing down Main Street and out to the edge of town. Eddie is on his knees, hugging Marley's feet as the board glides to a stop.

Marley hops off.

Eddie crawls from the board on his hands and knees. "What is this, Bob? What is this place?"

Marley doesn't move. His finger points toward a collection of gravestones shining against the pale moonlight.

Eddie turns to face Marley. "Before I go closer, tell me. Are these the things that *will* be—or are they only the things that *may* be?"

Marley's finger stays still, pointing the way.

Among the weeds, in an unkempt section of the graveyard, one stone rises above the others. It is of polished marble and its engraving reads: *HERE LIES EDWARD "EDDIE" SCROOPS.*

"But why show me this if I am past all hope?"

Marley shakes his head sadly.

"I can change! I *will* change! I will honor life in my heart and keep the joy of summer all year long." Eddie crawls toward Marley, wrapping his arms around Marley's legs. "I don't want to die! I wanna live …"

Eddie Scroops finds himself alone on the beach at sunrise, clutching a broken umbrella in his arms.

"I wanna live!" He sits up and blinks twice. A perfect wave breaks thirty yards out to sea.

Eddie stands and brushes the sand from his body. He looks around and sees nothing except the broken umbrella, its ribs bent and broken, bright orange canopy torn.

I'm still alive.

When Eddie checks his shorts for the key to the condo, the only thing he finds is a business card crumpled in his back pocket. Eddie looks at the card and begins to laugh hysterically. "Of course, of course!" He practically skips back to the condominium, bounding up the stairs like a man half his age.

The condo is unlocked, and Eddie moves quietly, so as not to wake his still-sleeping family. He grabs his wallet and cell phone and heads back to the boardwalk, business card in hand. After explaining his story to the kind owner, Eddie persuades the gentleman to meet him at the entrance.

"Which one? Which one was my wife looking at?" The owner shows Eddie the three pieces of jewelry his wife had been examining the previous night. "I'll take it!"

The owner points to the three items. "Which one, sir? Which one would you like?"

"All of them, my good man. I'll take them all." Eddie points to another piece, a necklace with what looks like a little surfboard hanging from it. "And that. I'll take that doohickey too."

That morning in the little condo overlooking the ocean in Rehoboth

Beach, Eddie bursts through the door wearing surf trunks and flip-flops, surfboard dangling from his neck. "Happy Summer! Happy Summer!" he cries, giggling to himself.

Tim was the first to emerge, all bedhead and bleary-eyed.

"What are you waiting for, sleepyhead? Go get ready; grab your board. I thought we were gonna ride some waves this morning."

Tim looks at his dad, then looks at the computer on the table. "What about work? I thought you had to work."

"Work? No, this is vacation, my good man. Now be a good lad and run along, the waves are four feet high and clean."

Mary is leaning against the door frame of their bedroom, wearing rumpled gym shorts and a T-shirt. "What happened to you last night? Did you even come to bed?"

Eddie leads Mary into the bedroom and shuts the door. "I'm sorry," he says softly. "I'm sorry. And I'm going to spend the rest of my life making it up to you." He trots out of the bedroom and returns with three boxes, all beautifully wrapped. "Happy Anniversary, Mary."

As time passes, Eddie Scroops is as good as his word. He spends time with his son and showers his wife with gifts and affection. He volunteers as a tutor to help adults earn their GED. Scroops even brings a little bit of the summer spirit into his company, implementing Aloha Shirt Fridays to end each work week.

David Strauss grew up visiting the beach, spending his summers in Clearwater Beach, Florida, and Ocean City, Maryland. He spent his college years living and working in Ocean City, where he delivered pizzas on his bicycle. David has had poetry and/or short stories published in *Damozel* and *Dirt Rag* magazines, and in *The Boardwalk, Beach Nights, Beach Life,* and *Beach Pulp*. He has also published two novellas, *Dangerous Shorebreak* and *Structurally Deficient*, through CreateSpace. He teaches US History until he can retire to the beach with his wife.

Dreams We've Lived

By D.M. Domosea

The walls at Seaside Pointe Nursing Home in Rehoboth are an inscrutable color. They could be faded yellow or yellowed white, and the dated fluorescents humming above me shed no light on the matter. The entire facility smacks of obsolescence, a twentieth-century relic struggling to survive past its relevance. I've only talked to my interview subject once over the phone, but I've already lumped Ms. Conrad into this assessment. She even admitted that they came into this world the same year—1974—making them both ninety years old.

I pause outside the open door to room 118. The usual pungent hospital odors coming from within are laced with more subtle, yet pleasant, aromas: saltwater, warm sand, and marsh grass. It's a mix I know well from spending time in Rehoboth Beach, trolling for local-interest stories to fill the *Cape Gazette*. I spot the source of the scents sitting on a cheap laminate credenza—an electronic fragrance diffuser used to mask the miasma of antiseptic and ammonia. I'd probably employ the same tactic if I lived here.

An elderly woman sits in a hoverchair near the window by the bed. I can't make out her features—the bright light from the window blanches her silhouette—but from the dip of her head, I assume she's sleeping. I reach through the doorway and gently rap on the wall next to the frame. I don't want to startle her, but neither am I making a second trip here simply because it's nap time.

Her head pops up, and she rotates her hoverchair to face the door. "Oh! Is it three o'clock already?" She places something small she'd been holding onto the tray next to her bed. "Are you the young man

I spoke to on the phone?"

"Yes. I'm David Wellington. Thank you for taking time to meet with me, Ms. Conrad." I stride into the room, cross the worn linoleum floor in five steps, and hold out my hand.

She waves off the formality and motions to the chair opposite her. "Please, call me Emma. The staff calls me Ms. Conrad out of respect, but it makes me feel old."

"All right, Emma. So long as you call me David."

I take the opportunity to study her as I settle into the chair. She looks all ninety of her years. Her hair hangs in delicate white strings from her scalp, like hastily spun spider webs or the tatters of a once luxurious tapestry. Dunes of ivory wrinkles surround pale blue eyes, but the apples of her cheeks are still smooth and taut.

I activate the voice memo app on my SmartBand. "Do you mind if I record us?" I gesture at my wrist, and she gives a quick nod.

"So, Emma, as I explained on the phone, one of my columns for the *Gazette* focuses on beach antiques and collectibles. Your nurse's aide, Adri, told me about your beach badges, and I'd like to learn more about them."

"Tags," she corrects me. "Folks south of New York always called 'em tags." She guides her hoverchair over to the bed and tugs at a plastic bin sitting atop the blankets.

"Yes, tags. What were they for exactly?"

"They served as access passes to the Jersey beaches, before they closed the Atlantic coastline for the Restoration Project. Beaches here across the bay never used 'em. Access was always free south of Jersey." She removes the lid, lifts the box, and flips it over. "These all come from Cape May."

A cache of colorful buttons cascades onto the blue knit blanket with the clack and clatter of brittle plastic. Each badge is only slightly larger than the half dollars we'd once used before everything moved to eCurrency.

I skim through the pile and pick up one with a Victorian house, and then another with a crane standing in faded marsh grass. I marvel at the amount of detail the designers put into something so transitional, so impermanent. Except for the collection before me, these types of throwaway trinkets have long disappeared into decades-old landfills.

My hand lands on another, this one a squashed circle engraved with a red-and-white rescue board leaning against a lifeguard stand. Two people sit in the stand, forever scanning the blue waves beyond them. Much of the paint has rubbed off from handling.

"Looks like you got more use out of this one—1994?" My brow raises with the question.

Emma reaches for the tag, and I place it into her shaky palm. Her skin is cool and tissue-thin, trailed with blue veins and brown age spots.

"The year 1994." She smiles, closing her hand over the tag. "Three glorious sun-filled weeks in July and one perfect day." Her eyelids drop as she bows her head. Her breathing slackens to a sleeping pace.

This is what Adri warned me about. Apparently, Ms. Conrad falls asleep whenever she holds one of her beach tags. Triggered narcolepsy, she called it.

Somewhere above us, the muted cries of seagulls offset the silence in the room. They must be on the roof of the facility, though I hadn't noticed any when I pulled into the parking lot. Not surprising, as their presence has become white noise to me in the seven years since I moved to Rehoboth. Another waft of sun-dried sea grass drifts through the room.

Emma opens her eyes after several minutes and releases a long, contented sigh. "I'm sorry," she says, "I didn't mean to leave you like that." She places the tag on the bedside table next to one she must have been holding when I first arrived.

"Can you tell me about that year at Cape May?"

Emma looks out the window, as if her story is written in the sunbeams that pour through the glass. "That's the summer I met my husband, Jacob." Her voice catches at the memory of a man who exists now only in her mind. "He'd stumbled onto my blanket by mistake. Practically fell right on top of me. He apologized over and over, but I couldn't see past his eyes. He had the richest brown eyes, lined with lashes that'd make a Greek goddess jealous."

"Love at first sight?"

She chuckles. "Not quite. But by the time the sun set that day, I knew. One kiss was all it took."

"Was that the perfect day? Meeting him for the first time?"

"That was a wonderful day, but our last one at the beach … now *that* was perfect. Jacob and I spent from sunrise the previous day to sunrise that final morning together." A wistful smile stretches her thin lips. "Sometimes I think, one day, I might just stay there with him."

I find her remark strange but chalk it up to post-nap confusion. "You're fortunate to relive those memories with such clarity. I barely remember what I ate on my date last weekend." I pick a diamond-shaped tag from the bunch. It shows a whale's tail breaching the water. "How about this one—2004?"

She winces but takes the tag and drops her head again. I sort through the bin as I wait, hoping that whatever dream this one conjures doesn't take too long. The fragrance of seashore air is joined this time by the heady scent of Old Bay, probably wafting in from the facility's kitchens. My stomach growls, so I make a mental note to stop by Fin's Fish House on the way home.

More faint cries echo through the room, but this time, the source is a young child. Likely visitors down the hall. I sympathize with the kid, dragged to this somber place to visit a grandparent they hardly know. The wailing stirs Emma. When she opens her eyes, tears well in the corners. One spills down her cheek as she grabs for a tissue to dry her face. "I'm sorry. Look at me, an old woman crying her eyes out."

"Was it a sad memory?"

"Oh, they're more than memories, David." She looks past me, ensuring we are alone, before she continues. "Do you want to know a secret?"

I lean in, a willing recipient of all Rehoboth gossip. "Of course."

"These are not just obsolete pieces of plastic," she says, waving the whale tag at me. "They're portals to moments in the past. When I hold one in my hand, I return to the time I wore it at the beach."

I rub my chin and nod. "I see. And where did this one take you?"

"Not just where, David, but when. This was the summer my son nearly drowned. He stayed at the beach with my in-laws while we returned to the cottage to steam blue crabs for supper. We'd just put them in the pot when my niece came running up the dunes, screaming for us. The lifeguard on duty saved Ethan, but still, I don't like to relive that day. Unfortunately, it's my strongest impression from that summer, so it's the day I most often visit when I hold the tag."

"When you say visit, you mean dream about?"

"No. I mean visit. I told you, these aren't dreams or memories. They're more than that, and these are more than old beach tags. They're gateways. Snapshots of time I can hold in my hand. And yes, I really do travel there. I feel the sand under my toes and taste the salty mist on my tongue. I see my family. I can talk to them again and hold them. I just can't change the fundamental events of the day, which is why I don't visit 2004 often." She tosses that tag next to the other two on the tray.

Damn. Does Emma truly believe she travels through time on the wings of sixty-year old plastic? Adri said Emma was generally healthy and still mentally sharp. That she experienced light depression from time to time but didn't suffer from the typical declines of old age. Maybe this notion of a physical escape to happier days is how she sustains herself in this dreary place.

The skepticism must show on my face. Emma maneuvers over to the bed and begins scooping tags back into the plastic bin. "Perhaps I shouldn't have shared this with you."

"I'm sorry, Emma. I'm just trying to understand what these tags mean to you. Wherever it is you believe you go when you hold one, I can tell you that your body stays here. I've watched you fall asleep twice now, so you must be dreaming. Vivid dreams, sure, but it's the only thing that makes sense."

"More sense than that there might be some power you don't understand? That some connections between our past and present are so strong, we can traverse them if only we have the right key? Reality is more than what we smell, hear, and touch with these flesh and bone vessels of ours, Mr. Wellington."

The fact she reverted to my last name meant I'd offended her, which isn't what I'd wanted. Frustrated, I shuffle through the tags until I find what I'm looking for.

"All right, then. This one is from 2033. My family spent a few days here at Rehoboth that year. It was our last trip as a family before they closed the beaches. So what do I do? How do I revisit that summer?"

"Just hold it and let the moments wash over you, like waves at the beach."

I squeeze my eyes closed and grip the tag in my hand until the plastic corners dent my skin. At first, I try to clear my mind, to empty it of the self-conscious awareness of how stupid I feel. When that's unsuccessful, I instead try to recall that summer at the beach. I was only six at the time, so the memories are blurry, spare, and incoherent, like looking at a ship on the horizon through the wrong end of a spyglass.

"It's not working for me." I'm disappointed, even though I know better than to expect the impossible.

"It's about both time and place, David. I imagine you would need to have stayed at Cape May for it to work." She takes the tag from me and grimaces before chucking it back into the bin. "That wasn't a great year for me, either, if it's any consolation."

"I've only been to Cape May once since they reopened the coast in 2052, but access was free."

"Yes, they stopped charging once the Restoration Project was complete. I guess they figured we'd learned from our past mistakes. That's why my collection stops at 2035," Emma says, shaking her head. "I lost Jacob a few years after that. Then the kids moved away—one to England, the other to San Diego—and had kids of their own. I moved to Rehoboth after they reopened the coast, but by then, I was hoverchair-bound and unable to go by myself."

I want to reach for her hand, to provide the nominal comfort of a stranger's touch. I settle for comforting words instead. "I'm sorry for all you've lost."

"That's the best part of the magic in these tags, though, isn't it? Those days on the beach with my family were never lost." She lifts her eyes to mine and searches them for either belief or understanding. I'm not sure what she sees in my face, but she finally sighs and relents. "It's alright, David. You don't need to believe me. Maybe I am just dreaming. But what is our past but dreams we've lived. Or, maybe a life that we've only dreamed."

We tacitly agree to leave it at that. I ask her a few more follow-up questions about tag usage through the years, and she obliges me by posing for photos with her collection. I place several of the more colorful tags—including the one from 1994—in her fragile hands for a close-up. The image is both simple and poignant.

I promise to return and show her the story once it's published. She thanks me for visiting and asks me to put the tags back into the credenza. As I tuck the bin into one of the bottom cabinets, I notice that the diffuser I'd seen earlier is empty and unplugged.

* * * * *

The day my story is published, I return to Seaside Pointe to share it with Emma. I'm eager to talk to her again, as I've been unable to reconcile a few details from my last visit. When I'd signed out of the log, I noticed I was the only visitor in the building that afternoon. No families. No small children to cry. The dining menu posted nearby listed spaghetti for dinner, not seafood, and not a single seagull loitered outside the building. And of course, the scent diffuser had been unplugged.

Emma's story about the special nature of her tags—magic, she'd called it—is unbelievable, but I cannot explain having experienced the exact sounds and smells she described from her dreams. That left me at the crossroads of impossible and inexplicable. I hoped another visit with Emma would steer me in a definitive direction. Practical though I was, part of me—that part that yearned to revisit just one sunny day from that final beach vacation with my family—wished for the impossible, even if it didn't apply to me.

I turn into her room, expecting to find her sitting next to the sun-filled window, asleep with a tag in her hand. Instead, the shades are closed and the hoverchair is gone. An orderly in pale-green scrubs pulls undergarments and loose socks from a drawer of the credenza—the top of which has been cleared off—and tosses them into a large gray garbage can, while another man removes sheets from the bed. A pit forms in my stomach as I ask the question I know has an unpleasant answer.

"Where is Ms. Conrad?"

"Are you friend or family?" asks the man stripping the bed.

"Neither. I interviewed her two weeks ago for a story. I told her I'd come back to show her when …" My voice falters. There's no point in continuing.

The other orderly, a burly young man with a blond goatee, pulls the bin full of beach tags from the credenza and heads for the garbage can. "They found her sitting there by the window, clutching one of these, a week or so back. The docs declared her brain dead, so her family took her off life support three days ago."

"She passed away yesterday morning, surrounded by family. It was peaceful," the other man adds. His Jamaican lilt carries a note of compassion missing in his younger counterpart.

I swallow past the lump in my throat as the younger man pulls the lid from the clear bin. I stop him before he tips them over into the garbage.

"Her family doesn't want those?"

"Nah, they took anything worth anything with them last night before they left. Said to donate or dispose of the rest. Why, you want them?"

"No. At least, not all of them. Maybe just one, if you don't mind."

The orderly shrugs, balances the bin on the edge of the garbage can and tilts the opening in my direction. I hasten over and dig through the plastic, looking for the 1994 beach tag. It's missing. Perhaps still clutched in fragile hands that now lay stiff and cold on a steel table. I don't like to think of Emma that way, so I envision her instead on that sunny beach from long ago—her perfect day—as she spends an eternal summer sprawled on a blanket, flirting with a man who would become the love of her life.

"Looking for a specific year or something?" The man's question is clipped with impatience.

I come across the one from 2033 and latch onto it. "Got it, thank you."

The orderly runs his own hand through them. "So weird, all this single-use plastic. Not even recyclable. What were they even for?"

"They were like tickets to the beach," I say. "Back when they used to charge for access. They stopped making them thirty years ago."

"You're both too young to remember, but they were still around when I was a kid," the older man adds. "My family spent a week at

Cape May back in 2020."

"In 2020, huh?" The orderly with the goatee digs around the box, pulls one from the jumble, and tosses it to him. "There you go."

The older man catches the tag and studies it, stroking it with his thumb. "I remember that vacation." He sits on the stripped-down bed and rubs at his eyes. "Man, it takes me right back. Like I can feel the saltwater stinging my eyes." He pauses for a moment, tilting his left ear to the ceiling, and asks, "Do you guys hear seagulls?"

I smile at the possibility of the impossible as the faint scent of saltwater and summertime tickles my nose.

D.M. DOMOSEA HAS AN UNQUENCHABLE THIRST FOR GEEK-WORTHY SPECULATIVE FICTION IN ALL FORMS. HER WORK CAN BE FOUND ONLINE AND IN VARIOUS ANTHOLOGIES, INCLUDING *BEACH PULP* FROM CAT & MOUSE PRESS. SHE IS CURRENTLY IN THE QUERY TRENCHES WITH A MIDDLE-GRADE SUPERHERO NOVEL AND EYEING UP THE NEXT MAJOR PROJECT FROM HER OVERFLOWING STORY NURSERY. D.M. LIVES WITH HER FAMILY IN THE DWINDLING WOODLANDS OF MARYLAND, WHERE SHE IS STEADILY LOSING THE WAR AGAINST PET FUR. YOU CAN FIND HER ON THE WEB AT WWW.DMDOMOSEA.COM.

JUDGE'S COMMENT

This is a wonderful story with diverse but well-blended elements. The narrative was moving and hit all the right notes for me: nostalgia and aging, the concerns about our environment and our beloved beaches, and a "just the facts" reporter surprised by a little magic. This futuristic story is a bit outside what I normally read for pleasure, but it stuck with me, which I think speaks to the strength of this piece. There was just the right amount of every ingredient here and I think the author nailed the recipe for this short story.

Sisters of Land and Sea

By Kim DeCicco

This is a tale of two sisters, born twenty minutes apart. They were as close as twins could be; they knew each other's thoughts, could finish each other's sentences. But when it came to appearance and dreams, no two sisters were further apart.

Margaret, the elder, had blue eyes like their mother and ebony hair—hair so dark, in fact, that ravens considered her one of their own. They perched outside her window and watched as she tossed and turned until dawn. The sea roiled and roared in Margaret's dream, and a dark figure emerged from its depths. This figure never had discernible features and left her filled with dread.

Little Louisa, however, had dark, wide-set eyes and pale brown hair—so pale, in fact, that field mice mistook it for a parent's fur and curled up in her hair once she fell asleep. The water remained calm and serene in Louisa's dream and while she also saw a faceless figure, she woke peaceful, ready for a new day.

The girls lived with their uncle, as one parent had died when they were seven, and the other they had never met.

On the morning before their twelfth birthday, Uncle announced that they would visit their Rehoboth beach house. Their mother had left written instructions, "Bring the girls to the water's edge at midnight the day they turn twelve. Have them look to the ocean and wait. Their future depends on it." No explanation, no clues.

"I'm not going," Margaret said.

Louisa rose from the breakfast table. "I'll pack my things."

"Why don't you want to go?" Uncle asked Margaret.

"It has something to do with the dream. I'm sure of it."

"Dream?"

"The one we have every night," Louisa said.

Uncle looked from one to the other, "How long has this been going on?"

"Since the night Mom died," Margaret said.

Louisa nodded in confirmation.

"Tell me," Uncle said, as he placed a reassuring hand over Margaret's white-knuckled fist pressed on the table.

With a deep sigh, Margaret took Uncle's hand in hers. "It's always the same. I'm on a stormy beach. Wind and rain slash my face, and waves crash against the shore. The sky is dark, whether from the storm or night, I don't know, but it's scary." Uncle squeezed her hand in encouragement. "Then, from the sea comes a shadow, big, like a man. It has no features and, although it moves toward me, I see no legs or arms. It stops a few feet from me, then I wake up."

Uncle gathered Margaret into his arms. "I wish you'd told me sooner."

"The first night we had the dream," Louisa said while sinking back into her chair, "I told Margaret mine was the same." She looked at her sister. "That wasn't true. Mine is nice."

"What?" Margaret straightened. "Why did you lie?"

"You were so upset. I wanted you to feel better."

"It's been five years." Margaret shook her head in disbelief. "Why haven't you said something sooner?"

"When?"

"Maybe the next day?"

"The day we found out mom died?" Louisa asked as she stood.

"Well, then, a week later."

"You had that dream over and over, were upset each time. How would telling you mine was nice help?" Louisa lifted a hand in offering. "I've wanted to tell you for years. I didn't know how."

"That's crap."

"Margaret, enough." Uncle said, as he lay a hand on her shoulder. She moved away from his touch and dropped into her chair, crossing her arms.

"Louisa, sit. Tell us your dream," Uncle said. "Then we'll work it out."

"The sea is calm." Louisa focused on the circles she began tracing with her finger on the table. "Waves lap at the shore and a full moon shimmers across the water. A figure with no features or limbs rises from the ocean in mine too. I also wake up just as it reaches me"—she peeked up at Margaret— "but I feel safe."

Margaret's jaw dropped. "Why isn't yours scary?"

"I don't know."

"Why do I get this? Wasn't losing mom enough?" She shoved from her chair and ran upstairs.

"I'm sorry," Louisa called as she made to follow. Uncle stopped her. "Give her time."

"Can I come in?" Louisa asked from the doorway.

"I guess," Margaret said, as she picked lint from her quilt.

Louisa sat on the edge of the bed. "Do you hate me?"

Margaret looked at the ceiling, "No." She pinned Louisa with a stare. "I'm not happy, but I don't hate you."

"I really am sorry." Louisa reached for her sister's hand. "I never meant to hurt you."

"I know, but I *really* don't want to go now."

"Uncle said he won't risk our future by staying." She gave Margaret a grim smile. "He also said the trip might stop our dreams"—she squeezed her sister's hand—"or we might find out why they're different."

Margaret paced the room after Louisa left. Frustrated, she kicked her school backpack. A bag of crackers fell out. She broke them up and tossed them out the window. Might as well give the ravens a treat if she had to go away. She stretched out on her bed and pressed her hot cheek to the cool pillow, hoping a dreamless sleep would come and let her forget the morning. A few minutes passed and she heard one, then another, and finally a third click on her window. Upon investigation, she found three small stones on the sill, each shaped like a seashell. The ravens were telling her to go.

Louisa went outside to the old shed and poured a handful of dry oats near its entrance. She knew the mice would enjoy them. One mouse slipped from under the door and sat down to eat, then out came another. A third darted out and back, then finally settled in with the others. Louisa noticed something white under the door. The mice scattered as she pulled out a nibbled scrap of paper covered with faded script. It read: "Tell them I love them. Tell them I'm sorry. Tell them their father was—" The mice had eaten the rest. Louisa ran back to the house.

"Uncle!"

"What is it?" Uncle said, as he emerged from his study.

"I found this." Louisa handed him the paper. "Mom wrote it."

Uncle read the few words and rubbed the back of his neck. "You're right."

"What's going on?" Margaret asked as she came downstairs.

"I found a note from Mom. Is this the start of her instructions, Uncle? What did she write about our father?"

"This isn't from her instructions. She said she loved you, of course, but she didn't mention your father." He rubbed his eyes. "So much in one day," he said to himself. "Girls,"—he looked up—"I need to sort out everything for tomorrow. Leave this for today. We'll talk more on the ride." He gave Margaret the scrap and returned to his study.

"What should we do with it?"

Louisa tugged the braided cord around her wrist. They'd each made one from embroidery thread found in an old shoe box once stored in their mother's closet. "Put it behind the photo of Mom we keep on the mantel?"

* * * * *

Louisa, having already supplied the mice with more oats and a large strawberry, loaded her bag in the car. Margaret leaned against the oak tree that shaded the driveway. The ravens, gathered in the branches above, exuded soft caws. Margaret ignored them. She was still upset about going. Uncle came out and they all got in the vehicle. Four hours and they'd be in Rehoboth Beach, at a house owned by the family for several generations, but not used by the three of them since the night the girls' mother had walked into the sea, taking her own life.

They drove quietly for the first hour. The next brought small talk about the weather and scenery. They stopped for gas, ate peanut butter sandwiches, and were back on the road by four.

"Girls," Uncle began, "I need to tell you what your mother said the morning before she died. She told me how she met your father."

Margaret and Louisa, both in the back seat, bolted upright.

"She'd been vacationing at the beach house alone," he said. "On her first evening there, a seal came up to her while she was swimming in the ocean. It circled around her, then dove under to pop up on the other side. It barked, almost like a laugh, she said, and then dove down to nose at her feet. She said this happened three nights, but on the fourth evening, the seal wasn't there. She figured it had moved on."

Uncle looked at the girls, rapt and waiting, through the rearview mirror. "Your mother told me that after her swim on that fourth night, she lay on her towel to gaze at the stars. She must have fallen asleep, she said, because she startled awake when drops of water hit her face. A man, in ill-fitting swim trunks, sat near and flicked water at her while smiling with all the charm in the world." Uncle saw the girls' astonished faces. "Her words, not mine."

"They're great words," Louisa said.

"Well,"—Uncle cleared his throat—"your mother saw him every night for the rest of her stay. A month after she returned home, she realized she was pregnant."

Margaret shot out, "What was his name?"

"What did he say when he found out?" Louisa said at the same time.

"Your mother never told me his name and, well, he didn't know about the two of you until you turned six."

"Why not?" they both shouted.

"He left no way to be reached." Uncle saw a parking lot and pulled over. Once stopped, he turned to the girls. "Your mother asked for a number or address, but he said he had no phone or permanent home. He said the best way to find him was to come to the shore on summer evenings. Your mother assumed he didn't want further involvement. Do you understand?"

The girls blushed. They'd seen things in movies, heard whispered gossip from friends who'd overheard parents talking, and, of course, that awkward conversation with Uncle two months ago when they'd both begun their woman's cycle.

"Didn't she take precautions?" Louisa asked.

It was Uncle's turn to blush. "She said she had." He adjusted his position. "Your mother went back every year on the same week she had meet your father. It wasn't until the year you turned six that she found him. He was thrilled when he heard about you and said he would be happy to meet you there, at the beach, but that was as far as he could go. Your mother was livid." Uncle smiled at the memory. "She ranted about men when she returned home, and for most of that year."

"I remember," Margaret said, "but then it stopped."

"Yes." Uncle shifted, started tapping his fingers against his leg. "She'd found out she was ill."

"What?" Louisa said. "You said she drowned herself because her heart was broken."

Margaret just stared.

"She did. I'm sorry." Uncle looked out the window. "Both things happened. Her heart was broken"—he turned back to face them—"because she knew she'd have to leave you. She found out she had advanced cancer, only a few months to live. She didn't want you to watch her die."

"More lies," Margaret said.

"She didn't want her illness to be your last memories of her."

Margaret threw her hands in the air. "What's with this family? She died alone and we were left without the chance to say goodbye. How is that better?"

"I agree," Uncle said. "I would have stopped her if I'd known. She told me about her illness that same morning she spoke about your father. I talked about treatments, but she just stared off into space." He sighed. "When I woke the next day, she was gone and all I had was a letter explaining that I was now in charge of your care. I called the police, but it was too late. She was already dead."

They sat quietly for some time; Louisa gazed out the window, silent tears running down her cheeks, and Margaret labored to get a full breath as she clenched and unclenched her hands.

Uncle stirred. "Let's finish the drive."

"Are we going to meet our father tonight?" Louisa asked.

"That's what I expect," said Uncle.

"He sounds like more trouble than he's worth," Margaret said. "Why do we need him?"

Uncle eyed her through the mirror as he prepared to get back on Route 1. "Your mother wanted you to meet him. What you do after that is up to you."

They arrived at the Rehoboth house by six-thirty. Bags were hauled in and windows were opened to catch the ocean breeze. Everyone gathered on the back deck to take in the view. The warm air, the growing shade, and the rhythmic breath of the sea lulled away their stress about the coming night and soon they all fell asleep.

Margaret startled awake and found the sky was dark. She shook Louisa. "Did you have the dream?"

"Yes. You?"

"Yeah, but this time the figure was definitely at man. His features were still blurry, but he had a face and limbs."

"Mine too." Louisa sat up. "I'm sure he's our father."

Inside, Uncle had prepared a meal from supplies they brought, but no one had much of an appetite. The clock's tick was a reminder that midnight was fast approaching. Margaret cleared away dinner. Louisa went in search of a blanket to use on the beach.

Fifteen minutes before the hour, they walked down the deck stairs and across the sand toward the ocean, a fully risen moon guiding their steps. Uncle spread the blanket a yard from shore. They sat and watched the sea.

"Is that a seal?" Louisa asked a few minutes later, when a head began to bob in and out of the waves.

"It sure is," said Uncle, his eyes wide.

Margaret walked into the water, up to her knees.

"Careful," Uncle called, as he and Louisa moved closer.

The seal barked and dove, then surfaced again, three, four, five times, Then the seal dove and stayed down.

"Did it leave?" Louisa asked.

No one answered because a head appeared again. It got higher in the water as it moved forward. A neck, then shoulders, appeared.

"Oh, my God!" Margaret gasped, as she stumbled back and onto the sand.

A hand pushed wet hair from dark eyes. A torso gleamed in the moonlight as he rose from the sea. He held what looked like a wet suit across his groin. Sturdy legs carried him to the water's edge.

"Hello, daughters," the man said. He nodded to Uncle. "Brother."

Mouths agape, the three just stared.

"May I borrow your blanket?"

No one moved.

"Please?"

Uncle stepped back and reached down without taking his eyes off the man. He flung the blanket forward, showering everyone with sand.

"Thank you," the man said, as he wrapped it around his waist. He placed the suit at his feet, where its shape was fully discernible—a finned tail, flippers, and a whiskered snout.

Louisa knelt to examine it. "This is the seal's skin. Did you kill it?"

"No, it's my skin. I took it off so you could know me in my human form."

"What are you talking about?" Margaret asked, her arms wrapped tight around her chest in an attempt to stop shaking.

"I'm a selkie." At their blank looks, he continued. "You must know. A seal who becomes human by shedding its pelt. Didn't your mother tell you?"

"Their mother is dead." Uncle moved closer, his fists ready to swing. "Is this how you're going to explain not wanting to be their father? That you're some kind of sea creature?"

"I'm sorry to learn of your mother's death," the man said to the girls. "She was kind and beautiful." Turning to Uncle, "I wanted to be their father, but I can't be a human one because I *am* a sea creature. Selkies can't live on land for any length of time. We need the water."

"Ridiculous," Uncle said.

"But Uncle"—Louisa stood, tugged his arm—"the note. The mice ate the words that would've explained this." Louisa turned to the man, "Are Margaret and I selkies too?"

"Maybe. Some children inherit the trait."

"Do all selkies go around impregnating women?" Uncle said, his anger palpable.

The man raised an eyebrow. "We come when called—seven tears cried into the sea at high tide will bring us to land—and we engage with the lonely who walk the shoreline or swim in the ocean. Sometimes children result."

"Elise wasn't lonely," Uncle said.

"Are you sure? Selkies hear the heart's call." The man turned to the girls. "Elise, your mother, was lovely. Warm, humorous, playful. I couldn't stay away. And, look at the result!" He smiled at them. "The two of you." He then addressed Uncle, "I'm sure Elise wasn't lonely once she had the girls."

Uncle deflated. He knew it was true.

"How will we know if we're selkies?" Margaret asked.

"Once you've turned twelve, go into the ocean. You'll either change into a seal or not."

Margaret looked at her wet feet. "I guess I'm not a selkie. I'm twelve today."

"I guess not," he agreed.

Everyone turned to Louisa. She inhaled deeply and took a step toward the sea.

"Wait!" Margaret grabbed her arm. "What if you change? We'll lose you too."

"She can visit every year," the man said. "We both can."

Margaret enveloped Louisa in a fierce hug. "Don't go," she pleaded.

"I have to," Louisa said. "I feel a need for the sea vibrating through my bones." She pulled back, wiped the tears from Margaret's face.

"This is why our dreams are different. Don't you see?"

Margaret's tears came faster. "Yes, because you gain a father while I lose a sister."

"You will always have us both, Margaret," the man said. "Just not every day."

Uncle caressed each of the girl's heads, "If this is Louisa's future, Margaret, then we have to let her go."

Margaret hugged Louisa again. "Meet me here on our birthday?"

"You couldn't keep me away."

"OK," Margaret said, as she wiped her eyes and released her sister. "Then go be a selkie."

Louisa kissed Uncle. The man waved farewell then retrieved his pelt. He offered Louisa his hand, and together they stepped into the ocean. Moonlight shimmered briefly off Louisa's hair, and then they dove underwater. A few yards out, a pair of smooth heads surfaced, their dark, wide-set eyes looked back at Margaret and Uncle. With a bark, they dove again and were gone. The blanket lapped against the foamy shore.

At the water's edge, Margaret stared at the receding waves. Uncle tucked the soaked blanket under one arm then embraced his niece. "Are you alright?"

Margaret's gaze lifted to the night sky and she thought about her ravens back home. "I guess I will be. It helps to know I'll see Louisa again"—she gave Uncle a half smile—"and to know the dream won't come back."

Water rushed over Margaret's feet. A piece of seaweed clung to her ankle. She bent to remove it and saw it was tangled with wet, braided thread. Once the thread was freed, she tucked her sister's bracelet in her pocket; something for the mice to remember Louisa.

KIM DECICCO IS A WRITER OF FICTION, NONFICTION, AND POETRY. BORN AND RAISED IN NEW YORK, SHE MOVED TO DELAWARE IN 2004. A PREVIOUS CAREER IN MUSEUMS, AS WELL AS HER LOVE OF MYTH AND FOLKLORE, COMPEL HER TO CREATE STORIES INFUSED WITH HISTORY AND OTHER-WORLDLY FLAIR. THIS IS HER FIRST PUBLICATION.

Dreaming in Stick Figures

By TJ Lewes

Ms. Getz stood in the driveway of her sprawling Victorian, scowling, with one hand on her walker and the other flailing at insects, when Terrance pulled up Friday morning. He took a deep breath before exiting, his car door squeaking loudly.

"You're late, Terrance. It's already 8:13 and we still have a lot to do for tomorrow's yard sale. What's wrong with you? You look terrible."

"Sorry, Ms. Getz. I ain't been sleepin' so good. I keep havin' bad dreams with stick people. But, look what I gotcha. I found this half-used bottle of bug spray in the trash and thought of those mosquitoes that keep bitin' ya. Here, spray some on so they don't getcha, while I start gettin' together that stuff ya pointed out in the garage yesterday."

Terrance immediately set to work, depositing the folding tables and items for sale in an empty stall of the large garage. Ms. Getz remained outside, contemplating the bottle of dumpster bug spray. Terrance could only write his name and count money, surviving by doing odd jobs for the folks in town. He had nearly nothing, yet he shared everything and never complained. She sprayed herself liberally, her frown disappearing.

"Ms. Getz, whatcha want me to do with the beach stuff? There's a ton of it back here under a tarp. Ya don't plan on surfin' anytime, do ya? Ya want me to add it to the yard sale stuff?"

Ms. Getz pushed her walker slowly into the far corner of the garage, where decades earlier her family had stashed an array of beach toys, surfboards, chairs, and umbrellas. She could barely make out her companion in the shadows, but she could tell he was sweating despite the holes in his shirt.

"That depends, Terrance. Is there anything you could use? Perhaps your granddaughter would enjoy going to the beach with you, especially on a day like this."

Terrance's eyes widened, appearing like twin moons before he grinned, baring a galaxy of yellowed teeth. He laughed heartily.

"Ms. Getz, I ain't never been to the beach and I ain't got no mind to start now."

"You've lived less than ten miles from the ocean for over sixty years and you've never gone to the beach, Terrance?"

"No, ma'am. I don't swim and all that water scares me. Anyways, I got several other jobs lined up for today. Whatcha want me to do with this stuff, then?"

Ms. Getz looked over the pile sadly, years of happy memories left to decay. Her husband had died, her children had relocated, and at eighty-two, she was moving into a retirement home where little would fit. She knew it was time to part with her past, but she paused a moment before answering, two little stick figures running through her mind.

"Do me a favor, Terrance, leave me one bucket, one shovel, the two green chairs, and the striped umbrella. Put all the rest with the sale items before you leave. Use the tarp to cover the furniture we set up yesterday. Here's your money for helping today. I will see you at six a.m. tomorrow for the yard sale. Wear your good shirt and don't be late. Oh, and thank you for the bug spray."

Ms. Getz shuffled away, the legs of her walker clicking against the macadam. Terrance finished the job, then climbed wearily behind the wheel of his Dodge Aries. It took several tries to turn over the engine before he could rush to his next job.

* * * * *

Terrance arrived promptly the next morning to assist Ms. Getz with the yard sale. He yawned widely as he walked toward the garage but got to work immediately setting up tables and displaying the goods as Ms. Getz affixed price tags. Before they finished, the first of many eager shoppers approached.

It was late in the day before the last bargain hunter disappeared, leaving behind nothing more than a lamp, some books, and a few tchotchkes. Terrance boxed the items to donate to the thrift store, then joined Ms. Getz inside. They rested together at the kitchen island, one of the only places to sit left in the house.

"Here, Terrance, take your money for today and have some lemonade. You must be thirsty after all that work."

"Thank ya, Ms. Getz."

Terrance slipped the money into his pocket and drank the lemonade slowly as he looked at the bare walls and empty countertops. Through the window he could see the sold sign swinging in the wind. He cleared his throat before speaking.

"I 'spect ya won't be needin' me no mo' after this."

"Actually, Terrance, I do need you for one more important job. Come Monday morning at eight a.m. Don't be late."

* * * * *

It was over ninety degrees when a fatigued Terrance arrived a few minutes before eight on Monday morning. The Lincoln Continental that Ms. Getz usually kept covered in the garage was gleaming in the driveway. By the time Terrance parked his car and yawned himself up the driveway, Ms. Getz had lumbered outside to meet him, her purse hanging from the handlebar of her walker.

"Good morning, Terrance. Today I need you to be my chauffeur.

We'll take my car."

"Aight then, Ms. Getz. Here, let me get that door for ya. Where ya wanna go?"

"You'll see. I'll direct you as we drive. Let's go now before traffic gets heavy."

Within fifteen minutes, Terrance and Ms. Getz were on East Savannah Road in Lewes. Ms. Getz directed them straight past Beebe hospital and over the canal bridge, to the end of the street that emptied into a large parking lot. The smell of sea air was strong and Terrance began to fidget in the driver's seat.

"Ms. Getz, whatcha thinkin' bringin' me here."

"Simple, Terrance, I need your help. I want to sit at the bay awhile and I can't take my walker on the sand. Everything we need is in the trunk. Now, let's go."

Before Terrance could argue, Ms. Getz had struggled out of the passenger seat. She waited by the trunk as Terrance grudgingly complied. Soon, Terrance had set up the two green chairs and the striped umbrella. While Ms. Getz read her book, Terrance stared at the wonder before him, his fatigue fading.

The bay stretched calmly into the distance, with only tiny ripples instead of the monstrous waves Terrance had imagined. It was low tide, leaving small pools of shimmering water along the shore, where seagulls foraged for breakfast. On the horizon, Terrance could see a large ship.

"What's that, Ms. Getz? Looks like a boat."

"That is the Cape May-Lewes Ferry. It goes from Lewes across the Delaware Bay to Cape May, New Jersey, where my retirement home is. You can drive your car right onto the ferry, or park and ride across as a foot passenger. Now, help me to the water's edge. I'd like to dip my toes in."

Terrance continued to watch the ferry as he helped Ms. Getz walk across the sand. Before he knew it, cold water lapped at his feet. He tried to retreat, but Ms. Getz held firmly onto his arm.

"Come now, man. It's less than two inches of water and you're over six feet tall."

"Ms. Getz, ya know I don't swim."

"You don't need to swim; you just need to walk. Now stop complaining and roll up your pants so they don't get wet."

Terrance swallowed his response and focused on his hems. The cool water felt wonderful on his hot skin, and the sand massaged his sore feet. He wiggled his toes, enjoying the novelty of doing nothing. He closed his eyes as Ms. Getz pulled him farther, until the water reached his ankles.

"Ms. Getz, far 'nough I think. What 'bout sharks?"

"Terrance, any shark that can swim in six inches of water is too small to hurt you. Take me a little farther. I'm hot."

Ms. Getz dragged Terrance several feet farther until the water reached his knees. He gulped heavily and dug his heels in, refusing to take another step. Without a word, Ms. Getz sank into the water, allowing it to envelop her up to her neck. She closed her eyes and waited.

For several minutes, Terrance stood stock-still beside her. At last, the relentless sun beat him down into the refreshing water. He sank slowly, every muscle tensed for retreat, until at last he settled himself on the bay floor. Even sitting, the water only reached his chest. Little by little, his breathing slowed.

The currents moved his body forward and back. At first, he resisted their pull, but soon he found himself leaning with them, relaxed by their monotony. The tension he always carried in his shoulders began to recede, and his arms floated weightlessly. Terrance started to doze, but then the water splashed his chin. He opened his eyes to find Ms. Getz smiling at him.

"It's wonderful here, isn't it, Terrance? You know, most of my happiest memories with my family were made at the beach. I can't thank you enough for bringing me here today, and for everything you have done for me over the decades. The tide is coming in. Let's walk back."

Terrance stood and turned to face the beach. He was shocked to realize that they were at least thirty yards from the shore. The small pools had reconnected with the bay, making the water stretch far up the sand. The water reached his waist and his heart began to race. Ms. Getz grasped his arm firmly.

"One step at a time, Terrance. We got out here together, and we'll get back the same way. Let's enjoy the journey, OK?"

Terrance nodded. Slowly, he and Ms. Getz trudged toward shore. With each step, the water level dropped, until it was comfortably around his ankles again. As happy as he was to reach the shore, he felt an odd sense of loss as he stepped onto the dry sand.

Ms. Getz and Terrance sat together on the chairs once more, drying in the baking heat of the midday sun. Around them, the beach had filled with families. Small children played gleefully in the water as parents lounged in the shallows with them. At its deepest point, the water only reached the necks of the few adults who ventured to the marker buoys. Terrance smiled.

"It's a lovely beach, isn't it, Terrance? Shame we have to leave. Help me with the chairs, please."

"OK, then, Ms. Getz. Ya need me to do anything else?"

"Yes, Terrance, come tomorrow morning at eight to say goodbye."

* * * * *

That night, Terrance fell asleep before nine and didn't wake until nearly six the next morning. His mind was filled with his beach memories, and he got out of bed feeling energized. For the first time in many years, he took a walk and enjoyed the sunrise. He delighted in the feathered orchestra, laughed at the frolicking squirrels, and admired the brightly painted landscape near his house.

He arrived promptly at eight to find Ms. Getz sitting on the bench near her front door, a large gift bag at her feet. She smiled warmly as he approached, beckoning him to the empty seat next to her.

"Good morning, Terrance. You look well rested."

"Yes, ma'am, for sure. Last night was great—I still got them stick-people dreams, but at least they weren't no nightmares this time."

Ms. Getz's smile brightened. She laughed as she presented the bag to Terrance.

"This is for you."

"For me? Nah, Ms. Getz, Ya don't gotta give me nothin'. It's my honor to work for ya all these years."

"Please, Terrance, accept it and open it now, so I can explain the things inside."

Terrance slowly pulled the large bag toward him. Inside, he found a beach bag, two towels, a bucket, a shovel, an iPhone, and two envelopes. He looked at Ms. Getz quizzically as she retrieved one of the envelopes from the bag and pulled a pen from her purse.

"You have two more jobs to do for me this week, Terrance. First, you must take the title of the Lincoln to the DMV and have it transferred to you. The title is inside this envelope. We'll do the paperwork here now before I leave so there is nothing to worry about. Second, you must take your granddaughter to our beach in Lewes. Use that cellphone to take pictures to send me. The chairs and umbrella are inside the trunk, and everything else you need is inside the bag."

"Ms. Getz, I can't accept all this."

"You can and you will, but promise you'll FaceTime me so I can see how you're doing. It's all set up on the phone. And maybe you'll even take the ferry and visit me once in a while. Now, sign your name here. My taxi is arriving."

Terrance was in a daze as he scribbled on the line Ms. Getz indicated.

Before he could fully grasp what was happening, Ms. Getz hugged him tightly, then disappeared inside the taxi. He sat on the bench a long time after she left, the car title grasped firmly in his shaking hands, tears streaming unnoticed down his cheeks.

That day, he mowed the yard for Ms. Planchock, power-washed the Rettig house, and took out the trash for Mr. Otte. It was nearly dark when he finally got home and took the gift bag inside. He looked through the contents once more, laughing at the bucket and shovel and shaking his head at the title of the Continental. As he pulled out the towels to admire them, the second envelope fell onto his lap. It was thick, heavy, and tightly sealed.

With his old pocketknife, Terrance sliced the edge of the envelope. Inside he found a stack of hundred-dollar bills. Shocked, he dropped the envelope, scattering the money across the worn linoleum. He quickly went to the window to make sure no one was around, then double-checked the lock on his front door, before gathering up the cash and gift bag and running upstairs.

He sat on his bed for several minutes, breathing deeply, before he counted the money with trembling hands. It came out to twenty thousand dollars. Never in his life had Terrance seen so much money in one place, and he had certainly never imagined it being in his bedroom. He slept with the cash in a bag under his pillow that night, and woke up excited, his stick-figure dreams melting into the daylight.

First, Terrance used the new cell phone to call his son. He made plans to pick up his granddaughter, Lakeia, later that day. Next, Terrance drove to the bank and opened a savings account. He held the deposit slip like a trophy as he exited.

Afterward, Terrance went to the DMV. He was nervous as he waited, but within minutes he was the proud owner of a Lincoln. Finally, he took the car to pick up his five-year-old granddaughter for their trip to Lewes Beach.

Lakeia clung to his leg as they walked into the water, but Terrance stood strong. Within minutes, the little girl overcame her fear and they played together in the bay for hours. Later, Lakeia and Terrance built a sandcastle under the shade of their striped umbrella. Terrance took and sent many pictures that day; he and Lakeia were smiling in all of them.

That night, Terrance made his first call ever on FaceTime. When Ms. Getz appeared on the screen, smiling radiantly, Terrance felt his heart might explode with joy.

"Good evening, Terrance. What a lovely surprise. I am so glad you called me. I enjoyed your pictures very much."

"Ah, Ms. Getz. I can't tell ya how happy Lakeia was today. She said goin' to the beach was a dream come true. Ya made my dreams come true too. Thank ya, Ma'am … for evrythin'."

"There's no need to thank me, because I care about you, Terrance. You helped me for many years, and now it's my turn to help you. I hope to see you soon."

"Good night, Ms. Getz. Ya will, I promise ya that."

Terrance fell asleep content. He knew that he could face his fears for the sake of people who cared about him, like Ms. Getz and Lakeia. He would continue to take his granddaughter to the beach and would even ride the ferry just to visit his dear friend for as long as she lived. That night, the stick figures left his dreams forever, leaving only the vivid images of his joy in their wake.

TJ LEWES, A TWENTY-YEAR VETERAN TEACHER OF SPANISH AND ENGLISH AS A FOREIGN LANGUAGE, STUDIED IN SPAIN, TRAVELED EXTENSIVELY THROUGH CENTRAL AND SOUTH AMERICA RESEARCHING, TAUGHT AND TRAVELED THROUGH CHINA, AND IS AFF-CERTIFIED IN SKYDIVING AND RESORT-CERTIFIED IN SCUBA. LEWES WAS ONE OF ELEVEN PROSE WRITERS CHOSEN FOR THE DELAWARE DIVISION OF THE ARTS 2018 WRITERS' RETREAT, AND HER UPCOMING WORK, "THE ROOSTER IN THE HENHOUSE," WILL BE FEATURED ON THE DELAWARE DIVISION OF THE ARTS ANTHOLOGY COVER. LEWES IS CURRENTLY COMPLETING HER FIRST NOVEL AND PENNING SHORT STORIES.

The Dolphin Whisperers

By Nancy North Walker

It gave new meaning to *rock 'n' roll*.

It hit her like a rock, and she rolled and rolled. Couldn't tell top from bottom. Finally felt sand beneath her. She sprang up, gasping for air, grateful to see blue sky.

Before she could think, a second one walloped her from behind, knocked her flat, and deposited her on the shore. She lay there like a beached whale, in front of hundreds of people on Rehoboth's town beach. *Way to go, Julie*, she thought. *Way to make a grand entrance your first time in the ocean.*

She heard someone running, breathing hard, so she cracked open an eye and saw two long shin bones and a pair of red swim trunks beside her.

"You OK?" The voice was surprisingly deep and soothing.

She scrambled awkwardly to her feet and saw a tall, lanky lifeguard with long, wild, straw-colored hair parted down the middle and a long nose covered with a white triangle of sunscreen. He reminded her of the scarecrow in *The Wizard of Oz*.

"I'm fine. Just humiliated." Warmth filled her cheeks as she brushed sand off her legs. "Championship swimmer fails first attempt at bodysurfing."

"Well, Indiana, the wave cycle's pretty tough today … even for strong swimmers." His eyes turned to half-moons as he smiled. "Do you have much experience with the ocean?"

"Not much. How'd you know I'm from Indiana?" She cocked her hip and shaded her eyes from the late June sun to get a better look at him. He had a long, oval face with moss-green eyes and a goofy, triangular grin. He had to be at least six-foot-five. She was five-eight, and he towered over her.

"Cuz you're broadcasting it?" He sprouted dimples as he pointed to her swimsuit.

She looked down at her crimson swimsuit with the gold seal across her chest and burst out laughing. "OMG! I forgot. I'm wearing my old Indiana University swimsuit. Now I'm super-embarrassed."

"What brings you to Rehoboth Beach, Miss Hoosier swim team champion?"

"I'm transferring to University of Delaware this fall and working as a summer intern at the UD marine science center in Lewes."

"Let me guess. You're a marine biology major and want to study dolphins."

"How'd you know?"

He bent down closer and pretended to whisper. "The dolphins told me you were coming." He winked, stood up, and chuckled. "Seriously, I have a sixth sense for dolphin lovers. It's a kindred spirit thing. Congratulations on that Sharp campus internship. They're hard to come by. A bunch of us lifeguards are UD marine biology majors or grad students. I'll be a second-year grad student this fall."

"Cool! I'd love to pick your brain sometime about how to navigate the curriculum … bodysurfing too."

"OK, Indiana. I'm off in an hour. Meet me at my lifeguard chair. I'll show you how to read the waves safely for a great ride. After that, we can get a bite to eat and talk. In the meantime, don't go in the water above your knees."

"Was that an insult?" She crinkled her nose. "But sure. Sounds like a plan. And … what's your name?"

"Pete. And you're Indiana, right?" He gave her an impish grin and ran back to his lifeguard chair.

That was serendipitous, she thought, as she wrapped her towel around her. *How great to meet a fellow marine biology major and someone who's into dolphins.*

Julie decided it was time to retire the crimson one-piece and went shopping on Rehoboth Avenue. She returned to Pete's lifeguard chair right on time, sporting an aquamarine bikini with a racerback top and feeling much more beach-worthy.

"Hey, Indiana! Almost didn't recognize you without the crimson and gold. Ready to learn how to read and ride the waves?" His sunscreen triangle was gone now, and he looked more surfer dude than scarecrow.

"Yes, but I must confess. I've been hanging out on the bay beaches in Lewes. This is my first day in the ocean … ever."

"No worries, Miss Hoosier pool queen, I'm a bodysurfing warrior and surfboard king. You found the right teacher."

They stood on the shore awhile and Pete taught her how to analyze the wave cycles to find the ideal waves for bodysurfing. He told her to always keep her eyes on the waves, rather than the shore, and to go underwater when a wave was cresting, unless she was well positioned to bodysurf it. If it wasn't cresting, he said, she could float on top.

They dove in and swam to a spot Pete said was the perfect bodysurfing zone. Her class ended a half hour later with the two of them riding a four-foot wave in perfect parallel, springing up into high-fives when they reached shore.

"That was exhilarating! I had four good rides."

"You did very well for a rookie. So … have you ever eaten raw oysters?"

"Nope. We don't do those in Indiana. But I'm game to try."

"Ever seen a dolphin in the wild?" Pete pointed to the ocean and reached for his backpack. "There's a pod about a hundred yards offshore, heading south." He pulled out two pairs of binoculars and gave one to her.

She took one look, then jumped up and down, squealing like a five-year-old who just rode a bike for the first time. "They're gorgeous. Atlantic bottlenoses, right?"

He nodded. "One of eight species in Delaware."

"So, which is your favorite?"

"Striped dolphins, because they're acrobats. But bottlenoses are a close second, because they love to bodysurf."

They watched the dolphins surface over and over, sometimes three or four abreast, until they disappeared from sight. Pete said he counted twelve in the pod, including one calf and two other young ones. "You'll be a pro at sizing up the pods by the end of the summer."

They headed to a noisy oyster bar just two blocks off the beach that was packed wall-to-wall with happy-hour fun seekers. Julie sampled her first Dogfish Head beer and her first oyster. She loved them both. After their dozen oysters vanished in minutes, Pete suggested they head to the quieter south end of the boardwalk, where they could sit and talk and watch for dolphins.

Over the next few hours, Julie and Pete swapped life stories between dolphin sightings. Pete was a Rehoboth Beach native who had grown up in and on the ocean. He joined the junior lifeguard program when he was five and became a certified lifeguard when he was sixteen.

"Surfing is my favorite sport, but I played basketball in the off season and was the star center at Cape Henlopen High. UD offered me a basketball scholarship, but I took an academic scholarship instead."

"So, how did you become interested in dolphins?" Julie asked.

"When I was three, my dad took me out in his two-seater kayak, and I had my first dolphin encounter. I was hooked. Now, my dream is to become a marine biologist and study dolphin communication. How about you?"

"It's Penelope's fault."

"Who's Penelope?"

"She was the bottlenose I got to feed at the dolphin show at the Shedd Aquarium in Chicago when I was eight. I threw her a fish and she jumped up and caught it. Then she flipped her nose up twice, like 'c'mon, more'! Kept on begging until the pail was empty. The crowd was still laughing when the aquarium lady signaled her to swim away. From that day on, I read every book I could find about dolphins, and, later, every scientific article. Then, in 2013, India declared dolphins 'non-human persons.' That was the clincher. I decided to dedicate my life to expanding human knowledge of dolphins."

Pete fist-bumped her. "You really are a kindred spirit."

"I'm a farmer's daughter. I spent my childhood in the barn cuddling baby pigs, lambs, colts, puppies, and kittens. My parents dreamed I'd become a veterinarian. They can't understand why a farm girl from Indiana, who'd never even seen the ocean, would want to move to Delaware to study sea creatures. But they've supported my passion for dolphins one hundred percent."

Pete smiled. "Now I'll let you in on a secret. I have a group of lifeguard friends—we're all marine biology majors—who share your passion. We call ourselves *The Dolphin Whisperers*. We jump in our kayaks most Sundays for sunrise dolphin encounters. We're going out this Sunday. Want to come? I still have my dad's two-seater kayak."

"I'd love to!" She found herself jumping up and down again like a kid. "That's why I transferred here."

Dawn was breaking that Sunday when Pete arrived in a rusty red pickup truck with an orange-and-yellow kayak sticking out the back. The malodorous scent from two buckets of bait fish greeted Julie as she jumped into the cab. Pete flashed her a sheepish grin. "Sorry about the smell … dolphin magnets."

Five more whisperers were waiting for them at Gordons Pond beach alongside their orange, yellow, and blue kayaks. Pete introduced "Indiana, aka Julie" to the gang: Mike, Josh, Matt, Hannah, and Emily.

Pete shared Julie's story and said she was a true whisperer. "Definitely obsessed like us."

Emily's brown eyes sparkled as an ear-to-ear smile overtook her pixie-sized face. "Why else would we all be here at the crack of dawn?" *She must be Delaware's tiniest lifeguard,* Julie thought. She felt like a big-boned, brown-freckled, Midwestern Amazon next to her.

It was a perfect summer morning. Pale pink light scattered across tissue-thin clouds. Julie jumped in behind Pete as they launched their kayak and did her best to keep up with his long, powerful strokes as he led the way.

A few minutes later, they saw them—several pods gliding their way north about two hundred yards ahead. Everyone stopped paddling. Pete turned around and gave a thumbs up. "I count at least fifty, mostly bottlenoses." He pointed to hundreds of fish leaping in the water. "Breakfast."

Most of the dolphins swam right past them, intent on forming a tighter and tighter circle around their prey. But a few smelled the buckets of bait fish, swam up to them, and poked their heads up close to the boats.

"Well hello, Miriam!" Pete leaned over and gave a fish to a dolphin whose dorsal fin was jagged and missing the tip. "I knew you'd be here first." Pete explained that injured and aging dolphins and mothers with babies would come to the kayaks for fish because they had trouble competing for food with full-grown, healthy dolphins. He said Miriam's dorsal fin and flippers probably had been damaged by a boat propeller and she was a frequent visitor to their kayaks.

"I've got Baby Bruce and his mom over here." Emily tossed fish to a small bottlenose dolphin and his healthy, full-size mother. "Wow! He's grown a lot in the last two weeks. He's going to be huge."

"Here's Billy Bob." Mike pointed to a twelve-foot dolphin who looked like he'd survived a few wars. He appeared to be blind in one eye and had nicks and scars all over. Mike threw him a handful of fish. "We think he's toward the end of his life cycle, forty years old, maybe more." Billy Bob tipped his nose back and forth asking for more. "I'm a sucker for this old guy." Mike's lips curved into a boyish smile as threw Billy Bob another fistful of fish.

"Lotta chatter today." Matt removed his headphones, turned up his speaker, and stuck his hydrophone deeper in the water. Julie felt her jaw drop as she heard squeaks, clicks, and the signature whistles dolphins use to identify themselves. Hannah and Josh said they recognized a few of the whistles. "The Cowboy" and "Angel" were in the area.

Moisture filled Julie's eyes. She felt like she'd been transported to some magical biome, where humans and dolphins were soulmates. A small squeak caught her attention. She turned and saw a calf resting at its mother's side. The baby was asking her for a fish. Tears rolled down her cheeks.

Pete nodded. "Go ahead! Old enough to ask, old enough to try." Julie dipped her hand in her bucket, found a tiny fish. The baby took it gently from her hand, tipped his head back and swallowed it. Then it splashed its flippers in the water, asking for more. Julie handed it another.

"I think it's a female. Maybe ten days old. Not a bottlenose. Pale underside, black eye patch, light gray strip down the side. They're striped dolphins. What do you want to name them?"

Julie looked out at the pink sky for a moment, a feeling of contentment swelling her soul. "Lily for my little sister and Loreen for my mom."

The rest of the morning, between visits from their special friends, the whisperers watched the dolphins dive, surface, tail slap, and breach as they herded, then feasted on, schools of fish. When their fish buckets were empty, the whisperers returned to shore for lunch and afternoon bodysurfing. Later that evening they met at Mike's favorite Mexican restaurant for tacos and margaritas. Julie fell into bed that night feeling as if she had found nirvana.

That was the beginning of the best summer of Julie's life. The whisperers included her in bonfires on the beach, bodysurfing rallies, beach volleyball tournaments, nightclub crawls, and, best of all, their dolphin encounters. By midsummer, she felt as close to them as her high school friends, maybe even closer.

One evening in late July, Emily and Hannah invited Julie to join them for dinner. Over dessert, they asked if she'd like to share their apartment when school started. She said she'd love to. *I must be in some kind of dream*, she thought. *I can't believe I'll be rooming with people who are as passionate about dolphins as I am.*

Her internship at the marine science center got more interesting too. She was assigned to a team working closely with MERR, the non-profit in Lewes that handled first response and veterinary care for beached sea mammals and turtles. MERR had responded to a higher-than-average number of strandings on Delaware beaches since January. They wanted to know if something was awry, or if this was just an off year, Julie's supervisor said. He asked Julie to analyze data from the past several years to see if any patterns emerged. Julie loved the project and MERR's dedication to dolphins and other sea life. The whisperers were already MERR volunteers and she became one too.

A ringtone jarred her awake early one workday morning the beginning of August. It was Pete. MERR needed volunteers to help with a dolphin calf stranded on Gordons Pond beach. "It's a striped dolphin. I'm worried its Lily. I'll pick you up in ten minutes."

They were the first to arrive and recognized the stranded baby dolphin as Lily. Julie filled a large bucket with sea water, knelt beside her, and splashed seawater on her skin. Pete dialed MERR's executive director. "Two-month-old striped. Need a vet over here right away."

A familiar whistle pierced the air. It was Loreen. She was swimming tight loops close to shore, like an anxious mother pacing a hospital waiting room. Julie went to her, armpit deep in the water, rubbed her back. "Help is on the way. Lily will be just fine."

A half hour later, the veterinarian pronounced Lily well and the volunteers eased her back in the water. She sounded a happy squeak, swam to her mother, slapped her tiny tail, and off they went. The vet speculated Lily had accidentally beached herself while being chased by a shark.

The rescue cemented Julie's bond with Lily and Loreen, and the pair popped up at her kayak whenever Julie went on a whisperer expedition. Lily grew fast and by mid-August she was swimming on her own, leaping, and breaching.

Soon it was late August, and Julie worked long days wrapping up reports for the team. The evenings were long too, as she, Emily, and Hannah drove back and forth to Newark setting up their school-year apartment. It was a hectic time, and the whisperers missed their dolphin encounters. They agreed they'd try to get one more in over the Labor Day weekend and aimed for sunrise on Monday.

It was wishful thinking, though, and one by one, most of the whisperers were called to serve Labor Day lifeguard duty. By Monday morning, Julie and Emily were the only two left for the dolphin expedition.

Emily picked Julie up in her old Volkswagen Beetle, with Pete's two-seater kayak strapped to the top. Julie hopped in the front seat, greeted by the scent she'd come to love: fish buckets.

"You still want to go? There's a tropical storm brewing off the Carolinas, but I'm game if you are." Emily's big brown eyes sparkled, as they always did before a whisperer outing.

Julie scanned the ocean conditions app on her smart phone. "Should be OK early this morning. Three- to five-foot swells. We've done that before. Rougher seas as the day goes on, though."

The weather was postcard perfect when they arrived at the beach. Blue sky. Cotton-puff clouds. The waves were three feet high, as predicted, but Julie noticed they packed more energy than usual. She texted Pete and Mike: "We'll be kayaking where you can keep an eye on us. Could be a little rough out there!" Pete replied right away with a thumbs-up emoji. Then she and Emily grabbed the fish buckets and life jackets and launched the kayak.

Paddling was tougher than usual, and it took them a while to find a pod of dolphins. When they finally did, Julie couldn't believe her eyes. They were bodysurfing. At least a dozen bottlenoses, bodysurfing. She and Emily began whooping and paddling faster. Finally, they were close enough to stop paddling, pull out their binoculars, and enjoy the spectacle.

Suddenly, Emily poked her hard from behind yelling: "Paddle! Paddle!" Julie turned and saw an eight-foot wave building to a crest. Within seconds she heard a powerful whoosh, saw the water curling around her, and felt herself tumbling. It was the rock 'n' roll all over again, only this time it was much worse. A feeling of hopelessness overwhelmed her as she watched the life jacket she had failed to buckle float away and realized the water was too deep for her to find and push off the bottom.

Then, something familiar touched her hand. It was skin, but not human. It was a dorsal fin. Loreen's. She grabbed it and, in a flash, air filled her lungs. Dazed, she clung to her dolphin friend. She found comfort in the sound of air rasping through the dolphin's blow hole as Loreen rested on the surface.

A distinctive whistle sounded to her right, and she spotted Lily pushing something orange toward her—her life jacket. Then she noticed another life jacket bobbing twenty feet away. It was Emily. She was waving her arms and pointing to their upside-down kayak, which seemed to be moving on its own. But it wasn't. Miriam and Billy Bob were pushing it. She bent down and kissed Loreen on the head, lifted her life jacket from Lily's nose, and buckled it around her. She swam to Emily and high-fived her. They grabbed ahold of the kayak and gave love-pats to Miriam and Billy Bob.

They had just turned the kayak over when they heard a lifeguard whistle and saw Pete and Mike swimming toward them, towing their red lifeguard rescue cans.

"You two OK?" Pete's voice was raspy, his breathing jagged.

"We're fine, thankfully." Julie winked at Emily and pointed to the dolphins swimming around them. "We had a little help from our friends."

The four whisperers came together for a group hug when, suddenly, they heard a splash, and saw something gray launch like a rocket from the water. It was Lily, leaping over them in a perfect arc, six feet above them.

Julie saw Pete's jaw drop, then his eyes turn to half-moons as he sent a big splash of water in Lily's direction. "Show off!"

A CREATIVE WRITING NOVICE, NANCY NORTH WALKER IS HONORED TO BE PART OF *BEACH DREAMS*. THE INSPIRATION FOR HER STORY, *THE DOLPHIN WHISPERERS*, CAME FROM A MAGNIFICENT SIGHT THAT GREETED HER THE FIRST MORNING OF HER FIRST DAY IN REHOBOTH BEACH. FROM THE ROOFTOP OF THE BOARDWALK PLAZA HOTEL, SHE SAW DOLPHINS WEAVING THEIR WAY NORTHWARD FOR AS FAR AS THE EYE COULD SEE. IN THE MORNING LIGHT IT LOOKED LIKE AN INVISIBLE HAND WAS HEMMING THE COASTLINE WITH SILVER THREADS. IT TOOK HER BREATH AWAY, AND SHE AND HER HUSBAND DECIDED THAT DAY TO MAKE REHOBOTH THEIR RETIREMENT DESTINATION. THEY BECAME FULL-TIME RESIDENTS IN 2017. NANCY JOINED THE REHOBOTH BEACH WRITERS' GUILD AND BEGAN TAKING THE GUILD'S CREATIVE WRITING CLASSES. ALTHOUGH SHE HAD MADE HER LIVING AS A BUSINESS WRITER AND RETIRED AS A COMMUNICATIONS VICE PRESIDENT FOR A FORTUNE 500 COMPANY, CREATIVE WRITING WAS NEW TO HER. INSPIRED BY THE PASSION OF THE FABULOUS WRITERS WHO TAUGHT HER CLASSES, SHE BEGAN TRYING HER HAND AT CRAFTING SHORT STORIES IN THE SECOND HALF OF 2018. THE FIRST FOUR SHE SUBMITTED FOR PUBLICATION, INCLUDING THIS ONE, WERE ACCEPTED AND PUBLISHED IN THE FALL OF 2019. SHE LOOKS FORWARD TO TAKING MANY MORE CREATIVE WRITING CLASSES, WRITING MORE SHORT STORIES, AND GROWING AS A WRITER.

Four Corners

By Chris Jacobsen

The little girl held her grandmother's hand as they stood and watched her grandfather dig a small hole in the ground. When he was done, the grandmother, a stocky woman with graying hair, bent over and with reverence nestled a *pysanka* into it. She committed the design to memory as a splash of dirt hid it from view. The grandfather then led the small family on a lengthy walk to the next area, where again he dug a small hole. A light spring breeze mingled the fragrance of local flowers with the sharp scent of distant mountain pines and encouraged strands of the little girl's hair to escape the confines of its braid down her back. Again, the grandmother withdrew from her basket a carefully crafted *pysanka* and placed it into the tiny ditch. A bird sang, as if to acknowledge the ancient custom taking place.

Another long walk along a furrowed edge brought the group to the next site, where the process was repeated. The child did not completely understand the significance but understood that what was taking place was important and that she should be on her best behavior. Just as her little legs were about to give out, the trio marched to the spot where the final hole would be dug. As the last egg was buried under the fertile soil, the grandfather offered a prayer.

"May these offerings, handcrafted with love and faith, beseech a blessing upon all that is contained within the four corners of this field, that other hands may come and reap the daily bread of an abundant harvest. Amen."

The grandmother synchronized her "Amen" with that of her husband's. The little girl quickly mimicked what her elders had just said.

* * * * *

Tasha switched off the lights on her ISOP bicycle, leaned it against the side of her hosts' home, and carried her helmet into the bedroom she shared with another ISOP girl. As a full-time university student in Kiev with excellent grades, she had been eligible for acceptance into the International Student Outreach Program.

Tasha changed out of her clothes and flopped her thin frame onto the single bed, her long, dark hair splayed over the pillow. Her roommate, Nadia, was also from Ukraine. A proficiency in English was another ISOP requirement, but when it was just the two of them, they spoke their native language. Tasha didn't know if it lessened her homesickness or made it worse.

Tasha's parents had been thrilled that their daughter was going to the United States, but Baba, her grandmother, was most excited that Tasha had been assigned to Rehoboth Beach. Being a farmer's daughter, and then marrying a farmer, she had been tied to the ground and had never had time for frivolous vacations. Having seen a postcard of a beach, Baba asked her father over and over if he would take her there, but his response was always, "If you want water, go to the river and bring home some fish for dinner."

Tasha liked her job at Candy Kitchen, on the busiest corner of the boardwalk right across from the beach. The hours were long, but the pay was decent. Most weeks, she took advantage of the free meals provided by area churches. It gave her an opportunity to visit with students from other countries. Many were like her, abroad for the first time on a J1 visa. ISOP also offered field trips such as attending a local baseball game or a day-long outing to Philadelphia or DC. The organization wanted to make sure the ISOP experience was not all work and no play.

Although work took up much of her time, Tasha made sure she

wrote a letter to her grandmother each week, sending it by snail mail because Baba did not own a computer. In turn, Tasha received a letter each week with news of her farm, friends, and neighbors. She would read the letter over and over.

Tasha missed Baba and wished she could share this experience with her. She smiled as she recalled asking Baba if the beach was at the top of her bucket list. Baba had let out a laugh and said the only buckets she'd ever known were the one full of soapy water for washing the floor, the one she used to carry fresh milk from the cow, and the dented one she hauled outside to sling feed to the squawking chickens. She doubted she would ever own a bucket that contained a beach!

Baba's hands showed that she was used to hard work, having been raised in the very same small, but comfortable, farmhouse that she now shared with her husband. It sat nestled in a valley within the foothills of the Carpathian Mountains. Tasha lived in the city with her working parents, so at the age of five she began spending the entire summer on her grandparents' farm. Tasha reveled in the rustic atmosphere of the countryside. She could run around in the wide yard, play with the barn cats, and help feed the chickens. It was during that first summer that Tasha was taught the sacred craft of her heritage and found her passion.

Tasha had been intrigued by the many brightly decorated eggs displayed in Baba's living room. Some stood on egg stands, while others were nestled in teacups or glass bowls. Timidly, she asked if she could hold one.

Her grandmother pulled Tasha close and kissed the top of her head. "Yes, you may. Which one would you like?"

Tasha pointed to an egg with a yellow, green, orange, red, and black star design. Baba removed it from the shelf and placed it in her hands.

"This is a real egg so be very careful with it."

"Is there a chick inside?"

"No, this was a raw egg like the ones we eat for breakfast. It is quite old, so the insides of the egg have dried out. If you shake it gently, you will hear the yolk rattle around inside. It's now a hard, little ball."

"How did you get all the colors on it?"

And so, Baba covered the wooden table with brown paper and told Tasha to kneel on a chair. She then gathered several eggs, a candle, and a writing tool, and placed them in front of the girl. At the other end of the table, Baba set out several jars of dye.

"I was about your age when my mama taught me how to do this, just like she was taught by her mama, and so on for many, many generations. What you are about to learn is the art of writing *pysanky*, our traditional Ukrainian Easter eggs." She handed Tasha a wood-handled implement with a small metal funnel attached at one end. Into the funnel she put a bit of beeswax. "Now, we use this *kistka* to write on the eggshell. We call it writing because the designs and symbols we put on the egg are a message, like a little letter, which we give to a friend or loved one."

Intently, Tasha did as she was told. She held the funnel near the candle flame to melt the wax. She practiced writing straight lines on the curved surface and waited patiently as the egg went through its progression of dyes.

"The wax will protect whatever color is underneath even when the egg is dyed another color. At the end of all the waxing and dying, we will melt the wax off the entire egg and the colorful design will be revealed."

Tasha wrote several eggs that summer and could not wait to show her parents when they picked her up.

"When you come back next summer, my Tasha, we will write more *pysanky* together."

* * * * *

Two young children entered the Candy Kitchen with an older woman. Tasha knew right away the woman was their Baba, which made Tasha yearn to be with hers. This was the first summer in fifteen years they would not be spending together.

It made Tasha's heart heavy to think that Baba would never have the chance to go to a beach. She tried to send the beach to Baba by taking pictures with her iPhone, even though they couldn't convey what it felt like to wriggle your toes in the sand, be lifted by the swell of a wave, or take a long walk along the water's edge.

While Tasha spent most of her free daytime hours on the beach, she dedicated her evening hours to staying connected to home by writing letters and working on *pysanky*. Her host family had given her a table and chair in the basement where she could set up her supplies without disturbing them.

Writing *pysanky* helped soothe her. She relished the moment when all the waxing had been completed and it was time to melt it off. Holding the egg close to the flame, little by little, section by section, Tasha patiently watched the wax become shiny and then, with a smooth stroke of a tissue, she wiped off the wax and revealed the colorful design in all its glory. A coat of varnish would keep it beautiful for years to come.

＊ ＊ ＊ ＊ ＊

Tasha recalled the summer she turned twelve. She and Baba were writing *pysanky* at the long table.

"Do you remember when you were very little, and you came to stay with us on the farm for a week?" Baba asked. "It was springtime, when the women write *pysanky* and the men plant the crops."

Tasha filled the petals of a flower with wax as she thought. "Is that when we had to do all that walking?"

Baba laughed, her one good eye twinkling. "Yes. It was the day we planted the four corners."

Baba held her *kistka* to the flame as she pushed away an errant lock of gray hair. She deftly laid down more strokes on her egg. "When I was a small girl, the eggs we planted were written by my mother. But one year, my mother, who was sitting in the very spot where you are now, said that she thought my designs were so well done, that I should be the one to write the four corner eggs that year." Baba's eyes shone with the memory of the honor. "I felt so very grown up."

Tasha looked up. "So, your eggs are buried in the corners right now?"

"The ones from last year, yes, but the ones from that first year, no; it was such a very long time ago that they have disintegrated. But, over the past few summers I have watched your work get better and better. Your designs are well balanced, and your execution is more precise than mine was at your age." She put her *kistka* down and turned to face Tasha, "I was wondering if you would give us the honor of writing the four corner eggs this summer. We would save them until next spring and ask your parents to bring you out so you can be the one to plant them."

Tasha filled with pride. "Really? You want to use my eggs?"

"If you would be willing."

"I know! I could use the wheat symbol. And maybe a sun and some stars."

"As long as they are written with love and faith, they will be perfect."

Tasha blew out her candle, slipped out of her chair and hugged Baba's wide girth. "Thank you," she whispered.

* * * * *

It was Tasha's day off. Although it was early morning, the sun promised to be a scorcher by afternoon. Hopping on her bike, she first pedaled to the post office out on the avenue to mail her weekly letter. She hoped there would be a letter from Baba soon. The past two letters had been shorter than previous ones and the handwriting seemed to have more of a sprawl than usual.

There were just a few remaining weeks of ISOP. Tasha had gotten a flowered sundress and a cute pair of sandals as souvenirs for herself, along with a tie-dyed T-shirt because it was made using the same wax-resist method that she used for her eggs. But now she needed to get something for her family. Her parents were easy; a Rehoboth T-shirt for her father and, for her mother, a pair of dolphin earrings from Valhalla, her favorite store. To Baba, she would give a miniature beach: a vial containing sand and tiny seashells.

The day's mail did not contain a letter from Baba, and there was none the next day, either. Tasha had gone from being disappointed to being worried. It was not until the following week that a letter arrived, but it was written by an unfamiliar hand.

She tore it open quickly and looked to see who had signed it. It was from her grandfather.

"Your Baba was ill with a bad cold. She used her home remedies, as she had done so often in the past, but her cough turned into pneumonia. Although the neighbors brought soup and laid hot compresses on her chest, Baba passed away."

Tasha suddenly needed to sit down. A rush of coldness swept through her body as her heart beat faster. She continued to read.

"The family understands how difficult it is for you to get this news while being so far from home. Once you return, you will be able to visit her grave. Baba wanted you to know that she loved you very much. Her last words were to tell you to be brave and enjoy the beach for both of you."

The chill would not leave Tasha's body. Had she known when she left home for Rehoboth that it would be the last time seeing her precious Baba, would she have gone? Part of her said no but the other part knew how important it was to Baba that Tasha take advantage of such a wonderful opportunity. She dragged herself upstairs to her bedroom and collapsed onto the bed. What would her world be like without

Baba in it? She was the embodiment of love, safety, comfort and joy. Tasha's chest heaved with every sob. Her throat seemed to spasm as she gulped for air through her tears. How could she continue to write *pysanky* without Baba's guidance, encouragement, and enthusiasm?

The final days of ISOP had arrived. Tasha worked her designated hours but then spent every free moment writing eggs as a way for her to commune with her grandmother. She heard the whisper of the elderly woman's voice, from long ago, telling her how to use her *kistka*, how to keep her hand steady, how to choose her color schemes. Tasha's heart swelled as she realized that through *pysanky* she would never lose her connection to her grandmother; after all, isn't that how the custom had survived, one generation passing it on to the next, and then to the next, and so on?

That night, Tasha got a pencil and paper and sketched several ideas for an egg. At a certain point, she lit the candle, reached for her *kistka* and took a deep breath. She wanted this egg to be perfect, in its design, in its message, in its execution. Midnight came and went before the ISOP student could no longer keep her eyes open.

The following day, Tasha worked her scheduled hours. It was an easy choice to forgo the beach so she could write a few final eggs before returning home. Her roommate, Nadia, tried to cajole her into going to some farewell parties, but Tasha could not be swayed. These eggs were of the utmost importance to her, and with the limited time she had left, she did not want any distractions.

* * * * *

When Tasha finished her final egg, she began to clean up her supplies. She would take home her *kistka,* but the candle had burned down to a stub, so it was not worth saving. The dyes had to be poured down the sink. Tasha folded in the legs of the table and leaned it against the wall. She took a deep breath as she looked around. This work area had been a gift she had not expected; it had allowed her to continue her craft and given her the space she needed to begin to work through the loss of her Baba.

It was past midnight when she mounted the basement stairs for the last time. She began to pack up her belongings. Some of her *pysanky* she would take home, others she would give to her host family and friends when she said her goodbyes.

But before she boarded the bus to JFK airport, there was something she needed to do.

She set her alarm to go off at an early hour. It was still dark, but in the east, the sun was just making its appearance. Tasha put on a sweatshirt, grabbed a yellow plastic sand pail into which she had placed the items she would need, and headed for the boardwalk. She scanned the area in both directions and, seeing no one, she took deep breaths to steady herself.

She headed down the ramp to where the boards met the sand. With a little blue shovel, she dug a hole. Although the sand fought back to reclaim its place, Tasha continued until she was satisfied with the depth. From the yellow bucket she removed a *pysanka*. She had drawn a boardwalk around its middle, and above and below it, little pictographs of a white bench, a mint ice cream cone with chocolate bits, a slice of pizza, and a carton of Thrasher's fries. Gently, she placed the egg in the hole and covered it with sand.

Tasha turned and, parallel to the boardwalk, marched fifty paces in the sand. She knelt down and dug another hole, placing in it the next *pysanka*, upon which she had drawn a large yellow sun beating down on sand dunes, with swaying grasses, a sand castle, and a colorful beach blanket. She scooped up sand and sprinkled it over the egg.

Next, she turned and walked fifty paces toward the water. The egg she now buried in the wet sand depicted the ocean with cresting waves, their edges white with foam. She had drawn a shoreline scattered with seashells. Gulls swooped in the air, one aiming for a crab exposed on the beach.

The chill of the ocean kissed Tasha's bare feet as she counted off the last of her steps, bringing her in line with the first egg she had planted. Again, she used the shovel. She lowered the final *pysanka* into the salty sand. She stood and looked at it, her hazel eyes starting to mist as she offered a prayer.

"May these offerings, handcrafted with love and faith, beseech a blessing upon all that is contained within these four corners, that it be delivered unto Baba so that she will finally be at the beach. Amen."

Before burying it, she peered once more at the egg, which showed two women holding hands, one young and one old, running toward the ocean.

FOR QUITE SOME TIME, CHRIS JACOBSEN HAS WANTED TO WRITE A STORY CENTERED ON WRITING *PYSANKY*, THE UKRAINIAN WAX-RESIST METHOD OF DECORATING EGGS. SHE LEARNED THIS CRAFT FROM A UKRAINIAN FAMILY THIRTY-FIVE YEARS AGO AND HAS LOVED DOING IT EVER SINCE. IN JULY 2019, SHE ATTENDED HER THIRD PYSANKYUSA RETREAT IN WILKES-BARRE, PENNSYLVANIA, WHERE SHE FOUND HERSELF IN A ROOM WITH ONE HUNDRED PEOPLE WHO SHARED THE SAME PASSION. SHE WAS IN HEAVEN.

CHRIS LIVES JUST OVER THE STATE LINE IN DELAWARE COUNTY, PENNSYLVANIA. SHE HAS THREE GRANDCHILDREN, AGED SIX MONTHS TO TWO AND A HALF; ANOTHER SLICE OF HEAVEN!

SHE HAS HAD STORIES PUBLISHED IN *THE BOARDWALK, BEACH LIFE, BEACH LOVE,* AND *BEACH PULP,* PUBLISHED BY CAT & MOUSE PRESS. CHRIS WORKS PART-TIME FOR A VETERINARIAN. SHE HOPES TO DRAW INSPIRATION FROM HER EXPERIENCES THERE TO SUBMIT A STORY FOR THE UPCOMING BOOK, *SANDY PAWS.*

This moving and poignant story provides the unique perspective of a student worker visiting Rehoboth from Ukraine who finds a special way to honor the grandmother she loves who had always dreamed of seeing the ocean. "Four Corners" turns the theme of beach dreams on its head, making us imagine instead what it may be like to dream of one day simply seeing a beach, let alone what we might wish to do once we arrive at its sandy shores. Authentic and stirring, this story left quite an impression on many of the judges.

What Would My House Say?

By Sarah Barnett

May 30

I can't wait to get home. Sometimes I think the only reason to travel is for the pure pleasure of returning to my own space. I recline my plane seat slightly, close my eyes, and daydream about entering my front door.

My living room looks exactly as I left it, a stage set ready for anything. I'll drop luggage, reset the thermostat, open the fridge, and reassure myself I won't starve.

My daughter, Mindy, and I took a getaway trip to San Francisco. Mindy and her husband, Ted, have decided on a "trial separation." I've been mostly on my own since my husband, Sam, died fifteen years ago. The last man I dated was Darrell, whom I met at a senior singles "happy hour." We drifted apart over a year ago.

"We need to escape," Mindy had told me on the phone. So, we did—toured Alcatraz, ate dim sum in Chinatown, wandered through the Museum of Modern Art, and tried not to think about what we might be missing back home. Mindy's daughters, Jennifer, twenty, and Alicia, seventeen, spent the week in my house in Rehoboth, enjoying beach time and taking care of Wally, a shepherd-mix rescue I acquired when I decided to sell my other home in the DC suburbs and live near the beach full time.

As my plane lands in Philly I mentally rehearse each step—trek to baggage claim, grab suitcase from carousel, bus to parking lot, and, finally, the drive home. I'll detour to Wilmington to buy supplies at Trader Joe's. A text from Mindy tells me she's landed at Dulles and is on her way to Arlington. Jennifer and Alicia will have left my house and are headed back to their mom.

To buy:

fresh flowers, cheese, crackers, salad fixings, coffee, frozen cheesecake

May 31

What would my house say if it could talk? I want it to say "dream house." But as I pull into the driveway after a trip to the supermarket, I notice those small things that make it the not-my-dream house: an overgrown forsythia bush about to blanket a living room window, the shaky stair railing leading up to a porch that's pleading for a coat of paint, the came-with-the-house blinds on the windows that always feel dusty to the touch.

It's not all negative. I love having breakfast on the back porch while I listen to a mockingbird's showy song or geese honking overhead. The hot tub I had installed when I moved here permanently provides hours of soaking pleasure and delicious conversations when Mindy's here or when friends come for a women's weekend. The layout of the house works too, with my bedroom and bathroom on the first floor.

But (isn't there always a *but*?) that leads to another drawback, perhaps bigger than those other fixable flaws. Lately, the house feels too big, as if I'm swimming around in one of my mother's dresses. I could lop off the second story and never miss it. Well, I *would* miss the giggling of my granddaughters and their friends as they settled in for the night, the splash of the shower and roar of hair dryers in the morning. But Mindy and the girls and my son, Ben, rarely visit these days. Occasionally, I wander upstairs to flush toilets, straighten the bed where Wally snoozes in the afternoon, and adjust blinds to let in some light.

What would my house say?

"Call a handyman."

"Find a roommate?"

June 8

We knew it would happen; we just didn't know when. This morning, the rumble of heavy equipment behind the house announced the destruction of much of the wooded area bordering the community to make way for new homes. I walk out front with Wally to see neighbors—Terry, Mitch, Anita—gathered to survey the damage.

"They're supposed to leave a seventeen-foot border," Terry says. "We'll have *some* trees." She leans down to scratch Wally's ears.

"Not nearly enough," Mitch says. Wally sits in front of Mitch and whines softly. Mitch pulls a small bone-shaped treat from his pocket and tosses it in the air. Wally snags it with a gulp. In addition to spoiling Wally, Mitch maintains bird feeders and puts out food for the animal residents of our former forest. He also shovels my driveway when it snows. I repay him with homemade brownies.

"We're thinking about moving," Anita says. "Anyone else?" Anita and her wife, Jenny, live across from me. They've been here only two years.

We answer in unison, "Where would we go?"

As I walk Wally around the neighborhood, I think about Anita's question. I'd always dreamed of living near the beach. How can I fault others for wanting to live here, too? But what will happen to the deer, foxes, squirrels, and birds that shelter in those woods? Where is their dream home?

To think about:

Stay or go?

June 10

To escape the bulldozers, I take Wally to the beach around eight a.m. so he can romp with other dogs before people arrive for the day. I unfasten his leash. "Go." He tears after a yellow Lab about to race into the ocean but pulls up short when his feet hit water. Wally's not a swimmer, which is OK with me, because he won't need a full rubdown before I can put him in the car.

We begin a walk along the shoreline. He dashes ahead. When I blow my dog whistle, he whips around and sprints back to me for a treat. He'll do anything for food.

I'm examining the shells at my feet when I hear a loud "No!" I look up to see Wally racing down the beach, a bakery bag in his mouth. The bag's owner stands, red-faced, hands on hips. "That your dog? He stole my doughnuts."

I can't decide whether to stop and apologize or run after Wally. "I'll be right back," I say, and scramble after the dog. I grab him, snap on the leash, and start picking up bakery remains. After putting the stuff in a trash bag I carry for dog cleanup, I tramp back to see if I can placate the injured party. He's wearing sunglasses, so I can't read his expression.

"I'm so—"

"You need to pay me for my food," he says, cutting off my apology.

Not what I expected, but the gray hair and beard tell me he's older. A senior citizen myself, I identify with grouchy. "Of course. My wallet's in the car. I'll be right back." It's a three-minute walk to the car, where I open the windows partly, park Wally in the back, and return to the scene of the crime, wallet in hand.

But … he's disappeared. Beach chair, cooler, frustrated doughnut consumer—all gone.

To do:
Take Wally to obedience school
Carry pocket money

June 13

I drive around looking for a place—my place. I cruise newer

communities that have winding streets and strategically placed ponds with spouting fountains. Is that what people want? Houses crowded together; front porches flanked by pretentious columns. The homes have an Identi-Kit look, as if assembled by ten-year-olds from jumbo Lego sets.

The area called Forgotten Mile appeals to me. It has an unplanned, lived-in vibe that seems homier—the way my living room looks on a Sunday afternoon—books and magazines lying around, sandals under a chair, a throw pillow that slipped to floor when Wally jumped up to lie next to me on the couch.

I find my "dream" bungalow on a shady side street, the neighborhood a mix of smaller, older homes and larger, newer ones. In the not-so-distant past I might have fantasized about meeting someone "available" (age appropriate, single, smart, funny), who lived in one of the elegant newer homes. We'd hit it off and … well you get the picture.

But I'm over this fantasy because *now* I'm daydreaming about living in this dowdy, but cute (i.e. small), house with a shady front porch, olive-green shutters, and a postage-stamp yard. I imagine the ornamental trees I'd plant, the porch furniture I'd buy, the brighter color paint for the shutters and front door.

But there's a pickup truck in the driveway and a bike on the porch. That house is not available.

To think about:

Do I really want to move?
Why did I dream decorate a house that's not obtainable?

June 15

I stop at The Point for coffee on the way home from our morning beach trip. Wally lies under our outdoor table searching for crumbs. I look up and there *he* is. Doughnut guy, holding a large Styrofoam cup. No sunglasses today; his eyes almost match the facial hair.

"You here to collect?" I put down my latte and reach for my purse.

He shrugs. "I wasn't sure it was you. I … uh … recognized the dog."

"Yeah. He's memorable, all right." When he doesn't say anything, I try, "Look, I'm *really sorry* about what happened. My dog is … I mean was … a stray. I found him at a shelter, but he probably lived on the streets for a while, so whenever he sees a chance to eat …"

"He grabs it. In this case, my doughnuts. I got it." He reaches down, holds his hand under Wally's nose, and when that seems all right, scratches behind his ears. Wally's about to roll over and offer his belly.

Maybe it's his gentle way with the dog that lets me say, "I owe you a doughnut or two." I hold out my open bag. "Will a sugar cookie do?"

He straightens up and smiles.

"I'm Nancy," I say. "Have a seat." *Did I really say that?* In my before-the-beach life, I would have called it quits at a cookie. *Who am I?*

"Roger." He pulls out a chair. "Listen, you're probably wondering about my disappearing act."

I nod.

"I guess I was embarrassed. I overreacted. It was just a couple of doughnuts. A dog. I like dogs." He reaches into my bag and pulls out a cookie.

To do:

Make brownies for Roger?

June 16

My third obedience class with Barb, the dog trainer Terry recommended. We steer Wally through the farmers' market in Grove Park. Barb has placed tempting treats on the path. Each time Wally lunges for one, I'm supposed to firmly say, "Leave it," then give him a treat from my pocket. It's working; Wally is focused on me, not on snacks on the ground. After ten minutes, it's working too well. Wally will lunge at anything—a stray coffee cup lid, an overturned berry basket—then he'll back away and look up at me expecting a treat. "I'm not sure this will translate to the beach," I tell Barb.

"Give it time," she says.

To Buy:
Large box of dog treats

June 23

During our chat at The Point, Roger and I discovered we had much in common. We were both widowed, both missed the same things about living near DC (like museums and the theater), and we both liked to travel. But when he said his wife died a year ago ("eleven months and thirteen days"), I pushed away any thoughts of a romantic relationship. *Good*, I thought. *I don't want to be in a relationship right now.*

Women in their thirties worry about their biological clocks. I'm approaching a different deadline. (*Deadline*? Interesting word.) Seventy. An age that feels like a window closing, a door slamming, an expiration date.

I'm pretty sure I'm the oldest person in yoga class, and when some of us go out for coffee afterward, I think everyone in the place is younger than I am. At the movies, on the boardwalk, and in restaurants, I see plenty of couples and women in groups, but few single men my age.

Sam and I were married for twenty-eight years. After he died I didn't long for romance. Then I met Jake at a singles dance. Jake, who I thank every day. If he hadn't ditched me ten years ago, I wouldn't have escaped to the beach house and the life I've loved since.

It seemed there was always time. Time to meet someone, time to get to know him, time to fall in love. But now I'm not so sure.

So why *did I* ask Roger to lunch at the ferry terminal? I didn't feel sorry for him. Not exactly. Still, I remember that when I was first widowed, friends, even people I didn't know well, invited me for coffee, to the movies, to take a walk. Simple activities that helped me through difficult days. Also, perfect summer weather was forecast for the day: low humidity, a light breeze, temperature in the seventies.

Over sandwiches, I tell Roger about my "dream house" hunt. He notices me eyeing the townhouse community on the bay near the terminal.

"Think you could live there?"

"Why not?" I say with a laugh. "Wherever I go, I imagine myself living there. I've put myself in a walk-up apartment in Greenwich Village, a condo in San Francisco's Union Square, a cottage in the Maui hills."

Without missing he beat, Roger rattles off his list: "bed-sit in Notting Hill, rent-controlled apartment in Brooklyn Heights, flat above a shop on Boston's Newbury Street.

The ferry horn gives out a long, ear-splitting blast to announce its departure. "If I lived here, that would definitely mess up my afternoon nap," I say.

To forget:
Townhouses near ferry terminal (too big for one person, too loud for me).

July 1
Demolition behind our homes is complete. Construction yet to begin. The wooded area looks sad, skimpier than I thought it would. Trees that were once tightly packed and impenetrable now look fragile and lonely. Will the area look even bleaker in the fall when the leaves are gone? How will it look when the new homes are built?

To do:
Find the autumn photo I took of the woods when I first moved in.

July 4
When my grandkids were younger the holiday meant dinner on the boardwalk, watching fireworks from the beach, then driving home in teeming traffic with sleepy children in the back of Mindy's minivan.

A few years later, with no company coming, I would decide to treat the holiday like a snow day. I'd stock up on movies from the library, enjoy a leisurely breakfast, wear my pajamas until mid-afternoon.

My next-door neighbors, Terry and Carl, started the holiday barbecue tradition two years ago. "Fireworks are for summer people and tourists," Terry said with her usual candor. Now the neighborhood cookout keeps me in the kitchen most of the morning preparing potato salad and brownies. Roger will bring beer and soft drinks.

The six families that live on our cul-de-sac gather in late afternoon. The teenagers ignore the volleyball net Carl set up and huddle in a corner of the yard while they study their cell phones.

"Done any house hunting lately?" Anita says, as she begins unwrapping hot dog and hamburger rolls.

"Nothing serious. You?"

"Jenny and I looked at some nice houses down the road. Seacrest or Beachview … something like that. But with all the new homes they're building in that area, we're worried about traffic."

"Traffic's a problem here too." I say. "Sometimes I try to cross that main road with Wally, to walk someplace different. Many drivers ignore us. One guy had the nerve to wave to thank *me* for waiting for *him*."

To do:
Renew house hunt?

July 7

Through the thin border of trees, I now enjoy the sunset each evening—an unexpected (and literal) bright side to the recent destruction of our forest. Random pink streaks in the sky deepen gradually to a rich, rosy glow. Soon, the lower portion of the sky gleams gold and rose and orange. The sparse trees seem etched against the sky, each branch sharp and distinct, as in an Ansel Adams photograph.

Luminous sunsets vs. the protective darkness of trees.
Delaware Beach Life *photography contest?*

July 18

Mindy and I tour some open houses. One home was the right size, but the yard was a deal breaker. Instead of grass, the area was hardscaped with white pebbles. "Isn't that great?" the real estate agent said. "No grass to mow."

"Not great for a dog," I said as we left.

"What about a senior living community?" Mindy says later, as we sit in the hot tub.

"Not for me. Not yet anyway." To change the subject I say, "Guess what? Darrell called last week."

"Really? What did he want?"

"Just checking in, I guess. He sold his condo in Dewey and bought a really nice house in town, close to the beach."

"Wait. Doesn't that fit into that idea you had? That fairy tale scenario in which you get to live in a really terrific house?"

I never should have told her about that. Still, I've done enough soul-searching to say, "You know what? I'm over Darrell and I'm over that fantasy too. The last thing I want is to live in someone else's dream house. Maybe I can fix what's wrong with this one."

We clink wine glasses.

To do:
Call handyman.

August 7

At the beach near Gordons Pond, three generations of family members, all wearing white shirts and khaki pants, mill around while a photographer sets up. Dad corrals three preteens playing a competitive game of keep-away. "Can you kids please pretend you like each other for thirty seconds?"

Mom comes over to pet Wally. "We had a dog that looked just like that." She strokes his back. Wally wags his tail, but his eyes are on their picnic basket.

"I hear that a lot," I say. Wally is your generic dog—black and tan markings, floppy ears, melting brown eyes.

"You live here?"

When I say yes, she tells me they're looking for a second home, someplace they can live in retirement when the kids are grown. "It's something we've dreamed about."

I hear that a lot too. In every conversation with friends or people I meet casually, someone almost always mentions how lucky we are to live in this beautiful place.

To do:

Check with dog trainer. Wally's beach behavior somewhat improved, but he still needs to be leashed when picnic baskets are lying around.

August 20

Almost fall. Change is in the air. The good news: Mindy and Ted are back together after couples counseling. They'll visit Labor Day weekend. It'll be different. Jennifer, who turns twenty-one next month, will bring her boyfriend, Nathan. Mindy mentions they'd like to sleep together "if it's OK with you."

My granddaughter is an adult now, so this was predictable. I tell Mindy, "I plan to wave you all upstairs and say, 'make yourselves at home.'"

To do:

Check upstairs bedrooms and bathrooms for linens, towels, soap, etc.

August 23

Another surprise. A couple of weeks ago I told Roger about the bereavement group that meets at the senior center. When he went to sign up, he met Cynthia, who ran the reception desk that day. He's taking her to dinner this weekend.

"I wonder if people will think it's too soon to date," he said, when we met for coffee.

I didn't know what to say, so I recycled the advice the people gave me after Sam died: (1) There's no schedule; (2) Janet (his wife) wouldn't have wanted him to be alone; and (3) don't worry about other people. Take care of yourself.

To do:
Join senior center?

September 4

Labor Day weekend. All this movement, but I seem to be staying put. For this weekend at least, I love that my house can hold my whole family. Nathan went to the deli this morning and bought bagels for everyone. Ted and Mindy act like newlyweds, each always checking to see where the other one is. Ben, who usually brings a date, arrived without one but with several tubs of homemade ice cream, his new hobby. He'd packed them in dry ice. Alicia is planning a group volleyball game in the community pool this afternoon. Everyone has an assigned task for dinner, which will be on the back porch if the weather cooperates. So far, so good.

What would my house say?
"Feed the birds. Invite friends for a fall weekend (Jazz Festival?). Enjoy the sunsets."

Before retiring to Delaware and discovering the joys of writing creatively, Sarah Barnett had careers as teacher, librarian, and lawyer. She is vice president of the Rehoboth Beach Writers' Guild and enjoys leading FreeWrite!s, teaching writing classes, and dreaming up story and essay ideas while walking her dog on the beach. Thirteen years of experience as a Rehoboth Beach homeowner provided background and details for "What Would My House Say?" She thanks her dog, Blue, for inspiring the character of Wally and the doughnut incident. Sarah's work has appeared in *Delaware Beach Life*, *Delmarva Review*, and other publications. She won first place in the 2013 Rehoboth Beach Reads Short Story Contest for her story "The Summer of Your Discontent," which was published in *The Beach House*.

JUDGE'S COMMENT

This charmingly low-key short story offers a slice-of-life portrait of an older-but-not-old widowed woman, living full-time in her dream house at the beach. Her children and grandchildren visit, she is briefly drawn to a widower she meets while walking her dog near the ocean, and her neighbors and she consider moving when a developer removes most of the dense woods that provided seclusion to their houses. But like the dreamed-of ideal of life at the beach, her daily life moves calmly, even contemplatively, with time to revel in the rose, gold, and orange sunsets, which are now visible from the back of her house, through the thinned-out trees.

Beach Dreams

2019 REHOBOTH BEACH READS JUDGES

Tyler Antoine

Tyler Antoine is the program librarian at the Rehoboth Beach Public Library in downtown Rehoboth. A graduate of the English and Creative Writing undergrad program at Temple University, Tyler spends much of his spare time reading short fiction and writing his own poems, a few of which have been published by literary magazines such as *Painted Bride Quarterly*, *bedfellows*, and *Mad House*.

Stephanie Fowler

Stephanie Fowler attended Washington College, a small liberal arts school in Chestertown that is renowned for its writing program. There she was awarded the Sophie Kerr Prize, the largest undergraduate literary award in the country. Fowler won the award for a collection of short stories based on her native roots on the Delmarva Peninsula. She was inspired to start Salt Water Media, a company designed to provide tools, products, and services for indie authors. The endeavor evolved from her love of writing and her own experiences with publishing her novel, *Crossings*.

Lois Hoffman

Lois Hoffman is the owner of The Happy Self-Publisher and award-winning author of *Write a Book, Grow Your Business* and *The Self-Publishing Roadmap*. Her online course, Adventures in Writing Nonfiction, challenges aspiring authors to imagine what is possible and helps them realize their vision. She is a book coach, speaker, workshop facilitator, and brings the joy of authorship to determined writers through personalized writing, publishing, and author services. She also elicits countless smiles as a professional juggler (really) along with her husband, Michael, who perform as The Juggling Hoffmans. Lois lives with her family in Newark, DE, where she juggles her creative pursuits with enthusiasm and joy. You can find her playing with words online at WWW.HAPPYSELFPUBLISHER.COM.

Laurel Marshfield

Laurel Marshfield is a professional writer, ghostwriter, developmental editor, and book coach who assists authors of nonfiction, fiction, memoir, and biography in preparing their book manuscripts for publication. She has helped more than four hundred authors shape, develop, and refine their book manuscripts—by offering manuscript evaluation, developmental editing, book coaching, ghostwriting, and co-authorship—through her editorial services for authors business, Blue Horizon Communications, which is located in Rehoboth Beach, DE.

Mary Pauer

Mary Pauer received her MFA in creative writing in 2010 from Stonecoast, at the University of Southern Maine. Twice the recipient of literary fellowship awards from the Delaware Division of the Arts, Pauer publishes short fiction, essays, poetry, and prose locally, nationally, and internationally. She has published in *The Delmarva Review*, *Southern Women's Review*, and *Foxchase Review*, among others. Her work can also be read in anthologies featuring Delaware writers. She judges writing nationally, as well as locally, and works with individual clients as a developmental editor. Her latest collection, *Traveling Moons*, is a compilation of nature writing. Donations from sales help the Kent County SPCA equine rescue center.

Harold O. Wilson

Wilson lives with his wife Marilyn on Kent Island on Maryland's Eastern Shore. He is a writer and a radio host for Delmarva Public Radio. In addition to his novel, *A Taste of Salt*, Wilson's writings include *The Night Blooming Cereus and Other Stories*, a novella and short stories. He also publishes essays, poetry, literary criticism, and short stories on his website, www.haroldowilson.com. In addition to writing, Wilson hosts the monthly "Delmarva Today: Writer's Edition" for Delmarva Public Radio WSDL 90.7 and hosts the quarterly "Delmarva Radio Theatre," which airs on Delmarva Public Radio WSCL 89.5. Both programs are streamed at www.delmarvapublicradio.net and program podcasts are found on the same website. Wilson is fiction editor for *The Delmarva Review*, a literary journal published annually. He is a past president of The Eastern Shore Writers Association.

Want to see *your* story in a Rehoboth Beach Reads book?

The Rehoboth Beach Reads Short Story Contest

The goal of the Rehoboth Beach Reads Short Story Contest is to showcase high-quality writing while creating a great book for summer reading. The contest seeks the kinds of short, engaging stories that help readers relax, escape, and enjoy their time at the beach.

Each story must incorporate the year's theme and have a strong connection to Rehoboth Beach (writers do not have to live in Rehoboth). The contest opens March 1 of each year and closes July 1. The cost is $10/entry. Cash prizes are awarded for the top stories and 20–25 stories are selected by the judges to be published in that year's book. Contest guidelines and entry information is available at: *catandmousepress.com/contest.*

Also from Cat & Mouse Press

Other Rehoboth Beach Reads Books

Beach Pulp

From giant creatures to ghostly specters and from heroic superheroes to hard-boiled detectives, our beaches are in for a shock. Set in Rehoboth, Bethany, Cape May, Lewes, Ocean City, and other beach towns!

Sandy Shorts

Bad men + bad dogs + bad luck = great beach reads. The characters in these stories ride the ferry, barhop in Dewey, stroll through Bethany, and run wild in Rehoboth. Now available: *More Sandy Shorts*

Children's Books

Fun with Dick and James

Follow the escapades of Dick and James (and their basset hound, Otis) as they navigate the shifting sands of Rehoboth Beach, facing one crazy conundrum after another.

How To Write Winning Short Stories

A concise guide to writing short stories that includes preparation, theme and premise, title, characters, dialogue, setting, and more.

Online Newspaper

Jam-packed with articles on the craft of writing, editing, self-publishing, marketing, and submitting. Free. Writingisashorething.com

Come play with us!

A Playful Publisher

www.catandmousepress.com
www.facebook.com/catandmousepress

When You Want a Book at the Beach

Come to Your Bookstore at the Beach

- Fiction
- Nonfiction
- Children's Books & Toys
- Local Authors
- Distinctive Gifts
- Signings/Readings

Browseabout Books
133 Rehoboth Avenue
Rehoboth Beach, DE 19971
www.browseaboutbooks.com

Made in the
USA
Middletown, DE

76924424R00139